DROWNED VOICES

WHEN GUILT CANNOT BE SILENCED

THE DARK WATER SERIES
BOOK 2

MARIA FRANKLAND

AUTONOMY
PRESS

I dedicate this book to my Advance Reader Team who initially requested this sequel to Undercurrents. (Formerly called The Yorkshire Dipper.)

With thanks and appreciation for their amazing support of my writing.

This book is the second in a trilogy.

ALSO AVAILABLE IN THE DARK WATER SERIES:

JOIN MY 'KEEP IN TOUCH' LIST!

If you'd like to be kept in the loop about new books and special offers, join my 'keep in touch list' by visiting www.mariafrankland.co.uk You'll receive a free novella as a thank you for joining!

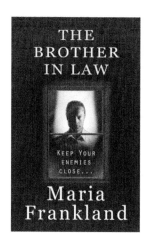

PROLOGUE

I HOPE my older brother knew what I thought of him. We fished, we got into scrapes, we watched sport, we played pool. What we never did was argue. Ever.

One minute we were walking side by side, the next Dean's life had been stamped out as though someone had slammed their foot on a spider. The might of the car had sent him hurtling over a garden wall, whilst I'd been mown to the ground.

Although I cracked my head on the concrete, I had several lucid moments prior to finally lapsing into unconsciousness. Time enough to glimpse the faces of the vehicle's occupants as they stared at the carnage they'd caused. Long enough to catch snatches of conversation such as 'my career,' 'my reputation,' 'prison' and finally, 'let's get out of here.'

Mum didn't visit me in hospital. She reckoned I'd be home soon enough. Besides, she was too busy grieving for her firstborn son. The one she thought *should* have survived.

As the subsequent weeks limped over one another, she could barely look at me, let alone speak to me. Until she finally threw me out of the house in a row about money for board. I left home beneath a cloud of guilt-fuelled hatred. And it's pursued me ever since.

PART I

WILL

1

THESE HAVE BEEN the most drawn-out five days of my entire life. The verdict was reached sooner than anyone could have predicted, so I'm not going to grumble on that front.

"Let's wait a few minutes, shall we?" I say as the collective in the courtroom stands, stretches and heads towards the exit.

"Haven't we spent enough time in this place? I could do with some fresh air." Eva also rises from her seat with a yawn and a stretch.

"I don't want to cross the path of the families, that's all."

"Why not?" The puzzled expression on her face intensifies. "Our family are victims of DCI Ingham as much as anyone else's, if not more. We've lost one family member like they have and we nearly lost Claire as well."

"But when all's said and done, me and Mark are still in the police. And no matter what compo the families have been awarded just now, they're still baying for blood."

Eva sits back down and squeezes my hand. "Let it go now love. It's over." Her hand on mine feels alien and I shake it off. It's as unexpected as the sunlight that filters through the slits in the wall. I suppose they can't have proper windows in here.

And we *never* call each other love. Not anymore. In fact, in these last five days, I've spent more time with her than in the last couple of years.

"It's not over though, is it - not yet." Not until I've been formally cleared and I'm back out there again, doing what I should be doing. For me, it's far from over.

I get my own way and we're the last to leave the room, apart from a few of the officials.

"Time to go." My sister Claire, sitting on the other side of Eva, nudges her.

Mark, flanked by our mother and Claire turns as we follow him to the door. "I reckon a beer sounds like a plan," he says.

"Mine's a coke then. I take it drinks are on you?" I slap his shoulder. I don't normally go into pubs, but I'll make an exception this time. "What did they say, four hundred grand?"

"It's hardly the price I'd put on my wife's life." He swings around to face me fully, surveying me as though I'm something he's stepped in. It's a look I've grown used to from my family over the years. I feel the smile fade from my face as Mum also glares at me.

"It's a bloody insult to Lauren's life." Brenda catches us up. I don't need to look at the expression Lauren's mother will be displaying – it's clear in her voice. And someone ought to tell her she's too old for plaits. It's how Lauren used to wear her hair. Brenda talks about Lauren endlessly, so I usually avoid being in her company.

I nearly say *she wasn't actually your wife* to Mark, but that would be callous, even by my standards. I guess she would have been by now though. Detective Chief Inspector Jonathan Ingham certainly put an end to that wedding day.

He's also carried the can for eight murders last winter, five the winter before and two attempted murders, one being my sister. Not bad for someone in a position of elevated office. It's certainly going to be interesting when we get outside this building. *Baying for blood* may well be an understatement.

I knew there'd be a crowd, but bloody hell. There's the media, of course. Everywhere. TV vans and reporters with stepladders, which makes my eyes hurt as the metal catches in the sun.

Huddles of women hold candles and wave placards as they jostle for position. I catch the words *we have had enough* and *justice for women* as I sweep my gaze over the throng of people. They've fastened photographs of each of the dead women to the town hall railings with a candle in front of each one. What they're trying to achieve here, I do not know. It's not as if this outpouring of who knows what can bring any of them back to life – what's done is most definitely done.

I see Lauren's work colleague at the front of the crowd. Lindy. My not-so-favourite news reporter. Our eyes meet and it's not a comfortable meeting. She's never had the highest opinion of me and never even spoke to me at Lauren's funeral. I wonder what Lauren told her about me.

A hush of sorts descends. The Chief Inspector of the Independent Police Complaints Commission ascends the steps and settles behind the assembled microphones. He glances down at some notes. He's written his speech quick to say the verdict has only just been announced. Perhaps he anticipated what was going to happen?

"I'm going to make a brief statement." He clears his throat and sweeps his hand over his thinning hair as he looks out at the crowd. "First, I want to clarify that we unequivocally accept the verdict of thirteen counts of murder at the hands of one of our serving senior officers, Jonathan Ingham." His voice is robotic, devoid of emotion. I notice that he's stripped Ingham of his DCI rank.

"Corrupt bastards." A male voice rises from the crowd and some jeering follows. I can see him being drowned out here. No. They're settling down again. Clearly they're interested in what he's got to say.

"It has been legally declared," the Inspector goes on, "that our trusted officer, holding a position of high office committed the crimes involved. This is one of the biggest failings in UK policing history and, whilst he acted alone, we accept that safeguarding policies and accountability procedures have been found catastrophically lacking."

Whilst he acted alone. Words I love to hear.

"Murderers." It's a female voice this time and she screeches the word with such venom that several people turn to the sound, but then avert their attention back to the unfolding statement. He's lucky. I've been at speeches like this where the speaker can't make themselves heard above the heckling.

"Thirteen women have lost their lives and the lives of many others have been changed forever. People have lost mothers, wives, daughters, sisters and friends. This force failed the victims *and* we failed their families." He pauses, seemingly for effect, clearly an old pro at delivering in these circumstances. "Today, I want to apologise *unreservedly* to these families and everyone else who has been affected."

He lingers again as more anger spews into the air. I wonder what they'd all do to me now if they knew about my involvement.

"These difficult proceedings have provided us with an opportunity to explore all the evidence and have enabled the jury to reach the unanimous verdict of multiple counts of murder.

"As for this police force, many lessons have been learned and will continue to be learned from what has happened." The Inspector raises his voice in keeping with the gradual volume lift throughout the crowd. "There will be immediate improvements in police training, communications, technology and supervision to ensure that nothing like this ever happens to innocent women again."

He's practically shouting as he concludes his speech – if it can be called a speech, that is.

"We shall now take some time to reflect on the implications of today's verdict, whilst recognising what has been suffered, and will continue to be suffered, by the families of the victims. Our thoughts are, of course, with them all."

He glances across at the photographs and candles as he steps away from the microphones and is ushered towards a waiting car on the side street for his getaway. His face bears a nonchalant expression as he dodges bellowed questions and more heckling. I'd have thought he might have answered some of them.

I'm still technically suspended, so am wearing civvies. Mark, however, is in full uniform, so I don't fancy us trying to get through this crowd unscathed. Not all of them out here will realise our family is one of the families the police bigwig just apologised to. One who's been through the same thing as the others. They'll just see the uniform and that will be that. Usually I feel invincible when I'm in uniform. Today must be the first time I've felt relieved that it's hanging in my wardrobe.

I poke Mark in the ribs to get his attention over the roar of the gathering. "I say we wait back inside for ten minutes – let this lot die down."

Mark nods and nudges Mum and Brenda back towards the revolving doors.

Mum tuts. "I thought we were going to the pub. Why's he calling all the shots?" She points at me.

I ignore her. It's my best defence. "Are we OK to wait in here until it clears out there?" I'm grateful to come back in. My ears are literally buzzing.

The guard nods and gestures towards the seating area.

"Cheers mate. I'll just pay a call." I rub my hands together to warm them up as I stride towards the gents.

"You're Lauren Holmes's brother-in-law, aren't you?"

As I emerge from the loo, a woman steps out of the ladies. There's a familiarity about her that I can't put my finger on. She must sense how intently I'm trying to work out where I know her from, and she looks away, possibly feeling like a specimen under my microscope.

I'm immediately on my guard. No way am I speaking to any reporters. Maybe she's one of Lauren's work colleagues.

"Yeah? Well I was. Why?"

"It must be a really difficult time for you all." She gestures towards where everyone else is sitting. Somehow, she knows I'm with them.

"Erm, yeah, I suppose. Look, I'm not being rude, but my family is waiting for me."

She slides a card from her bag and presses it into my hand, sending a wave of something through me. My wife hasn't had that effect on me for years. "I can help you." Her composure doesn't match the affirmation of her words. There's a shake to her hand and a tremble in her voice.

I stare at it as I struggle to compose myself. *The Alder Centre. Counselling, Coaching and Psychotherapy.*

"Psychotherapy?"

"It offers more depth than the bog standard police counselling they'll have offered you and your brother." She tucks a stray hair behind her ear. "Like I said - as a family, you've been through a lot. We've helped a few in the force in my time at the practice."

"I don't think..."

"Just keep hold of it. You never know. I'm the practice manager, so call anytime you want." She smiles, but the smile doesn't reach her eyes. In fact, I'd say she looks more uncomfortable than when she first made her approach. Clearly, she fancies me.

"So what's your name then?"

"Suzannah Peterson."

As she walks away, I'm certain the offer of therapy is a cover-up. She obviously just wants me to take her number, or else she'd have collared Mark as well. He needs therapy more than I do. I'll have to mull this over. Perhaps I don't need any complications at the moment. We've all had enough drama lately. But Suzannah Peterson is definitely the sort of woman I'd go for. Dark hair, though I usually prefer women to wear it longer than she does, green eyes and everything in perfect proportion. I can't help but notice her arse as she pushes into the revolving door out of the foyer. She doesn't turn back.

Then, as might be expected, I sense Eva's eyes boring into me. I drop the card into my trouser pocket and head towards them all. Brenda and Claire are deep in conversation, Mark's engrossed in his phone as usual, and Mum must have gone to the loo whilst I was talking. She's hardly uttered a word to me today – just a couple of barbed digs from a distance. No change there then. Anger rises and I push it down.

"Who was *she*?" Eva's mouth hardens some more, and I resist the urge to tell her how unattractive jealousy makes her look. In contrast to Suzannah Peterson, my wife is totally *not* my type. She's too thin for a start, especially since she's started teaching bloody kettlebell classes. I tried to break my usual mould when I settled for her nine years ago with her mousy hair, small tits and all. I'm not keen on the Freudian thing where we're attracted to women who look like our mothers. The idea makes me queasy. Hence, I went for the complete opposite. But we can't run away from our genetics, no matter how hard we try.

"Oh, she's from some private counselling service."

"Why would she think *you* need counselling? Surely she'd be asking Mark?"

"She meant any of us, but you know Eva, it's all been near the knuckle for me as well. All the finger pointing, I mean."

"Ingham's the guilty one. At least it's official now."

"Despite his deranged wife's best efforts." I slam myself into the seat beside Eva. "When I think what the two of them have put our family through over the years. He might be gone, but she'll be out soon enough..."

"Give over – you'll have calmed down by then."

"I wouldn't count on it."

"How she dared try to pin it all on you, I'll never know." Eva rests her hand on my arm. "I'm sorry if I was funny about that woman you were talking to."

"No worries."

"Maybe we can start getting our marriage back on track now all this is over."

I glance at her as we all get to our feet to leave, not sure whether she actually said those words or whether I imagined them.

"I've had enough of courtrooms to last me a lifetime." Mum chugs her wine. She's another person I'm not used to being around for any length of time – in fact, being in this close proximity with any of them is making me claustrophobic.

Even from the opposite side of the table, the wine reeks. I've never been able to stand the smell of any sort of alcohol. Especially after what happened twenty years ago. I've often tried to imagine the man my brother Dean would have become before Ingham and his intoxicated missus left him to die.

"At least they're both where they should be now," I say. "One rotting six feet under, the other in a prison cell."

Pat Ingham would be six feet under too if I'd had my way. Especially since she grassed on me. I'm sure I'll get my chance for retribution. Luckily, her squealing has fallen on deaf ears.

"I can't believe she only got three years for knocking Dean down." Claire tears open a bag of crisps and lays it in the middle of the table.

"Especially after lying for all these years." I help myself to a handful of Claire's crisps. I'd never do that. If I'd bought myself a bag, I'd be the one eating them.

"She should be dead in the ground alongside her husband." Mum pushes her greying fringe from her eyes as she looks from Claire to Mark. She never speaks or looks at me directly. Her grudge against me existed long before the accident. But that I emerged from being run over with just concussion, whilst Dean died almost instantly, was the final nail in the coffin, so to speak. And since then, her revulsion of me only seems to have increased. To use her words, *she knows who I really am.*

"It's a good job Ingham's in an unmarked grave." Mark fiddles with a beer mat. "After hearing all the hatred outside court..."

"I still can't get over the fact that you went to his funeral Mark." Claire drains her glass. "I needed that after the week we've had. I might have to get another."

"Closure." Mark looks thoughtful. "Anyway, it could hardly be described as a funeral. There were only the undertakers, me and Pat Ingham, and the coppers she was cuffed to. And a few ghouls who'd come for a nosy."

"Never mind courtrooms." Eva slides her purse from her bag. "I've had enough of funerals to last me a lifetime too - Lauren's, Chris Canvey's..."

"Can we not talk about Lauren's funeral please?"

Eva looks sheepish and I'm annoyed with my brother for shooting her down. Me and Eva might only go through the motions these days, but she's still my wife, and Mark should respect that. We're all wrestling with stuff in our own way. Only some need to talk about it more than others. Suzannah Peterson's contact card jabs into the top of my thigh and a wave of excitement shoots through me.

"At least that PC, what's his name, Chris, got commended for going in after Ingham," Mum says. "Richly deserved. It's a shame more police officers aren't made of the mettle he was."

It's another dig at me, I'm sure of it. "Fat lot of good when he's dead though."

Everyone looks at me, their expressions saying it all. "Sorry." I raise my palm. "It's true though, isn't it? According to Mark, DI Jones ordered Chris Canvey not to go in. He should've listened – they gave orders for a reason."

"It broke my heart to watch his poor wife going up to collect the medal." Eva's voice is an annoying whine at the side of me. We've totally allowed ourselves to settle into a life I'd never have chosen. Still, being a husband and father of one has been an excellent veneer and one that I must do further work on.

"Right, that's enough of all that." Brenda slams her glass down. "Let's change the subject now. Talk about something normal. I can't hear about any of it anymore."

2

DI JONES CLOSES the file and points the remote control at the screen facing us. "So Will, I'm pleased to inform you that this investigation is now concluded."

My head jerks up. "That's it? Really?" I expected nothing else, but to hear it said out loud sounds pretty good. When I consider how everything might have gone the other way.

"You're free to resume your normal duties."

"Straight away?"

"Your family's been through quite enough Will. I'm only sorry you've had to cope with the extra pressure of this investigation." He slides his chair back with a scrape. "I'm off to make a brew. Do you want one?"

"I most certainly do." I try to tone down the grin that has spread across my face. After all, they might have cleared me of any wrongdoing, but eight women still met their maker last winter, and five the winter before. It's hardly a grinning matter in front of a boss.

But I do feel lighter than I have in months. *The investigation is now concluded.* I'm bloody thankful for that. And more to the point, beyond thankful for my heavy sleeper of a wife who never knows whether or not I'm in bed once she's out for the count.

"No need to ask how your meeting went." Mark glances up from his screen as I tap on his door and poke my head into his office. "It's written all over you."

"It's done. Finally." I sink to the chair in the corner of his office and clasp my hands behind my head. "They've accepted that Ingham was solely responsible for all of them."

"We already knew that from the Inquest." Mark looks back at his computer. "It was hardly unexpected."

"Yeah, but to hear it, you know, officially."

"So, what did DI Jones say?"

"Just that all my alibis had checked out. I was either in bed, or on shift, as we knew all along." And the more I say this out loud, the more I convince myself as well.

"Patricia Ingham should have another charge added, I reckon. The whole thing will have cost the taxpayer a packet." Mark closes his eyes for a moment. He's certainly gained more wrinkles around them since Lauren died. "But I still wish we'd managed to pull her bastard of a husband out of that river alive. The moment they dredged him from the Alder... well that was it. He got the easy way out if you ask me."

"You and all the other families mate. But I don't think he'd have lasted long if he'd survived."

"If it hadn't been us dealing with him, he'd have certainly been finished off inside." Mark rubs at his temples. His hair has also receded. I reckon people would mistake him for the oldest out of the two of us these days. "A bent copper is one thing, but a bent copper who's killed eight women..."

"Not to mention five the year before." I let a long breath out. I'm still in shock that the whole thing is over, and normality, whatever that is going to look like, can resume. "Anyway, I reckon we should do something."

Mark frowns at me. That's all he does these days. "What do you mean, *do something*? About what?"

"To celebrate the fact that this shit is no longer hanging over me like some sort of noose. I can get back to work. Get back to living my life again."

"Lucky you." He's looking at me the way our mother usually does. Again. Like I'm an insect.

The lightness I was feeling becomes a shadow. "I'm only saying."

"Do I need to remind you of what I've been through? And what I'm still going through?"

"Do you not think it's time to get on with things?"

"Get on with what?" He slaps his palm onto the desk. "Bloody hell Will, you're as sensitive as a breeze block."

Everyone says that about me. Often, when I open my mouth in front of Eva at home, she looks at me as though I've just chucked a welly at a duck or something. "Life. Living again. Moping around every day isn't going to bring Lauren back, is it?"

It's true. I'm right. It's time for him to put it behind him. The inquest is over. "What *are* you going to do with all that compo anyway? It's a fair whack."

"I haven't given it a thought yet."

"Well I'd better let traffic know I'm back in business." I tug my phone from my pocket. "I still need a few extra quid for the holiday."

"You're not still on about going to Disneyworld after all that's happened, surely?" He shakes his head. "Does Eva still want to go?"

"Why wouldn't she?" Heidi's face swims into my mind. "I've promised both Heidi and Alysha. Heidi only ever mentions it, like... every day."

Mark's face falls even further. "I don't think I'm ready to let Alysha go, to be honest. Not to Florida. It's too far away."

"You could always come with us. Especially now you've got all that money. Come on, live a little."

"*Live a little!* My daughter's having to grow up without her mother. *All that money,* as you put it, is for her future."

"Ah, you'll meet someone else – of course you will. Alysha won't grow up without a mother. You'll pull someone again in no time."

Mark's frown deepens. "I don't want to meet anyone else."

"I really reckon you should come away with us." I don't say that another adult would keep Eva entertained as well. Two weeks in each other's company, even with Heidi and Alysha around is going to test us, especially after the way things have been.

"Florida's the last place I want to be," Mark says. "I've only just got through what should have been our wedding day."

I thought my brother was going to combust with misery that day. I got away after half an hour – but at least I showed my face. Eva had insisted on us visiting. In the end, we left Heidi behind to keep Alysha company. Mum had been there, and I hadn't wanted to be in her company for long.

DI Jones appears in the doorway, holding two mugs on either side of his pot-belly. "I saw you come in here, so I made you one as well Mark."

"Cheers Sir." Mark stands and takes a mug from him. "I'm honoured. Tea made by the boss. At least we can get back to day-to-day policing. It'll make a nice change to deal with a drugs raid or armed robbery."

"Yeah. The media frenzy should die down soon enough."

"I just don't know how long it'll take me to feel like a day-to-day person again." The chair creaks as Mark sinks back into it.

"Maybe you should get yourself onto the waiting list for

counselling with Police Care." DI Jones looks at him. "It can't do any harm, can it?"

"My sister's having counselling, but it doesn't seem to be doing much good. She struggles for a day or two after every appointment." Mark sips his tea.

"She's bound to." DI Jones sits in the chair facing me. "Claire had one of the closest calls I've seen in all my years of policing. How she managed to survive Ingham attacking her like that..."

I should mention The Alder Centre at this point. No waiting list there. And Mark's got the means now. But having checked Suzannah's credentials on their *who's who* webpage, I'd quite like to keep her all to myself. Especially with Mark being technically single now.

~

"How did your meeting go?" Eva is simultaneously stirring two pans as I stride into the kitchen. She's not even changed after the gym class she teaches. The curve of her arse in her gym pants should stir me, but it doesn't these days. I don't think it ever did – and it's not that I'm incapable of being stirred in certain situations.

"They've dropped all allegations – as I expected. I can go back on shift at last."

"See, what did I tell you? It was always going to turn out OK." She drops a lid onto each of the pans and turns to face me, smiling for a change. "But I hope you won't return to all the overtime you were doing before. Heidi misses you."

I note she only mentions Heidi. Eva's a decent woman, mostly. But now the investigation is completely over – I'm totally, well, *bored*. I'll get the holiday booked. It's time I had a go at being husband and dad. Whole-heartedly. Not that I really have to try at being dad. Heidi's the glue that holds me and Eva together. She's also the reason I occasionally regret who I am and wish things were different. But as I keep reminding myself, what's done is done.

No way would I stand for some other man hanging around my daughter, playing *daddy* to her, leaving me as the weekend dad. No chance. Heidi's mine. And so is Eva, really. When I want her, that is.

"I'm sick of telling you about your drinking. When are you going to listen?" I point at the glass at the side of Eva's plate.

"Will – come on. If I want a drink with my meal, I don't need your permission. I am an adult, you know" She takes a loud slurp, leaving a red wine moustache, which turns my stomach as much as the all-too-familiar vinegary stink of the wine.

I push my plate away as my anger rises and images of DCI Ingham fill my mind. He detested drinkers too after the accident that took my brother. Even then Pat Ingham was unable to stop drinking. She made him how he was and indirectly made me how I am. And Eva is showing signs of going the same way. I sometimes wonder if this is my fate. That I've ended up with someone who won't listen and thinks it's acceptable to drink, despite what I tell her to do.

"Are you alright Dad?" Even at eight, Heidi knows the signs. Guilt twists in my chest. She's the one thing in my life I'm truly proud of. She's unspoilt, untainted by life. And I truly want to be the father she deserves.

"Yeah. Just not hungry right now." I rest my hand on her forearm. She's about the only person that I can show any affection towards. At least with her, and perhaps with my niece, Alysha, I know they're not going to turn anything back on me like most females. Nor are they going to judge me. Unless they take after their mothers when they get older. Claire's certainly taken after our dearest mother – it's no wonder she's still single.

"I'm off to get my work gear ready for tomorrow. Just stick my dinner in the microwave, will you? I might have it later."

"Yes Sir." Eva pulls a face as though she'd empty the plate over my head if it wasn't for our impressionable daughter, watching our every move, as always. When Alysha's here, which she has been a lot this year, the two girls occupy and distract each other, but I'm aware of the effect we risk having on Heidi when she's on her own with us. I blame Eva for this. If only she'd listen.

I'm doing my best job as a father, which is more than could be said for my own parents. They were around, yes, although my dad worked long hours literally up to the day he died. To escape my mother, no doubt. They put a roof over my head, clothes on my back and food on the plate, but that was it. They only did what they were legally bound to do. With me anyway – the others got more than I did. I was the darkest of sheep to infiltrate any family. It's no wonder I grew up hating myself. And women.

3

I DROP my pocketbook onto the desk, which is the tidiest I've ever seen it. "I can't tell you how good it is to be back."

Sergeant Donaldson who's recently moved over to traffic peers at me over the top of his computer screen. "How's the family? And Mark?" He's avoiding eye contact and randomly moving things around on his desk. What is it with people when they're around me?

"I've come to work to get away from all that." I fire my PC up. Why does everyone still want to go on about it all? "Right, I might have missed flying up the M62 at a hundred and fifty, but I haven't missed the form filling."

He laughs, but it's forced. He probably reckons there's no smoke without fire after the recent investigations. Yes, I've been cleared, but I don't think anyone's treating me the same as before. I could tell by the lukewarm greetings I got as I entered the office.

It's like being the unpopular lad at school, not that I ever knew that. I was always bigger than everyone else. Most of the lasses fancied me as I had the edge. Most of them reckoned they could tame me. The other lads were either scared of me, jealous of me or picked fights with me, even from the years above. There certainly was no in-between.

I blame my *dear* mother for the fact that I've become so indifferent to others – and I've accepted that. But she'll never apologise for what she's done to me. Things have definitely got worse since my twenties, when *everyone* I come across seems to adopt a less than favourable way of seeing me. Particularly women.

Which is another reason why it felt good to be singled out by Suzannah Peterson last week. I lift the flap of the leather wallet Claire bought me for my last birthday, and check the contact card is still nestled amongst everything else. Something about the woman got me going, though it keeps bugging me where I've seen her before. I might wait until we get back off holiday – and then...

When I arrive home, I poke my head around the lounge door. Heidi's knelt in front of the coffee table drawing. She briefly looks up but continues what she's doing, evidently engrossed. I chuckle to myself at the tongue that curls up towards her nose, as it always does when she's intently focused on something. I was exactly the same as a kid, but Mum never affectionately chuckled at me and sat beside me and ruffled my hair as I do now with my daughter. It pleases me that she takes after me rather than her mother. Right down to our shared eye colour.

"So, what are you drawing?" I glance down at the page. She's good at art – takes after me with that as well.

"It's my homework." She slides the paper towards me. "I've got to draw a picture to go with my princess story. So I'm being an illustrator."

"How would you like to see a princess for real?" My chest

swells. Not every dad would do this for his daughter. "Along with a certain mouse and a particular duck?"

I'm warmed from the inside out as her concentration face becomes one of total excitement. "Do you mean...?"

I nod and open up the email from the tour operator. Confirmation of flights, park entry and the hotel. Being only eight, she takes a few minutes to sound out some of the words on the screen. But Heidi's a clever kid – obviously she doesn't get that from her mum either. "I thought you'd forgotten about it Dad!"

"As if I would. I don't make promises like that, then take them away."

"When are we going?" A smile spreads across her face. "I hope it's soon."

"A week on Saturday."

With a squeal, she leaps up and darts towards the door. "Mum! Guess what? We're going to Disneyworld!"

Instantaneously, the top stair creaks. Through the lounge door, I watch her descend them, a basket of laundry balanced on one hip. She's in her bloody sports clothes again. I know she teaches most days, but she could at least make the effort to get changed and try to look half decent for once. Maybe she will when I take her on holiday.

"What?" I'd be lying if I said I wasn't at least a bit pleased to detect a hint of a smile as she looks at Heidi. "Yeah, great, but you might have checked with me first?"

"I thought you'd be pleased." *Ungrateful cow.*

"I might not be able to get my classes covered at the gym. When have you booked it for?"

"Next Saturday Mum. I can't wait!"

"Next Saturday?" Eva's face drops. "But that's not going to give the gym much notice."

"Sod the gym. This is the trip of a lifetime, isn't it Heidi?"

"Can Alysha come too Dad?" She bounds back towards me. "Please say she can."

"I've booked her a ticket too, don't worry."

"Really?" Eva steps from the doorway and places the basket of washing on the sideboard as she looks at me. "Have you cleared that with Mark? I got the impression he wasn't keen on her going."

"Leave my brother to me." I switch my attention from her face back to Heidi's. "Don't worry Heidi, she'll be going."

"I guess Alysha needs a trip more than anyone, after the time she's had lately."

"I mentioned to Mark that he could probably use a break too, but he was having none of it."

"Perhaps we should ask your mum to come if Mark doesn't want to." Eva perches on the edge of the sofa and looks at me. "It might mend some fences."

"No thank you." I throw myself into the armchair and scowl at her. Why does she have to spoil everything with her stupid ideas?

"Heidi." Eva tilts her head towards the lounge door. "Maybe you could start choosing what clothes you'd like to put in your suitcase for next week."

Heidi rushes from the room, clearly in agreement with that suggestion.

"Why the hell would I invite my mother on our family holiday Eva?" I can't understand why she's even suggested it. "Haven't you noticed what a bitch she is around me?"

"You're just as bad towards her." Eva's voice is uncertain. She doesn't normally challenge me, but since Lauren's death and Claire's attack, she's developed a different air about her, like something's been awakened. And I don't like it.

"My mother should have stayed in the Midlands. Things were much better when we only had to suffer her company three times a year."

"Going away might have been a good chance for the two of you to spend some time together." Eva forever tries to be the voice of reason. "Without Mark and Claire around, I mean. She'd *have* to talk to you then. At least give it some thought Will."

"No chance. She only has anything to do with me because of Heidi."

Eva's eyes narrow. "Actually, I get on *reasonably* OK with her."

"That's because you don't know her like I do. How cold she is. How she's always favoured the others over me." Something inside me drops and the familiar darkness spreads through me. "How she treated me after Dean died. Great - thanks Eva. I was in a good mood after booking this holiday and seeing Heidi so excited. You always have to spoil things."

"I was just thinking – you know – after all this family's been through – well she's moved up here, hasn't she?" Eva gets up and stands in front of me. "That must count for something."

"She's moved up here because she's worried about Brenda being more of a mother to Mark and Claire than she is, after what's happened." I stare at the TV in the corner still blaring away with some crappy cartoon.

"Oh Will, that's not true."

"And more of a grandma to Alysha. They're all Mum's possessions, not *Brenda's*. That's why my mother's here. Open your eyes and turn that thing off, will you?"

She points the remote at the TV. "I don't agree with you." She pauses, as though deliberating over what she's about to say. "Look, don't take this the wrong way Will..."

"What?" I fold my arms.

She looks at the window, then back at me. "I've been mulling this over more and more..."

"What?"

"When we get back off holiday, you need to speak to

someone. All this jealousy over your siblings. It's doing you no favours – the whole thing is eating you alive."

"I'm not jealous of anyone." The barriers go up. Who's Eva to sit in judgement of me? "So get your facts right before you start."

"All this hatred towards your mother." She sits back beside me again. I wish she'd piss off and leave me alone. "Things have affected you more than you realise. It's in how you're acting all the time. You're not so bad with Heidi, but with me..."

"Here we bloody go." I work overtime to book a family holiday to Disneyworld, and this is what I get.

"You've said yourself that counselling's on offer through work if you want it."

"It's a load of crap through work. Anyway, I've heard that they blab to our superiors whatever we tell them."

"Don't be daft. They're not allowed to do that."

"I don't need no shrink. Right?" I've raised my voice, but I don't care. If I do decide to go to the Alder Centre, I don't know yet if I'll even tell Eva.

She visibly crumples in front of me. This used to get to me for the first couple of years of our relationship, but now it's as though I've lost all feeling. And all sense of conscience. The only person I could ever fear losing is Heidi. I also quite like being Uncle Will to Alysha. Out of anyone I've ever had in my life, only these two girls have meant anything to me since Dean. And even when they're older and doing their own thing, I'll do whatever I can to protect them from turning into some of the women I've come across. *Anything.* At least now I've been cleared, I can guarantee that I'll still be part of their everyday lives. It's been looking shaky lately. I was convinced the investigation against me would throw something up.

Eva shuffles towards the lounge door. The kick ass in her only lasts so long before I kick it out of her. I can say anything I want, and eventually she'll accept my way of thinking. That's not good for any woman. It's a sure-fire way for them to lose respect in my book. To be fair, she lost mine a while back. I'm really hoping this holiday will be a fixer for us. With her and Heidi beside me, I can forge my way to a more normal life. Without them, who knows?

4

ALYSHA'S FACE presses against the glass of their lounge window as I pull up alongside the gate. She leaps up as I wave at her. Heidi bolts from the passenger seat down the drive to be met by Alysha at the door. The cousins, both dressed head to foot in pink, jump up and down together whilst hugging on the porch.

I've started to consider since the investigation was dropped whether I should persuade Eva to get pregnant again – with a son this time. Someone who'll genuinely look up to me and carry the Potts name on. My dad would be pleased about that if he were still alive. It might have been one of the few things I could have done that would impress him. Until now, I've dismissed the idea – apparently sons are closer to their mothers in the normal scheme of things, although in my case, I got on a lot better with my dad – not that my relationship with my mum took much beating. Usually, it's dads and daughters – and nieces now, as Mark's not been up to much as a dad this year. He's spent most of the time palming Alysha off to either us or to

Brenda. And after all that, he's got the nerve to bellyache about us taking her to Florida.

Mum sidles up behind the kids in the hallway, pushing all my nerves to their edges before she even opens her thinning lips to speak. "Hello Mum." I offer a curt nod. She looks to be shrinking as she ages, so her still-enormous boobs and wide hips make her appear overweight. *Is it weird to notice things like that about your mother?* Anyway, I'm glad I got my height from my dad – Mark did too, whereas Claire took after Mum with her shortness and size three feet.

"I thought Eva would collect Alysha." Mum looks straight through me, like always.

"No. Where's Mark?" I'm not rising to her bait. Not this time.

She jerks her head backwards. "In the kitchen. Why? You're not stopping, are you? Haven't you got a plane to catch?" Her voice is gravelly even though she stopped smoking years ago.

"We've got bags of time. I'll just say hello. Mind out, will you?" I step past her into the hallway, proud of myself for not telling her to piss off.

Claire pokes her head from the lounge. "How are you doing? Those two are about to combust. Alysha's been doing my head in." She laughs.

She practically lives here now, my sister. I resist the urge to say it's about time she got on with her own life, instead of revolving it around Mark and Alysha. And Mum now. Claire claims not to feel safe at home after what happened, but I think it's just an excuse.

Mark's slamming things into the dishwasher as I walk in. He doesn't look at me either. Pathetic so-called family. Perhaps if things had been normal, and they'd at least *acted* as if they wanted me around, I wouldn't have done what I've done.

"What the hell's up with you?" I stride up behind him.

"Ah, you know." He carries on stacking the dishwasher

without looking at me. "Just a bit stressed about Alysha going away, that's all."

"What for? You've got two weeks of freedom. What are you going to do with yourself?"

Mark swings around to face me now. "In case you hadn't noticed Will..."

What I do notice is that he badly needs a haircut, and he plainly hasn't shaved for days again. He needs to sort himself out.

"Noticed what?"

"Look, you might think I'm being daft, but it's a big deal for me, this."

"What's a big deal?"

He sighs from his guts. "It's me and Lauren who should have been taking our daughter on her first plane journey. Not you and Eva."

Oh hell, he's going to start up about their bloody Maldives wedding again. Deflection needed. Mark takes every opportunity to wallow. At first, I cut him some slack. Now it does my head in.

"So what are you going to get up to whilst she's gone?" As Mum appears in the kitchen doorway, I repeat my earlier question to fill the silence.

"Get up to?" Her laugh reminds me of childhood. I always feel like a kid again around her. Inadequate. And on the outside. "That's a strange question to ask a newly widowed man."

"At least he's got you to take care of him." One point to me for civility.

She doesn't reply. Neither does Mark. I must have done something pretty terrible in a past life to have been born into this family. Now that life is returning to some kind of normal, their hostility towards me has intensified. Mark's certainly got worse since Lauren died, and I don't think that being in such close proximity to our mother is having a positive effect on him. She needs to crawl back under her rock. In other words, bugger back off to Derbyshire. Normally, I can cope with all this, but lately, it threatens to overwhelm me. I ask myself repeatedly – why this family? Why me?

"Anyway. I'd best be off. It's gone quiet out there, so no doubt those two are waiting in the car for me." At least, I've tried to make conversation with Mark.

"Keep in touch, won't you Will? Every day." Mark pushes the dishwasher door closed. "Text me when you land safely, and don't let Alysha out of your sight, do you hear me?"

"I know how to keep kids safe, believe it or not. We've got Heidi to eight years of age, unscathed."

"I'm sorry. It's just..."

"No worries." Not wanting to hear his explanation, I march past Mum without looking at her, and from the kitchen. I curl my head around the lounge door, where Claire is on the phone. From her tone of voice, she's obviously talking to a man. Someone should tell her that's she's making a show of herself.

She puts her hand over the mouthpiece. "The girls are in the car. I've put Alysha's case in the boot."

"Cheers. I'm off. Before I say something to mother dearest I might regret."

"Have a fab time." I'm aware that she doesn't join forces with me over the *mother dearest* reference, even though she's not as far up Mum's arse as Mark is right now. He makes me sick sometimes. Mr Perfect. Golden boy at work and now in possession of four hundred grand which has just landed in his lap. And he's not even happy about that. Nor has he even offered anything towards the cost of the trip to cover Alysha. I hope he's put some spending money in her bag. He's becoming as tight with his money as Mum.

· · ·

"Are you ready to go Eva?" I call into the quiet of our hallway, welcoming the smell of home after being in Mark's house. Before I went there, I was all buoyed up, anticipating our fortnight away. Now I'm as deflated as an old football. That's what they do to me – that's what they've always done to me.

"Yep, just help me with these cases, will you?" Eva dumps one at my feet.

I grab the hand luggage bag and the handle of the larger case, hoping I've paid for enough baggage allowance.

"Cheer up Will." She peers at me. "You've saved for this holiday for ages, yet you've got a face like a smacked arse. What's up now?"

I wait for her to wheel our third case through the door, then lock it behind her. Normally I'd be saying something sarky about the amount she's packed, but I can't be arsed. "Mark was being a dick... and as for my mother. Honestly, I wish she'd piss off back to where she came from."

"I'll drive." Eva plucks the keys from my hand. "You're too wired. Especially with the girls in the car."

I let her take them. I could give her the spiel about me being a traffic cop and being a far better driver, wired or not, than she could ever be, but what's the point? Besides, I feel crappy enough.

"Calm it you two." Even with seatbelts on, Heidi and Alysha are like jumping jacks on the back seat. "We've got a long drive to the airport."

I rest back in the passenger seat; the tension seeping from me as we leave Alderton behind us. When we get back, I'm going to distance myself from my family. Mum, Mark and Claire, that is. And Brenda. Not that she's particularly family. I guess I'll always have a certain amount of involvement with her though. She is Alysha's grandmother. And Alysha and Heidi are mostly inseparable. Another reason for Heidi to have a younger sibling. Well, a younger brother. I really wouldn't want another girl. I must do some research into how to guarantee that.

"You seem to have settled down." Eva gives me a knowing smile. "I reckon this break is exactly what we all need."

"Me too." I brush my hand over hers as she changes gear. It's most un-Will-like behaviour, and a flush rises up Eva's neck. It's amazing how my crumbs of affection make such a difference to her. If I'm going to get back any semblance of our former life, a facade for the outside world, I really need to make more effort with her. Yes, I might have got her more or less under control at the moment, but she may well rediscover that kick-ass that's still lurking in there somewhere. I keep seeing flashes of it. I'm going to broach the subject of a second child. Another baby would certainly guarantee a stay of execution for me.

"I'm certainly outnumbered on this holiday, aren't I?" I crane my neck to glance at the girls, who are engrossed in some electronic game or other. Full marks to Eva for that one.

"You'll need to be on your best behaviour then." Eva laughs. It's an alien sound these days. There hasn't been a lot of laughter lately.

"Perhaps when we get back, we could focus on having another male about the place." The more I consider it, the more the idea appeals to me. My birth family might be a pile of shit, but I can make my own family work... surely?

She's silent for a moment, which unnerves me. "You mean...?" Her neck's gone red and blotchy. It always does when faced with anything out of the ordinary. As we wait at the lights, she turns to me, and I notice she's wearing make-up. Yes – I really can make a go of things with her, so long as she puts in the effort as well.

"Well, I'm not on about getting a dog. Although that would be pretty cool."

"Dad. Dad. Can we get a dog? Please? *Please?*" That got Heidi's attention.

"Yes. Uncle Will. Please get a dog. It can be mine too when I come to stay." Alysha's voice turns from excitement to sadness. "I'd love a dog. It would keep us safe from bad men like the one that got my mum."

Eva's face clouds over, presumably at what Alysha's said, so I cup my hand fully over hers. "We'll see." We linger over the gearstick as she sets off again. I can do this. William Potts. Husband. Father. Uncle. Copper. Two kids and a dog. Family man. Pillar of the community. I rub Eva's hand just before she lets go of the gearstick.

"You're being very attentive all of a sudden." She frowns. I can see, even from the side, how etched in her head those lines are these days. "What on earth's got into you today?" She eases out onto the motorway. We're definitely on our way now.

"Now everything can be put behind us, I'm working out what really matters." I'm also wondering if we should move completely from Alderton. I feel so much better to be travelling away from there – but I don't say this to her. One thing at a time.

She blinks repeatedly, probably blinking back tears if I know her correctly. Maybe tears of relief. I've hardly been husband of the year lately. And that's an understatement. "You OK love?"

"Just relieved to have a bit of you back at last. You've been on another planet for months."

I smile. I won her over easily when we first got together. If I can just keep a tight rein on myself, we can somehow get back to that again. And at least if I get her up the duff, she'll be forced to take a break from the poxy fitness classes and the crappy lycra she wears. She doesn't need to work. I put the hours in for us all. She's more use taking care of the house and the kids. I can't believe I've just used the word *kids*. Looks like it's game on.

"Have I been on an aeroplane before Dad?"

"Yes. You probably can't remember it, though. You were only three."

The girls can't keep still as we stand in line at the foot of the steps up to the door of the plane. Their pink coats are making my eyes ache.

"I'm scared." Alysha stares up at the plane. At a glance, she and Heidi look more like sisters than cousins.

Eva reaches forward for Alysha's hand. "Don't be. Just be excited. Aeroplanes are really safe."

"Are they, Uncle Will?"

Mark's face flashes into my mind, and I remember what he said just before we left. For a moment, I agree, it's a shame that he's not accompanying Alysha for her first ever flight. *What has got into me?* Empathy for someone else, especially my brother, isn't exactly normal. "Yes, it is. Flying is actually the safest way to travel."

"But how does the aeroplane stay in the sky when it's so heavy?"

I remember asking exactly the same question of my dad at a similar age in one of the rare moments that I was stood at his side, queuing, like we are now. He'd given me the same knowledgeable reply that I now give Alysha, as Heidi listens in.

"Four forces keep an aeroplane in the sky," I begin. "The forces are lift, drag, gravity and thrust."

Eva rolls her eyes.

I'm glad my dad wasn't as distant as my mum always has been. He kept me at arm's length, but I never felt like an outcast with him. What could have been so bad about me as a kid for my mum's rejection? It plagues me at times, more so since she's moved up here. When I didn't have to see anything of her, I was able to bury it. Pretend it didn't exist. But now she's in my face, constantly.

I suppose I didn't help matters when I was young. I'd do anything possible to get her to pay attention to me. Being bollocked was better than being ignored. I'd be rotten to Mark and Claire, or I'd pinch something. Once I swiped a ten-pound note from Mum's purse, bought some sweets and shoved the change in our dustbin. She slippered me across the arse for that, but at least she acknowledged that I existed.

Maybe Eva's right. Perhaps I do need to talk to someone. It won't be Police Care though – I'm not wasting my time with that. It's a shame Miss Suzannah Peterson isn't one of the therapists at the Alder Centre, but she's the practice manager, so I'd see her in passing every time. I've checked her out on Facebook and she's a 'Miss' alright. She could be a tough nut to crack, but I do like a challenge. I catch myself. I'm supposed to be morphing into husband of the year and here I am, fantasising over some green-eyed brunette.

Alysha grips my arm as the aeroplane shoots into the air. "We're flying," she gasps, and several other passengers smile at her.

"So we've got this aeroplane, then another aeroplane and then we'll be in Disneyworld."

The girls cheer.

Eva ordering wine from the hostess trolley doesn't annoy me as much as it normally would. Although, alcohol abstinence would be another happy by-product of her falling pregnant. We'll start trying whilst we're away. I'll flush the pills away myself if I have to.

I never set out to be a father to two-point-four children and all that, but I've come dangerously close to finding myself with an alternative way of spending the rest of my life. And it would have been the rest of my life. There's no doubt about that. There were so many variables that might not have gone my way. Eva might not have corroborated my whereabouts. DI Jones could have been more thorough getting hold of the information about the timings and lengths of my night shift breaks. Ingham or Chris Canvey might have survived after I launched them into the Alder. One of the women could have survived and testified against me. And a myriad of other possibilities. I rarely let myself consider them, but I've been forced to lately.

Something Mark said a couple of weeks ago has lodged in my brain like a splinter. About a copper not surviving inside. He's bang right. I might handle myself in the normal walk of life. However, I've heard about life on the vulnerable prisoners' wing, which is where I'd have been locked up for certain – amongst the wife batterers and the nonces. As well as the risk to your safety, things end up in your food. Additives of the worst kind. I think I'd have chucked myself in the Alder, as opposed to seeing my days out like that. Which is why I've got to change. I've had a very close call.

I scrunch my eyes against these thoughts. I am where I am. Here, amongst my *true* family. I am the new Will; I am going to change and put the man I used to be firmly in the past. Miraculously, I've been cleared of all wrongdoing and now it's time to be someone completely different. I'm certain I can do it.

5

ALYSHA DIGS her fingers into my arm, like she did when we were taking off and landing a fortnight ago. "Uncle Will. I'm scared again."

They say time speeds up as you get older, and I can hardly believe we've already landed back at this drizzly English airport. That was the fastest two weeks I've ever known.

"There. One small bump, like I said. We're down now."

"You can tell everyone at school that you've been on four aeroplanes." Eva leans over me and ruffles the top of Alysha's hair.

"I'm going to write all about it in my journal."

"You like writing, don't you Alysha?" Eva smiles at her. "What a talented pair of cousins you are. You with your writing, and Heidi with her drawing."

"When I get big, I'm going to write stories for the news like my mum did to catch bad people."

"Oh – right."

I shiver as I gaze out at the grey sky. It's exactly the same weather as when we left. We're still dressed for the Florida sunshine rather than for the English murk of November. I'd like to say it's good to be home, but it's not at all. I've escaped myself for the last couple of weeks and I've been glad to. But now I'm back. I only hope I can keep this new Will up front and central. My alter ego has got to stay well under wraps. He's done enough damage over the last couple of years. And he could do me a lot more. As it is, I'm shocked I ever got into double figures. Anyway, I've definitely decided I'm going to get some help to be rid of him once and for all. I can't ever get found out. I can change – I know I can.

"We might as well wait here for a few minutes." Eva drains her wine. It's her third on the journey. "We're only going to be standing and waiting around whilst everyone else gets off."

"Good idea – I can't stand up straight, anyway. They build these planes for midgets." I make a mental note to check the house when we get back – any wine I come across is going down the sink. If she's fallen pregnant already, I hope that the wine doesn't hurt our little fella.

I tug my phone out. Apart from keeping Mark updated about Alysha, I've barely touched it in two weeks. I've been too busy with the girls. Eva and I have got on great too – it has been almost like it used to be. I persuaded her to bin the pills and we've got down to it as much as we used to when we were trying for Heidi. Somehow, I like Eva more when we're away from the usual routine. Maybe we should get away permanently. It's not as though my family would miss me. A sudden heaviness drags at my stomach at the reminder of my family. Right on cue, my phone beeps. It's Mark.

I've been tracking the plane. Make sure you bring Alysha straight home.

No plans to do much else. We're all knackered.

You and me both.

How come?

> Been doing overtime. Another two women drowned in the Alder on Saturday night.

Two women?

> Yup.

I'll ring you when we get through passport control.

> Why?

I want to find out more about it.

> Google it. It's been in the news. Anyway, gotta go. I need to make a phone call.

Shit. I Google *women, River Alder, Saturday,* and get a stream of results, mostly from last winter. Yeah, yeah, yeah – I know first-hand about all of those. I scroll back up again and hit the first link. Crap reporting from the Press Association. It literally gives what Mark's just told me and that's it. I press call on my phone. Straight to Mark's voicemail. I need to speak to him. Bloody hell.

"Come on. Everyone's nearly off now." Eva throws her wine cup into a bin liner held out by a passing air steward. I recoil as a couple of wine droplets land on me in its transit. I leap to my feet, nearly hitting my head, then wrench our cases from the overhead locker. I thrust one at Eva.

"What's up with your face? Who were you texting before?"

"Only Mark." Don't say she's getting possessive again already. We've only just landed.

"What on earth has he said to you? You've got a face like you've won the lottery and lost your ticket."

"Nowt much. He wants us to get Alysha straight back to him."

"And that's put you in a mood? He'll have missed her, won't he? Of course he wants you to get her straight home."

"Nah. I'm OK. It's just shit to be back. Really shit."

"Aww, Dad said a naughty word." Alysha and Heidi giggle as they trail behind us towards the exit of the plane.

I'll wait until I've found out the full details about the drownings before I say anything to Eva. She'll only go on and on about it all the way back, making assumptions and wittering on about Lauren. Since she pretended to be Lauren in the reconstruction after her death, Eva acts as though she knows it all.

Mark said it was Saturday when it happened. That's really thrown me. Saturday nights are the norm with the previous women, but this time, I was four thousand miles away.

"Can *you* drive back to Alderton?" Eva gives me a pleading look – the one that she thinks wins me over. Except it doesn't. Not anymore.

Talk about being back to reality. I've had two weeks of genuinely enjoying my wife's company and being on the job with her, morning, noon and night, but now we're home, all my irritations have risen to the surface and she's back to her usual mousy self.

"I'd rather you drove, Eva. I've got a couple of calls to make."

"To who? We've only just got back."

"It's work stuff."

"It can wait, surely. I'm too tired to drive."

"You've sat around on a plane for the last nine hours. How can you be tired?"

"I always find travelling tiring - plus I've probably got jetlag. Even the girls are flagging."

I glance around at them. They're certainly not bouncing around like they were on the outbound journey.

"Can you at least drive some of the way Eva?"

"Sure, if you'd like to risk me crashing into the central reservation. When I say I'm too tired to drive – it's because I'm too tired to drive. I'm not making it up, you know."

Eva's trying to find her defiant side again. I'm in two minds whether I want to encourage it or crush it.

"Alright. Alright. My work stuff will have to wait, won't it?"

"I agree. You're not even back at the station for a couple of days."

"Daddy!" Alysha flings herself at Mark as he opens the door. "I've missed you!"

I'm jealous of her enthusiasm towards him. I can't help it. First, she's been in *my* care for the last two weeks. Second, I never get any sort of welcome from my daughter to that extent. But I force the feeling down and glance back towards the car where Eva is fast asleep with her gob wide open. Very attractive. That's what wine does to her. The journey from the airport has passed reasonably quickly, although with all three of them asleep, my thoughts have been louder than normal. Sometimes I fear they're going to drive me insane.

"Are you not inviting us in?" I step forwards and Mark straightens up, blocking my entry. Alysha's clinging to his side as though she can't bear to let him go. Pissed off doesn't come anywhere close to how I feel right now. I take his daughter away and he can't even ask me in for five minutes.

"To be honest Will." Mark rests his hand on Alysha's shoulder. "I'd rather spend some time alone with this one. I'm sure you've lots to tell me, haven't you?" He moves his hand to ruffle her hair.

"Scary granny's not here, is she Dad?" Alysha's voice a whisper as she glances behind them.

"Don't call her that," he replies. "She'll be very upset if she ever hears you. And no, we've got the house to ourselves for a change."

Despite my irritation, the fact that Alysha refers to my mother as *scary granny* amuses me. They say kids have an innate sense of who a person really is.

I can't leave without finding out what he knows. "Before I get off, what about those women?" I shouldn't be asking in front of Alysha, but I have to know.

"What women?"

"*What women?* The ones who drowned on Saturday?"

"Oh, that." He peels Alysha from his side. "Take your bag in. I'll be with you in a minute." He looks back at me. "To be honest, them being fished out of the river has brought everything back." A shadow crosses his face. "I could've done without it happening – I should have listened to DI Jones."

"Why, what did he say?"

"He thought it was too soon for me. That to get involved would be too raw. It's hit Claire and Brenda pretty hard too, even though they were accidents this time."

"How do you know that?"

"Lack of injury again. Water in the lungs, meaning they were still alive when they went in. And they've gone in drunk. Mind you, this is all what we said last time."

"What else do you know?"

"Nothing much. Anyway – how come you're so interested? You're in traffic. It's nothing for you to worry about."

"Of course I'm interested. Especially after all that's happened. Who were they, anyway?"

"Mother and daughter, apparently. I don't know much more than that. There's a load of flowers down there again. The only difference, it seems, is it happened further downriver than before."

"Whereabouts?"

"Do we have to talk about this?" He shuffles from one foot to the other, clearly wanting to get away from me. "I'll be turning it over all night if I let myself. I'd better get Alysha a drink anyway. Catch you later Will."

He shuts the door in my face. I raise my fist to thump on it. He hasn't even thanked me for taking Alysha on holiday. Then I remember, I'm the new Will. I lower my arm and return to the car.

Eva's straight on with unpacking and laundry the minute we get home. I pace the lounge, watch the local news again, then take out my phone to ring Claire. Mark will have told her what he knows, even if he won't tell me.

"So what happened on Saturday?" I don't even say hello as she answers. "In the Alder?"

"Oh that." Her voice dips in contrast to the cheerful hello she answered the phone with. At least she sounded relatively pleased to hear from me. "Yeah, Brenda's all over the place."

"Why? Lauren died in the stream on the cycle path, not in the Alder. Brenda's always so dramatic."

"They were all at the hands of the same maniac though, weren't they? And what happened to me was close enough to nearly raise the death toll even higher."

"Well, it didn't, did it?"

"To be honest, what's happened on Saturday has got to me as well."

"Yeah, well, there's nothing Jonathan Ingham can do to you now, is there?"

"Brenda's convinced the last two winters are happening all over again," Claire continues. "To be honest, that's what I thought to start with, but the police are adamant that they're accidents this time."

"What do you know about it? Mark was being really cagey before. He wouldn't tell me a thing."

"I've no idea why he'd be cagey. You're probably reading something from him that isn't there. To be fair, he's only told me a few bits and pieces. He's not on the case this time."

"Such as? What *bits and pieces*?"

"That the two women were related - mother and daughter, as far as I know. They'd spent all evening in the Yorkshire Arms with a group of women and were worse for wear when they left."

"What time was that?" *Worse for wear.* Clearly, they had it coming.

"Well, according to Mark, they weren't pulled out until Sunday morning. The DJ was on, so it would've been busy in the pub. And how would I know what time they left? Anyway Will, I don't really want to talk about all this – honestly, it's really hard for me."

"Have they released any photos of them yet?" The photos will tell me all I need to know. If someone's cloning my way of doing things, and they look similar to the ones before, there'll be hell to pay.

It's reassuring to talk to my sister. She's always had a knack for bringing me back to myself. It does my head in though, that she and Mark are like conjoined twins. She's supposed to be my sister too, and perhaps if she'd been warmer to me over the years... all I'm saying is that it's not solely my mother's fault that I have such a downer on women.

"Last question, I promise."

"Last question about what?"

"The deaths. Have they named the women?"

"No, not yet – their families have only just been told. I probably found out they were dead before the families did."

"How come you were told?" Why did we ever come home from Florida? It feels like two steps forward, five steps back. My thoughts are as dark as the night closing in outside this window.

"You're not letting this go, are you? Mark needed to spill to me when they were pulled out – he was in a right state."

"He always is." Irritation coils around me.

"Don't be so insensitive. It's only been a few months since Lauren was killed."

"Nine months," I say, probably too quickly. Like an alcoholic being able to state how many days they've been dry. I could number the weeks if someone asked me to. "It's plenty long enough for him to have come to terms with it all, and to have moved on."

"Oh, have a heart Will. Honestly!"

"Well, that's my opinion. Anyway, if you hear any more about it, let me know, won't you?"

"Right you are." Her voice rises as though she's puzzled at me asking her that. "Though you'll probably hear about things well before I do. I only find out what Mark tells me. They're treating the deaths as an accident anyway, so hopefully nothing to get stressed about."

"Yeah – catch you later then."

"Did you have a nice..."

I cut her off then search again for *River Alder, women, October.*

They've now been named. Rosalind and Eleanor Speight. Age forty-three and twenty, and yes, it's being described as a tragic accident whilst they were taking a shortcut along the river. They were said to be heading home after spending the

47

evening in the Yorkshire Arms. As DCI Ingham would have concurred, they were *asking for trouble.*

A search on Google tells me they're new to the area, but what snatches my breath away is their photos. It's the long, dark hair and green-eyed combo again. Not to mention the fact that it was a Saturday, well the early hours of Sunday, the same as before. Someone's taking the piss here. I scroll through some of the comments. Last winter's dead women and those of the year before are being dredged up and the comparisons are being drawn. And it would appear that I'm not the only one who's flagged up the similarity in appearances with the two who've just departed. Someone's out to clone me. I know they are.

Other than that, it's the usual outpouring of shite on social media. Do-gooders who never even knew them, and people who did know them, but can evidently only be arsed giving them the time of day, now they're dead.

But who am I to judge? I wasn't arsed whether Lauren was dead or alive most of the time – not after she knocked me back time and time again, believing my brother was a better bet than me. At the time, I was shocked by my reaction and behaviour. Blonde-haired, and blue eyed, Lauren was the polar opposite in every way to the women that usually get my attention.

I've often told myself that it was a case of *what goes around comes around,* when DCI Ingham finally got hold of her and finished her off, especially when she'd been reporting on us and our so-called police failings. She was never going to get away with it, and Lindy, her line manager. She's lucky to still be here.

But despite my anger, I still went to see Lauren at the funeral home. I've told no one that – not even Eva. It's the one time I could really look at her without her challenging me and I needed to see her one last time. I even laid a rose across her chest. It's the first time I've ever done anything like that, which proves I'm not all bad. And at least my conscience is clear in terms of *her* death - I can still meet Mark's eye. That matters to me even if I have spent most of my life envying him and his ease with people, whilst I'm unable to really get on with anyone.

Our mother thinks the sun shines out of his arse, and he and Claire have grown up close; people even used to think they were twins when we were kids. He also gets on with Eva better than I do. But now, more than anything, I envy his sense of right and wrong. Deep down, I'd love that moral compass inside me instead of the voices. If I'm totally honest, I'd do anything to go back in time to before two winters ago.

At least I finished both Ingham and Chris Canvey off - the two people who knew too much and could have ultimately caused me a lot of problems. Ingham deserved what he got. And what he did to Claire, once he'd finished with Lauren, stepped way beyond any sort of boundaries. Getting blood thirsty with my sister was the wrong move. As he found out in the end. And Canvey, well, he'd just been in the wrong place at the wrong time. Unfortunate.

6

MY COLLEAGUE TYLER pats me on the back as I hang my jacket up. "Welcome back Will. The word is that you're back in business." He's grown a beard whilst I've been away. It looks shit, so I don't comment.

"Sure am. Back to full duty again." I drop to my chair and fire my computer up. "Before I get back out there though, I'd better check what fun and games have been going on in my absence."

"The usual." He pulls a face. "Good holiday?"

"Yeah. Not bad, thanks. Over too quick, as they always are. Plenty of action with the missus though." I wink at him, expecting him to be impressed, but he doesn't appear to be. That's the trouble with the world nowadays – everyone has to adhere to this political correctness crap. No one can say what they want to anymore. "Right, let's have a gander at these e-mails." It's the usual twaddle. Staff meeting agenda, minutes, targets, someone doing a sponsored event, reported figures... then...

You are invited to a brief event to celebrate the commendation of

Sergeant Tyler Wilkes of the traffic division, who cornered a dangerous suspect after a major drugs raid earlier this year...

I look at Tyler over the top of my screen, my jaw tightening. "How come you're getting the glory for this? I drove that night. It was *my* driving that cornered that perpetrator. You were in the passenger side."

"In between buggering off when we were supposed to be acting on the intel being passed over." Tyler's red-faced as he defends himself, apparently uncomfortable. "It was me that kept my mind on the job."

"But I was the one in the driving seat when we ran him off the M62. I should get some recognition as well." This is the story of my pitiful life. Passed over all the time. It's as though there's someone, somewhere, poking pins into a replica of me. I've always suspected that there's more to my life than mere bad luck. Someone's out to get me.

According to Ingham, before he met his sticky end, I only ever got promoted to Sergeant because of the dirt I had on him and his wife for all those years. I'm so pissed off. I want another kid, and yet, no matter what I do, I can't climb the ranks in this shitty police force.

"Take it up with DI Mills." Tyler shrugs his shoulders. "And don't blame me for accepting it. If they want to commend me, I'm not going to argue, am I? Who would?"

"Didn't you tell them I was driving that night?" I stand and tower over his side of the desk.

"They'd have known you were driving."

I'm pleased to see he shrinks away from me.

"But you've only just been cleared, haven't you?" He lowers his voice. "Of whatever it is they've cleared you of. They couldn't have commended you for *anything* whilst all that was going on."

I resist the urge to tell him how crap his new beard looks, just for the hell of it, and instead glance over to where DI Mills is talking animatedly in her office to one of the other sergeants. She's always reminded me of my mother, which is intimidating in itself. I should go in there and have it out with her over this commendation. But in the state of mind I'm in, I'd end up losing it. It's bollocks. I graft my arse off and the thanks I get is having to watch my usually lily-livered colleague, who prefers to let me take the reins when it's high speed, take the credit for *my* work.

By lunchtime, I've caught up on everything I need to, so escape the station to clear the buzzing from my head. If I don't get out, I'm going to explode. My hands, balled into fists, swing at my side as I wrestle with the existence I've returned to. If there's one thing guaranteed to get me reacting, it's bastards who shove me out of the way. I've had it all my life. I was angry enough about the current River Alder situation, but this with Tyler has forced me into a mindset I thought I'd left behind.

No matter what I do, I'm always the person dumped to one side - a scenario that's shadowed me since childhood. Dean, Mark and Claire got all the praise, even when it was me who'd done good. I might as well have not existed.

I need something to stop my stomach churning. I curse as I join the sandwich shop queue, where there are only two people serving. If they go any slower, they'll grind to a stop. After five minutes, I yell to everyone in earshot, *this shop is a frigging joke. I won't be back in here.* As I stomp away to find somewhere else, I remember I'm in uniform. Shit. I can do without being reported right now. Not when I've only just got the investigation against me dropped. Really, I need to lie low.

The next shop's food isn't as good, and the lack of queue reflects that. Still, I need fuel to keep body and mind together today. As I pay for my sandwich, my gaze falls on The Alder Centre's card in my wallet. Realistically, I *could* probably do with talking to someone like Eva suggested. This anger needs releasing and my past needs dealing with, once and for all. Who knows what I'll be capable of again if I don't sort myself out?

"Suzannah Peterson."

"It's Will Potts here – you gave me your card..."

"I remember who you are." Her voice is as sharp as broken glass, which throws me off guard. She was friendly enough when we spoke outside the court that day. Sometimes though, when a woman fancies her chances with me, the more aloof she seems to be. I'm not scared of a challenge, and, as I've proven time and time again, I'm happy to lie in wait.

"I thought I'd take you up on your offer of an appointment to talk things through."

"Right you are." There's a shuffling of paper. "I'll just check for you. Can you come for an initial assessment on Thursday? One of the psychotherapists, Daniel Hamer, has had a cancellation."

Daniel Hamer. I was hoping for a woman, but I can't tell her that. I can't even explain why myself. I guess I find women easier to manipulate. Yes, I mostly despise the lot of them, but they can't see through me in the same way other men can.

"Hello?"

"Do *you* not do appointments – yourself, I mean?" I wouldn't mind being stuck with *her* for an hour in a confined space.

"No – I'm not a qualified therapist. I'm the practice manager, like I said. So... Thursday?"

"Yeah. I've got the day off."

"Are you back on active duty now?" Her voice still has its chilly edge, but curiosity has crept into it. I'm thrown off guard again at the directness of her question – and the fact that she

53

seems to know so much about me. How would she have found anything out about me having been reinstated to active duty? I decide to sidestep the question. "Yeah. I've just been on holiday. First official day back today."

"Lucky you."

I wait for her to ask me where I've been, but she doesn't. She's definitely playing it cool. Either that, or she doesn't want to acknowledge the fact that I've got a wife and kid. Some women prefer to shut that out when they're embarking on an affair.

"OK then. Thursday at three pm."

"That's fine."

I'm puzzled when I hang up, thinking she'd have sounded more pleased at the prospect of seeing me again. Perhaps she's got someone in the room with her. Or maybe it's just her telephone manner. People can be very different on the phone to how they are in person. Despite that, I find myself looking forward to the appointment. As women go, Suzannah Peterson definitely represents the term playing hard to get. But there's few women I fail with.

I glance through the windows of the Yorkshire Arms as I pass. Being a Monday lunchtime, it's nearly empty, apart from the alcoholics of the town. And they all appear to be men. Women are more covert about their drink addictions, but I can sniff them out a mile away. After what happened to my brother, I hate the lot of them. Alcoholics, I mean. But my hatred towards women in general seems to be escalating too. The older I get, the less respect I have for them. I'm only too aware that Heidi will grow and become a woman, which is another reason I have to deal with this. Plus, I absolutely can't spend my life in prison – I've got to change. And I do feel lighter now that I've made that first step to get some help.

I pause at the spot on the riverbank where the flowers have piled up. I've no idea why people waste their money. The council will shift and bin them in a matter of days. I can't help but study the cards though.

Beautiful Eleanor. Gone too soon.

Tributes to a lovely mum and daughter. Words can't describe how much we'll miss you.

To the best mother and sister in the world. How will I ever live without you?

RIP lovely ladies.

If they hadn't been arseholed, they wouldn't be where they are now. They've only got themselves to blame. But what I can't get to grips with is who might have jumped onto my turf whilst I wasn't around. I don't buy the accident theory – not after the last two years. Not with what I know.

I stare at the surface of the river, reflective of the heavy sky. I lower myself onto a bench, feeling heavy myself at first, but after a few moments, a familiar dark excitement starts twisting in my gut. I really, really don't want it to settle, but it's found me again.

At least I've got the therapy session booked, which might straighten my thinking out. It would be a shame to break all the reformed family man promises I've made to myself.

I should run from here, move away completely. Stop thinking about it, stop letting the urges control me, stop allowing the voices to order me around. All I know is that if it wasn't for whoever is behind this... I can't have someone else working on my patch. This needs to be put right. I pull my phone out to check the rota for this Saturday. As luck would have it, it's my weekend off. But I'll have to be more careful than I was before.

"Sarge. How are you doing?"

I look up to see PC Ben Roberts striding towards me. "Yeah, not so bad thanks."

With his wide smile and dimples, he looks too young to be a copper. "I'm on patrol – I just needed to take a leak and get warm for a minute. It's handy, having the pub over there."

"Do you know much about the investigation?" He probably won't be able to tell me a great deal. He's not long out of training – he came up with PC Chris Canvey and I remember him from the funeral. Roberts has a look of Canvey, apart from the bum fluff on his face.

"No – not really. It's looking like an accident though – but just a shit coincidence after what Ingham did, isn't it?"

"Where were they pulled out?"

He gestures downriver. "PC Ryder's patrolling that bit. He's really struggling though." Roberts tugs his jacket more tightly around himself and rubs his hands together.

"How come?"

"He was good mates with Chris Canvey - they spent a lot of last year on patrol here. I remember him moaning about getting the crap jobs as a new PC."

"We've all got to start somewhere, haven't we? No CCTV then?"

"I don't have a clue. But if they're saying accidental death, then they must've seen something on the cameras to prove that." He shrugs. "Even so, I'll be telling my girlfriend to stay well away from here when she goes out, for the time being."

"Yeah, I don't blame you mate. I'll be doing the same with my missus. Catch you later."

·   ·   ·

My thoughts are swirling as I head back to the office. At least I'm out on patrol this afternoon. Manning a speed trap will give me plenty of thinking time – though that's not necessarily a good thing. I could do with being busy and distracted. It's when I'm alone that the voices in my head shout louder.

I keep trying to reassure myself that my previous actions were nothing compared to Ingham's. His attacks at the stream were premeditated, brutal, and drawn out. His victims died in fear and in agony.

At least my way of ending life is swift, perhaps to the point of painless after that initial slap onto the surface of the freezing water. That's partly why I choose the winter months. Not only am I under the cover of darkness, but I'm aware that heart failure will be almost immediate when suddenly submerged in the night-time temperatures of the River Alder. It's only four degrees in the daytime. Plus, drink anaesthetises things as well. That's the only positive property it has.

And above anything else, I'm providing a valuable service to society – ridding the place of out-of-control drunks like that bitch who snatched my brother's life, and ruined mine. And women like my mother, who continues to cast a shadow over every single day.

7

SUZANNAH PETERSON SHUFFLES papers as I sit facing her reception desk. I'm aware that I'm bouncing my leg up and down. *What's all that about?*

Like I've already suspected, she's probably got her eye on me as much as my eyes are on her. Why else would she have singled me out and offered me her business card outside court?

There's just the two of us in here and she seems somewhat uncomfortable – I expect she's wondering what to say. Perhaps I should do the talking.

"If I could just ask you to fill this form in with your personal details for the file." She plucks a pen from the pot on her desk then promptly drops it. She's seriously on edge. I guess attraction can do that to a woman – I remember Eva being a bag of nerves when we first met. She dropped food in her lap and spilt her drink. Before things between us became stale, that is.

I make sure our fingers touch as I accept the pen, my eyes not leaving hers the entire time. I notice her eye makeup and the curl of her eyelashes. She's clearly made an effort, knowing she'd be seeing me today.

Anyway, I should go along with this therapy process. I'm not just here for Suzannah Peterson. As Eva has suggested, it might not be a bad thing to talk to someone. Especially with the unwanted stirrings that have returned to me over the last couple of days and the voices becoming louder again. And no matter how hard I try to deny it, the way my mother looks at me still cuts me in half. My hatred for women runs through me like a stick of rock and rather than subsiding as I'm getting older, it's intensifying.

I must keep a lid on what I divulge during these appointments but can use the space to talk about my mother, losing Dean and other stuff. If I say too much, I think I can be reported. I hope these meetings will curb my compulsion to hang around outside the Yorkshire Arms, and stop it from getting the better of me.

I want to be normal – I really do, even though nothing gives me a hit like the power and control of ending a woman's life. The biggest buzz for me is that moment when they realise I'm not the nice guy they thought I was when I first went over to them.

Then it dawns on them that my asking if they were alright was a complete con. And I love it when they find out for sure that accepting my offer to walk them to the safety of their taxi or back into the pub has been the biggest mistake they'll ever make, not to mention the final one. That fear that creeps into their eyes when they realise what danger they're in. Well, there's no high like it.

But, as I keep telling myself, the life I must strive for is the one which includes two kids, a wife and a dog, and perhaps even Suzannah. She really makes me want to add 'bit on the side' to that list. If I carry on as I have been doing for the last couple of years, my luck will, at some time, run out.

I watch Suzannah as she rises from her desk and walks towards a filing cabinet. Her arse looks good in that skirt.

"Will Potts." A bearded man appears in the doorway and holds out his hand, putting an end to my mental undressing of Suzannah Peterson. I've noticed the lace of her bra beneath her blouse. Red.

"Yes." I rise and accept his handshake. He's around my age and looks trustworthy enough. I've got to be really careful about what I say, especially if the voices in my head start up whilst I'm talking to him. What they tell me to say might not be what I want to say. As long as I remain in total control, these meetings might really do some good for me.

"I'm Daniel Hamer. If you'd like to come this way, please."

I follow him up two flights of carpeted stairs, giving static responses to his small talk about traffic and the car parking in this area. He's more casual than I would have expected, both in appearance and in manner.

"OK Will, we'll get the preliminaries out of the way first."

"Right you are." I sit back in the easy chair and clasp my hands behind my head. "It's the first time I've done anything like this so I'm not really sure what to expect."

He launches into a ramble about fees, payment on account, length and frequency of sessions. He talks fast for a counsellor and in a strange way, also seems nervous. I'm more in control here than he is.

I stifle a yawn. "So what's psychotherapy going to do for me that the Police Care counselling won't?"

He blinks several times before speaking. "Counselling is often concentrated in one area. It focuses more on the here and now and how to get beyond and overcome certain issues. The sort of therapy we offer dives much deeper than that?"

"What do you mean?"

"There's more emphasis on the *why*. And much more focus on childhood and background. How the past is affecting the present."

"Right."

I guess talking about childhood will help me. It's definitely where all my shit started. Plus, it's safe territory to be in.

"Before we get started though, I must ask you to complete this." He passes me a form attached to a clipboard, which he's been clutching since we sat down. "This is to assess where you are now, in terms of your mental well-being, and what you perceive your main issues to be." He rummages in his briefcase, then offers me a pen.

As I complete the form, I'm taken aback to notice Daniel sliding his feet from his shoes and resting them on the carpet. It must be a ploy to help me relax or something. Though I'm not as relaxed as I thought I was when I first sat in this chair. What if he's able to get information out of me that I'm not ready to give?

Most of the questions I can answer honestly, though some of them are close to the bone. I tick *sometimes* or *often* on more of them than I might have first predicted. When I tick *never* or *not at all* to ones such as *I have been physically violent to others,* I'm not lying – after all, the form specifies feelings and behaviour over the last week.

"There, done." I thrust the form across the table like a boy would pass his Maths book back to a teacher.

Daniel rises from his chair. "Before we get to that, I must go through the confidentiality contract with you."

In his socks, he heads to a desk in the corner of the room. "Sorry, I thought I'd already attached one of these to the clipboard with the other sheet. Right..." He lowers back into the chair, crossing one leg over the other. "What this clause basically says is that you can talk to me about *anything,* and whatever you say is completely confidential. The only time I'd be duty-bound to repeat anything to anyone outside this room, would be if you appeared to be posing a risk to yourself or to someone else."

The accusing glint in his eyes as he glances up from the

page makes me uncomfortable, but I'm sure I'm imagining it. I'm even more paranoid these days than I used to be. The man's here to help. Sure, I'm having to pay for the privilege, but he's not going to judge me. And with his help, perhaps I can change – *without* having to tell him too much.

"The other time I'd have to break our contract of confidentiality," he says, squinting in the sunshine that's beating onto my back, "is if you were to impart a knowledge of a crime that might be committed, or one that's already been committed."

Again, his expression is pointed, and I squirm within it. *He knows something about me – I'm sure of it.* But how? He can't possibly be aware of anything. "Do you mind if we close the blind?" I say, rising at the same time as him and then sitting again to let him tilt the blind. It's *his* consulting room, after all.

I'm probably twenty years too late for this kind of help. Since Dean died, I've never, ever touched alcohol, but in between Mum kicking me out and starting my police training, I was smoking copious amounts of skunk weed and it did something bad to my head. I'm certain it did. Not that I'm ever going to admit to this to anyone else.

For a while back then, I developed Obsessive Compulsive Disorder, to the point where all my tins had to face the same way in the cupboard, and everything in my flat was colour ordered or alphabetical.

I was convinced people were out to get me. Really get me. I'd be scrutinising people as I tried to go about my life, certain that something might be added to a coffee I'd ordered. The worst thing, whilst I was smoking the skunk, was avoiding roads as I became convinced I'd be run over like my brother was. It's ironic really that I became a traffic cop.

I'd also draw conclusions and parallels about my life, which made no sense, such as why did girls only talk to me if they were in groups of three, and why had my name been shortened to Will? Might my life have turned out differently if I'd been known as William, Bill, or Billy?

The worst thing was the voices I had, telling me what to do. They mostly seemed normal, telling me to get out of somewhere or away from someone, but then at other times I'd get a strong sense that what I was hearing really wasn't normal. At first, they'd instruct me to tell others, particularly women, what I really thought of them.

The voices continued long after I stopped smoking the skunk. Eventually, they died away and had stopped up until the last couple of years. Now, they're back and their instructions have changed. I now must act on them. If I don't, something terrible will happen to me.

Anything I did in the time between the voices stopping and starting was because of my own voice inside my head. Obviously, I've never been able to talk about any of this to *anyone*. Eva doesn't have a clue. And I'd never have been accepted into the police if I'd seen a doctor and been put on medication when it first started. It's become my fiercely guarded secret, as even if it had come out later, I'd have been chucked out of the force on my ear, and I can't do anything else.

"OK." Daniel's voice breaks into my thinking, startling me. He strokes his beard as he looks up from the form I've filled in. "Your responses offer several possible starting points," he says. "We'll use this first session to talk about the main reasons that brought you here and if there's time, I'll also get you to explain the responses you've made on the assessment form. We only have an hour for each session."

I glance at the clock – we're twenty-three minutes in already. Bloody hell. I'm never going to get my head fixed with hour-long sessions. I might need to offer more money, especially with the thoughts I've been having over the last few days.

"OK. Right. So what brings me here... Well you might have heard from the news reports earlier this year about my sister-in-law being murdered by my colleague... Jonathan Ingham?"

"Your sister-in-law?"

"She was killed in the stream which runs into the river Alder, and then Ingham went on to attack my sister."

Daniel shuffles in his seat, his expression unflinching. "Yes. I can't imagine there's anyone in this town who hasn't heard the story. Talk me through what happened to you."

"It was what happened to my sister that affected me the most. Mark, our brother, had been looking for her all over the place and I completely dismissed his worry – I told him he was overreacting."

"So the attack on your sister, what's her name?"

"Claire." A version of her swings into my mind, but it's a younger, gap-toothed Claire, not the Claire she is now. Once again, I wish her allegiance had been more towards me over the years, rather than Mark.

"The attack on her affected you more than Lauren's murder? Why is that?"

The way he uses Lauren's name makes it appear like he knew her and makes me uncomfortable. "Claire's my flesh and blood, isn't she? I should have been able to protect her. In the end, it was Mark, my brother, who did. It's always Mark, never me."

I watch as he writes something. What I can't say is that what happened to Claire is probably the main reason I threw Ingham to his death. If it wasn't for what he'd done, I'd have probably let him make a run for it. We'd covered each other's backs for long enough.

Not Chris Canvey though – he'd heard *everything* that had been said between me and Ingham on the riverbank that night. Even though Canvey had begged for his life, saying he'd never tell anyone about what he'd heard, there was no way I was going to trust him. *No way.* Ingham, on the other hand, was cut out of a similar piece of cloth to me and had nearly as much to lose as I had.

"But wasn't Lauren your sister-in-law?"

"Nearly. But they didn't get married. Granted, it's been really tough on my niece and brother." I glance behind him at the wall art, which is a painting of a river scene. At that moment, a seed of suspicion is planted. *Has someone put it there on purpose?* They must have done.

"But her death hasn't been tough on you as well?"

His voice has an accusatory edge, I'm certain of it. I thought we were here to talk about me, not bloody Lauren. That's what I'm paying for. And I should drive this conversation, not him. But I decide to answer him this time.

"We didn't get on all that well, to be honest, me and Lauren – it was safer that way. We had history."

"Really? You had a relationship?"

"Not as such. We could've done though. When she first met Mark, it was obvious she was attracted to me. She fought it but it's always been there." An image of Lauren, laid in her coffin creeps into my mind. That's been happening a lot lately. It's like she's haunting me. I should never have gone to that funeral home.

"OK. I imagine you had to take on a supportive role with your brother after his bereavement."

"He's got plenty of people around him for support. I just take care of his daughter, my niece, from time to time." Then I think of Eva. "My wife's been more involved with it all. I let her take part in the reconstruction of Lauren's death, to help catch whoever had done it – my colleague, as it turned out."

"Detective Chief Inspector Jonathan Ingham." Daniel appears to be gripping the arms of his chair. "Yes – everyone certainly knows *his* name. He never actually admitted to what he was accused of though, did he?" Daniel stares at me intently,

65

like I know something he doesn't. I should definitely have insisted on a female for these sessions. I'm not sure about this man at all, and I don't like the way he looks at me. A silence falls between us. I really don't want to get into a discussion about Ingham and what he did or didn't admit to.

Daniel seems to get my unspoken message. "You mentioned before that you *let* your wife take part in the reconstruction of Lauren's murder? What's her name?"

"Eva."

Daniel writes this down. "Would she have still taken part if you hadn't *let* her, as you put it?"

"I don't know. But she wanted to. She and Lauren were close. All my family are close to each other." The usual tug of sadness merged with fury drags at my belly. It's a sensation I'm all too familiar with. "It's *me* none of them can stand."

"Tell me about that Will." Daniel is quietly spoken and seems more chilled out now. He'd be far from chilled if he suspected the truth about me.

"I've always been the family scapegoat," I tell him. "Right from being a kid. The rest of them were allowed to stay in the house, watch TV, help themselves to the baking tin..."

I glance at him, unable to tell if he's really listening.

"Go on."

"I'll never forget feeling like an outcast. Every single day of my life. If it hadn't been for Dean – that's my brother, who's dead now, I don't know how I'd have got through it."

"How did Dean make things better?"

"He'd sneak cake and biscuits out to me, or take the blame for something that was my fault, and well – Dean was the only person who thought anything of me."

"So why were things so different for you? Compared to your siblings?"

"My mother despised me. It was like I made her skin crawl. She'd make me play outside even when it was raining." The memories of all my time-killing tactics invade my mind. Watching TV screens through other people's windows as it was getting dark. Counting cars. Imagining who people might be.

"I remember not even being allowed off the street and I'll never forget that sense of having nowhere to go through the school holidays and weekends."

"Why do you think that was?"

Daniel doesn't seem as sympathetic as I would expect a therapist to be, especially with what I'm telling him. In fact, his eyes are marble hard – I don't understand it. He's loading emotion into his voice, but his facial expression doesn't match it.

"Take your time. I'm aware this is painful stuff we're bringing up."

I can't speak for a moment. I'm scared how my voice will sound. I've returned to eleven-year-old Will and I don't like it.

"I remember when I had a stomach bug. My mother made me go to school even though there was a chance I'd chuck up all over the assembly hall. All I wanted was for her to tuck me into bed and take care of me." I can't believe I'm telling all this stuff to this man. Once I open up, who knows what will happen. I need to be careful. I glance at the clock. There isn't much longer to go. Maybe I should keep the sessions to an hour. I've got to keep coming though, no matter how hard it is. I've got to keep fighting not to return to the other side of me.

"And what do you think her reasons were for not looking after you?"

"I have no idea." My shoulders droop. "I guess I was a difficult kid."

"In what way?"

"I don't know. But it got even worse when Dean died."

"What about now?"

"She's just moved up here, to Yorkshire. Rented a house and

put hers on the market. And she's as cold and distant with me as she always has been."

Her stony face flashes in front of me. Clearly they're needed for reproduction, but the world would be much simpler without the existence of women. Especially my mother.

"Where was she living before?"

"Derbyshire. And she should have stayed there. She only usually bothers with family a couple of times a year. Christmas and Easter."

"So why has she moved back? Is it because of what happened to Claire and Lauren?"

I nod. "I reckon she couldn't stand Brenda, that's Lauren's Mum, looking after Mark, my brother, as well as Claire, our sister and my niece." My voice sounds loud in the quiet of this room. It's totally alien – speaking about myself at length like this. "Plus, Mark's just been given a shed load of compo money. She's probably after helping him spend it."

"You mentioned your home life got worse after one of your brothers died." Daniel looks down at his notes. "Tell me about that."

I'm irritated that he doesn't acknowledge what I've just told him, but has instead jumped backwards twenty years. He must have his reasons. "I was a teenager. My mother told me straight to my face once, that I should have been the one that was killed in that hit and run, not Dean. I'll never forget hearing her say that. To be honest, at the time, I wanted to be dead."

I would expect Daniel to show a hint of sympathy now I've divulged this. But his voice stays even, and his face remains passive to the point of couldn't-care-less. Perhaps he's trained to respond in this way.

"What does your mother look like?" His pen is poised over his notebook. I'm not sure why this shit is important. I glance at his expectant face. Evidently it is.

"She was slim with shiny hair and high cheekbones when I

was young. Tons of perfume and makeup. Her face has become pointed as she's got older, and her hair a steely grey now."

And I remain as intimidated by her as I always was. It's something I really want to get beyond.

"Talk me through what happened to Dean?"

"A drunk driver killed him. Who just so happened to be the wife of DCI Ingham."

Now his face *is* giving something away. He looks interested for the first time since I sat in this chair. "Go on."

"Yeah. I saw Ingham's wife get out of the driver's side after they hit us. I was nineteen and Dean was twenty-one. They were talking about her getting done for drink driving. I was out of it, but I remember every word they said to each other."

"What did they say?"

"Ingham was panicking about losing his job for allowing his wife to drink and then get behind the wheel. Whatever they were saying ended with *let's get out of here.*"

"Then what?"

"I remember the slam of their car doors and a screech, then nothing, apart from waking up in the ambulance. I don't know how long we were lying out there."

"Why didn't you report them?"

"I did, of course I did. And as far as I can remember, the police did what they could, but never caught up with them." He's nodding as I speak. "I even did an e-fit, but Ingham will have known how to cover their tracks."

"I see."

"I didn't have a clue who the couple in the car were until I started my police training. Then I recognised Ingham straight away. You don't forget the face of a man responsible for your brother's death, do you? He didn't have a clue who I was at first."

"Why didn't you report him *then*?" Daniel glances towards

the door as there's a bang from the landing and footsteps die away down the stairs.

"If I could have my time over again, I would."

I wish that was the case. Part of me is proud of what I've done, but another part knows it's a compulsion that could easily land me in prison for the rest of my life. A vison of someone jacking off into a bowl of porridge enters my head, making me nauseous. No way can I end up inside.

"So, what did you do instead? Of reporting him that is?"

I swallow the bile that's risen in the back of my throat. I've found out why people resist these so-called talking therapies. "Eventually, I had to say something, so I stayed late one night and had it out with him."

I remember it well. Him leaning against his desk like he was the big man, but then, he seemed to shrink before my eyes when I told him who I was. "I didn't know how else to handle it. Who would've believed a trainee PC over a Detective Inspector as he was back then?"

"What happened next?"

"He warned me he'd finish my career before it even started if I breathed a word about what he and his wife had done. He reckoned I wouldn't have been able to prove anything, anyway." Which is true.

"I don't see how he'd have had the power to do that. Finish your career, I mean." Footsteps outside this room again make me aware of the world that continues to exist beyond the miserable confines of my own life.

"A couple of years had passed by then and the forensics capability wasn't what it is now."

"I guess so."

"And yeah, he had the authority to decide whether my probationary period was ended or extended. That's at best - at worst, he had the power to recommend that I failed completely."

"I'm surprised you didn't at least try to report him. After what he and his wife had done to your brother."

"I know that now." I take a deep breath. "The truth of it is that he promised to fast track me up the ranks and the pay scale if I kept a lid on what they'd done to Dean. There's a bit more to it than that, but that's the gist."

"So he was effectively *bribing* you?"

"I suppose you might call it that." I want to add that in the end we were blackmailing each other – take some of my power back here. But of course I can't say anything.

He's quiet for a moment, like he's mulling over his next question. "Did you have any suspicions about what Ingham was *allegedly* doing to all those women over the last couple of years?"

I don't like his sudden change of tone. "What do you mean, *allegedly?* The inquiry found him guilty."

"There was some doubt over the perpetrator though, wasn't there?" His gaze wanders around the room as he asks the question. I know *exactly* what he's getting at. He must be aware that I was under investigation. Suzannah certainly seemed to know something when I rang to make the appointment. I wonder again whether I should even be here. Maybe he's in league with Lindy from the Press Association. Perhaps what I'll say will end up splashed all over the front pages.

"Did the two of you talk about it?"

The two of us. I don't like the way he's lumping Ingham and me together. "Daniel." I take a deep breath and stare at him straight in the eye. "You don't mind if I call you Daniel, do you?"

"No, most of my clients call me by my first name." He can't hold my gaze and keeps looking away whilst fiddling with his shirtsleeve.

"Daniel. It's as though I'm being *interviewed* here. I thought this was supposed to be a therapy session. And I'm the police officer, not you." I laugh, but it's the least *amused* laugh I've ever emitted.

"It is a therapy session. Of course it is." He glances at his watch. "I'm just establishing some background with you. We need to go backwards to go forwards, as I said at the start." He's gabbling now. "Anyway, our time's nearly up for this week."

"It all just seems a bit..."

He cuts in. "Any kind of therapy is always difficult, especially to begin with." He places the clipboard on the table. I try to read what he's written, but I've never been any good at reading upside down.

"Great. I'm here 'cos I want to be helped with things, not to make things more difficult than they already are."

"In my experience of working with a variety of clients, as therapy roots things out and gets into a person's psyche, it can feel worse before it gets better. But it will be worth it."

"Really?" The idea of getting into my psyche isn't a pleasant thought. It wouldn't be for Daniel Hamer either if he had any idea who I really am.

"Might I suggest..." He sits forward and slides his feet back into his shoes. "That you bring a few photographs to our next session. One or two of you as a child, alone, and one with your siblings would give us something to work with."

I nod. *Worse before it gets better.* If things were to get *worse*, I may end up being somewhere I shouldn't be on a Saturday night.

8

SUZANNAH SLIDES the invoice across her desk towards me. "Cash or card?"

"Card." She has perfectly manicured fingernails – something Eva used to be meticulous about in our early days. "So how long have you worked here Suzannah?"

She casts me a strange look, clearly startled at my use of her name. "Since it opened. I helped set it up." She slots my card into the machine.

"But you're not..."

"A therapist – no. I'm a partner – I've already told you. I'll need to take payment for this and one on account for your next session. Ten o'clock next Monday?"

I nod. She has shot up in my estimation. I might not want a career-minded wife, but there's something seductive about it in other women. I tap my number onto the card machine.

"Will any of your other family members require an appointment?" She rips the receipt off and passes it to me. "What a dreadful business. And I can't believe there's been a further two drownings."

It might be my imagination, but she appears to be studying

73

me as I drop my wallet into the pocket of my coat. Ideas of what people may or may not be thinking of me keep intruding into my mind. "Yeah," I reply. At least my conscience is clear about the last two.

"So how did you get on Will?" Eva glances up from her book as I poke my head into the lounge. Her face is bathed in the lamplight in front of her, and I find myself once again hoping she's carrying our son. I'm yearning to abandon this dark side of me and need something to hang onto. There's much less chance that I'll revert to my old pattern if we've got a baby on the way. Especially a son.

"It was OK, I suppose. Early days." I'm not going into things with her, and only told her where I was going as she'd been quizzing me whilst I got ready. I glance around, then listen. Silence. "It's very quiet in here. Where's Heidi?"

"She's having tea at Mark's house with Alysha."

"How come?" Something within me darkens as I imagine Heidi being part of their 'happy family.' I didn't feel this bad about her being around there until Mum came back. I can't stand the thought of her spending time with my daughter.

Eva smiles. "It sounds as though she and Alysha conspired together at school." She reaches over to the coffee table and sips from a glass of wine.

"So I'll be the one picking her up, will I?" My voice rises along with my heckles. "Since you're on the drink, yet again."

"I'm having one glass of wine for goodness' sake." But she looks at me with a face that says *go ahead and stop me.*

"We're trying for a baby Eva." At least I've got that card I can play now. "You could already be pregnant." Despite my irritation, a wave of excitement passes over me.

"About that Will..." She rests her book on the chair arm and shifts her weight in her seat. Her furrowed brow tells me that whatever she's about to say will be something I won't want to hear.

"What?" I sit in the chair opposite, scanning her face for answers. It's too soon for a positive test already. It's not even been three weeks since we decided.

"I think we should wait a little longer."

"What do you mean?" It's like being thumped in the chest. "What for?"

"It's just, well, I enjoy work, and I'd be forced to give that up for a while and..."

"No chance Eva. No excuses. No way. We agreed."

"No Will. *You* agreed. You caught me at a funny moment and I just got carried along with the idea whilst we were out of our normal routine. But now we're back, I don't..." She shakes her head.

"You can't promise something like that, then snatch it away from me." I dig my fingernails into the palm of my other hand and try to keep my voice steady. "I won't let you."

"To be fair Will, if I've changed my mind, there's not a lot you can do about it."

There's too much confidence in Eva's voice for my liking. *What's got into her?* Maybe she's seeing someone else. I stare at her. Not long out of the shower by the looks of it, her hair is stuck to her neck like seaweed and her face is pasty. Nah, I can't imagine anyone else taking her on. She's no Suzannah Peterson, that's for sure.

"So how much longer do you want to wait then? If you can give me a timescale, perhaps I can live with it." Though I suspect I can't. This is something I don't want to wait for.

"I can't say Will. But I'm not saying *never*, I'm just saying *not now or in the foreseeable future.*"

I don't want to hear another word out of her, and I need to get away before I do something I'll regret. I slam the lounge door and storm up the stairs – taking two at a time. I'll give her *not now*. Yanking the boxes of her contraceptive pills from the bathroom cabinet, I stuff them into my coat. They're going and so is Eva if she goes back on what we agreed. I pay the bills here. She can piss off and I'll find someone else to give me the son I deserve.

"Will?" She shouts as I wrench my coat from the peg.

I've got nothing more to say to her. I bang the front door behind me and stride towards the car.

After a few minutes of driving, I pull up alongside a bin and hurl the pill boxes one at a time from the car window. I can only hope she's already pregnant from our holiday. But she could get rid of it. Bloody hell - if she did that, well I wouldn't be responsible for what I did to her.

I can't allow these thoughts. Once they start, they consume me and take over, and if the voices join in... I've proven already that I'm unable to keep what comes up in my head as fantasies, just for me. I'm compelled to act. I was doing OK until – *this*. If I end up repeating the last couple of years, Eva will be the one with blood on her hands. It will be *her* that forces me back to that way of life.

I point the car in the direction of Mark's house, suddenly needing to see Heidi. She's the only person in my life, well, there's also Alysha, who is ever pleased to see me. I've nowhere else to go, anyway. Most blokes make friends in the pub, so that one's obviously out for me.

Nor do I have any mates at work – just acquaintances. They're too busy taking credit for work I've done. Fury rises in me like steam from boiling water. How dare bloody Tyler accept a commendation when it was me driving that night? And how dare Eva wrench my chance to be a father again from me? For Heidi to have a little brother – I'll maybe get her on board – she'll be able to put some pressure on Eva. Why do bloody women hold all this power over us? Then they wonder why we have affairs... or worse.

〜

"You're early. We've not even had dinner yet." Mark holds the door open. He looks happier than normal. Back to himself even, just a skinnier version.

"Mum's not here, is she?" I peer beyond where he's standing, then back towards the street. She's the last person I want to see. My first therapy session has brought all the old feelings of rejection flooding back.

"No, but I'm expecting someone for dinner."

I slap him on the back as I walk in. "Nice one. It's about time you got back in the saddle. I thought you looked cheerful." Despite my inner darkness, my brother being normal with me provides a momentary lift.

"It's not like that Will. She's really just a friend."

I hook my coat over the banister and follow Mark to the kitchen. "Yeah right. Perhaps I should stick around and give her the once over."

"You're welcome to stop for dinner. As long as you can behave." Mark stirs a pan.

"What's that supposed to mean?"

"In any case, I don't think Heidi will thank you for dragging her away from here early. Or is Eva cooking for you?"

"No." *She's too busy drinking wine.* But I don't say that.

He gives me an inquisitive glance. "What's up? You haven't fallen out, have you?"

"Let's not even go there."

"That suits me fine. It's not as if I don't have enough of my own woes."

"I'll only stay for dinner if you're absolutely sure mother dearest won't show up." I can hear Heidi and Alysha shrieking

77

and banging in the room above us. I'll tell Heidi I'm here shortly.

"Mum's pissed off with me. She was supposed to be staying for dinner, but she's buggered off. Hence I've cooked enough to be able to invite you."

"Who, Mum? Pissed off with the golden boy? Never."

"I've booked a visit to see Pat Ingham." Mark keeps his back to me and lowers his voice. "Mum doesn't approve. Nor does Brenda, for that matter. In fact, to say Brenda doesn't approve is an understatement."

Bloody hell. For once me and Mum agree on something. "And neither do I Mark. What the hell would you want to see *Pat Ingham* for?"

"She sent me a visiting order and a letter – she reckons there's stuff she wants to talk to me about. Things she wants to clear up."

I glare at him. "How can you even think about sitting across the table from the woman who murdered our brother? And tried to frame me for everything her husband did?" It's a fair argument.

"Her *husband* also murdered my fiancée, remember? There's still a ton of questions about it all that I'd like to ask her. Plus, Pat Ingham was the last person ever to speak to Lauren. It'll give me some closure."

"Like hell it will. You might as well slice at yourself with a blade if you pay *her* a visit. Don't you think she's caused our family enough damage?" *Family.* Some bloody family.

I sink into a chair and watch my brother. As always, his shoulders sag and his head bows. He needs to get a grip and I must talk him out of this. It's pure madness. I'm surprised the authorities are even allowing Pat Ingham to send Mark a visiting order given the connection between them.

But if he gets blocked from going, he'll be able to use his status as a police sergeant, soon to be a Detective Inspector, to overcome anything that gets in his way. I'll have to be the one that puts a stop to this. I can't let him and Pat Ingham see each other – no way. There's far too much at stake.

"What's up with you Will?" Mark takes something from the fridge behind me, evidently trying to change the subject and deflect the attention back to me.

I twist around to face him. "What do you mean?"

"You've had a face on since you arrived. Well before I told you about the visiting order." Mark walks back to the cooker. He's had a shave, a haircut and has got out of his scruffy joggers for a change. Clearly out to make an impression on whoever is coming for dinner.

"Me and Eva had a few words, that's all."

"You've no idea how lucky you are that your wife is still here. The mother of your daughter. Don't fuck it up Will."

Mark doesn't swear often and as I open my mouth to respond, the doorbell goes.

"Honestly Will. Take it from someone who knows." He turns the gas down and strides towards the door.

Like I'm going to accept marital advice from Mark. I frown as I try to place the familiar voice which echoes through the hallway, then a click-clack of heels along the tiled floor. *Who is it?*

"Oh, it's you."

"A very warm welcome from Mr Will Potts, if I'm not mistaken. Hello to you too."

Out of anyone it could be, Mark had to go after bloody Sara. There's no denying she's got a resemblance to Lauren, which is probably the attraction. Similar long, blonde hair and blue eyes. Lauren was far better looking though.

I've no proof that Lauren bad-mouthed me in the past to her friend, but Sara's opinion of me has always been evident in the sneer of her mouth whenever we've encountered each other. Another woman who thinks it's acceptable to sit in judgement of me.

"Can I get you a drink Sara?"

Mark's almost acting like himself. It's weird after putting up with the grieving widow ensemble for all these months.

"A glass of white wine would be nice." She shifts on the chair so she's pointing the front of herself at him, flicking her hair behind one shoulder. What sort of woman comes onto their *dead* friend's partner?

Mark slides two wine glasses from the cupboard. "What are you having to drink Will?"

"I'm alright thanks."

"Dinner smells good." Sara's bracelets rattle as she reaches to take the glass from Mark. She's probably after all the money he's come into. "It makes a lovely change for someone to cook for me."

"You're the one whose boyfriend was already married, aren't you? Lucky escape there!" I actually mean him, not her.

"Will, give it a rest." Mark frowns at me as he rinses a jug out. "That's got nothing to do with you."

"I'd rather not talk about it anyway, if you don't mind." Sara sips her wine and smiles sweetly at me, though her eyes say *piss off.*

"Right." Mark flicks the cooker dials in turn. "That's all ready. I'm just going to pay a call then I'll bring the girls down for dinner." He grins as he walks past us. "Play nicely, you two."

"If I'd have known *you* were going to be here..." Sara's face darkens the moment Mark leaves the room. She's all perfume and makeup. And I can tell a mile off that she's here for far more than dinner.

"Shame. Am I interfering with your plans to hit on a

grieving widower?" I fold my arms and grin at her. "It's a good job I'm here to watch out for him."

"Shut up, will you?" She slams her glass on the table, and I cringe at the red lipstick smeared all over it. "It's not like that at all."

"So tell me, what is it like?" I lean back in my chair. "Lauren's dead. You've no business to be here, getting off with her partner."

"You're one to talk about hitting on other people's partners." She points at me.

Someone should warn her how much it winds me up to be pointed at. I wouldn't like her to find out the hard way. Or maybe I would. "What's that supposed to mean?"

"Lauren told me all about you. When she first met Mark, I mean. What sort of man tries to cop off with his brother's girlfriend? Like she'd ever have looked twice at you. You made her skin crawl." Sara half smiles and I want to wipe it clean off her face. "And you make mine crawl too."

"Shut your nasty mouth. That's not true - it was Lauren who came onto me."

"She told me everything. And I mean *everything*. And I'm warning you, if you keep giving me grief like this, I might decide the time's right to enlighten Mark about what his brother is really like." She drains her glass in two more gulps, then looks around, presumably for the bottle. "Lauren should have enlightened him herself. Who knows what stopped her?"

My jaw is clenched so tight it's hurting my head. I must get away from this bitch or I'm going to lose it.

"Mark, I'm off. I don't like the company you keep." I shout up the stairs. "You can drop Heidi off at mine when you're done. Eva's on the sauce too."

"But... I'm having a..."

I drown his voice with a slam of the door. What the hell has Lauren been spreading about me? If there's one thing I can't abide, apart from drunk women, it's women bitching about me behind my back. Eva learned that the hard way once when I caught her moaning to one of her friends about me. And she wonders why I prefer her to be where I can be sure of what she's up to. Loyalty's a big thing in my book.

9

It's like visiting an old friend. The right kind of weather too. Winter drizzle – the sort that keeps drinkers inside the Yorkshire Arms until late into the night. Most people would be enticed by the lamps and fire-lit glow about the place, but not me – I'd rather be on the outside, looking in.

Unlike the other Monday when I walked by, there's an uneven balance of women this evening, all in pairs and small groups - many of whom are extremely worse for wear. I can't understand it – unless they've been living on the moon for the last two years, they're aware of the risk they're taking.

The DJ's packing up, so it won't be long until the women start making their way home. If they get home, that is. I wonder how many of them are still heeding the *safety in numbers* message from last winter – perhaps the two accidental deaths from last week will put a stop to any easy pickings for me this evening. Or maybe they'll be too drunk to care.

This thought excites me and alarms me all at the same time. I should be nowhere near this place on a Saturday night. Yet it was as though a compulsive force lured me from where I lay in my warm bed and transported me here. Eva's been on the wine again, so won't have a clue that I've gone anywhere. Cleansing the world of drunks, of women like my mother and Pat Ingham has become my life's work. We're all given a purpose in life, and this seems to be mine.

If I could ever divulge to Daniel Hamer that my mother is at the root of this purpose, he might rightly wonder why she has never found herself over her head in the wintery river Alder, like the others. But I've got to be honest, there's a line you don't cross – and killing my mother would be like I'd murdered an aspect of myself. Even if she can't stand being in the same room as me.

I've got insider knowledge of a couple of the CCTV-free spots. About half a mile downriver to the north, there's an area outside a restaurant that went bust a few years ago. I've heard a rumour it's being turned into flats. There's a decent stretch on either side where the CCTV doesn't reach – nor is it particularly well lit. There's another place I've come across along the south path, the shortcut from Alderton centre to South Bank, going along the riverbank, and through the woods. It's less than a minute that someone would be out of the CCTV zone, but that's long enough for my purposes.

I recall that the lights around the Yorkshire Arms are on motion sensors, so I sit as still as the river is tonight. I've got the best seat in the house here. No one can see me unless I move, and I've got a perfect view of the pub doorway. Despite this continual battle with myself – it would appear that I'm back. The urge is too powerful.

A group of six women leave the pub, leaning into one another. It's nearly half-past one in the morning, so if they've been in there all night, it's no wonder they're staggering about. It infuriates me that anyone would want to sit, pouring poison down their throat for hours on end. That's bad enough, but losing faculty control, and the danger they become to the rest of society is something else. Not only that, I've seen the worst moods and violence from women in drink over the years. My mother being no exception, especially when I was younger.

I watch to see if one of the women separates from the group, but no, they're sticking together. My attention returns to the doorway and a lone figure with their hood up. After a moment, I can tell it's a man from the way he ambles towards Carlton Bridge, exuding a confidence that no woman in their right mind would around here at the moment.

A pair of women emerge a few minutes later. Damn – they've got a taxi waiting and I'm at the wrong side of the river to intercept. I used to hang around the empty building next door to the pub, but I'd be bang to rights there now. There's a motion sensor light right above where Lauren once parked up in the shadows, spying on me. Well, she didn't realise it was *me* she was spying on. She was very close to finding out though. There's a small part of me that will always be grateful towards Lauren – if it wasn't for her death, Ingham might never have been held responsible for *all* of them. That's the main reason I took the rose to the funeral home – out of gratitude.

My fists clench in my pockets as I suddenly recall Mark's plan to visit Ingham's wife in prison and what it might mean for me. Though, if she'd had anything concrete, I wouldn't be sitting here now.

I continue to watch, anticipation rising each time the pub door opens, then falling as the groups and pairs of women huddle together, all heading for the road rather than in either direction of the riverbank. I yawn, then shiver. This must be the universe telling me this isn't the life I'm supposed to lead anymore. Just another quarter of an hour, then I'm out of here. Back to my normality beside my snoring wife who's pulled the plug on the one thing that could've turned us around. This may well be on her conscience one day.

∽

"What are you so dressed up for?" Eva's eyes narrow with suspicion as I descend the stairs and scan the hallway for my keys. She screws her nose up. "Are you sure you've got enough aftershave on?"

"I've got an appointment, then I'm on a late." My gaze falls on the hallway mirror. Sharp Will. Sharp. My reflection tells the story of someone who hasn't gone near alcohol for many years, has never eaten crap, and has always worked out several times a week. That can't be said for most men in their early forties.

"You've got an appointment with who?"

"The therapy again."

"Is Mark going too?" She glances up from where she's rummaging in the under-stairs cupboard. "And I'm trying to find Heidi's book bag?"

"No. Mark reckons he doesn't need counselling. Besides, he's got enough people to talk to." I slide my arms into my jacket. *Not like me*, I want to say, but don't. "Heidi's book bag's in there." I point to the lounge. "Under the coffee table. I read it with her on Saturday night after you'd gone to bed." The fury I was feeling returns.

My stupid bloody wife, who had promised to try for a baby with me, spent Saturday evening drinking wine on her own after turning my advances down flat. Her excuse was she couldn't risk getting pregnant until she had another supply of her pill. She's mentioned nothing about me getting rid of the boxes from the bathroom cabinet. I'll deny it, anyway. It's because of her that I ended up outside the Yorkshire Arms again.

One day, when I turn up here, telling Eva that I'm shacking up with someone else, Suzannah Peterson, for instance, she'll be all upset and accusing me of *whatever*, when really, she'll be able to blame no one but herself. A woman who neglects her husband can only expect one outcome.

. . .

It's Daniel who opens the door to me when I ring the intercom. He's shorter than I remember, but I guess I mainly saw him sitting down throughout last week's appointment.

"Come in Will. The room's ready for you."

I glance into reception as we pass. "No Suzannah today?"

He turns to me before ascending the stairs. He's had a haircut and beard trim since last week. "Erm, no not yet. Why do you ask?"

I straighten my face up, quick. I don't need him knowing about my ulterior motives. "No reason. I expect you get used to seeing someone in a particular spot, don't you?"

"Well, since this is only your second session with us..." He laughs as he reaches the top of the first flight, but the laugh is as hollow as the whitewashed walls it bounces around. "I'd be surprised if you'd already got used to seeing anyone here."

"How many sessions do you think I'll need?" I follow him into the same room as before, feeling a surprising sense of ease as I lower myself into the chair and notice the river painting again. Yes, the picture might be a conspiracy, but it reminds me of why I'm here and what I'm trying to get beyond. It's the first time I've ever had the opportunity to open up about myself, and whilst I'm concerned I might say the wrong thing – it's also liberating to loosen some of the knots inside me.

"It's difficult to say." Daniel slips his shoes off again as he sits facing me. He crosses one foot over the other. He's wearing beige chinos. Dear me.

As I get comfortable in my seat, I realise that Carlton Bridge, next to the Yorkshire Arms can just about be seen from this window. Daniel hasn't closed the blind this time.

"So Will, before we get into everything, I'd like to know what you see the purpose of these sessions being. What changes do you want to make for yourself?"

If I answered that truthfully, he'd be running for the hills. But I'll have to give him some version of the truth. "I won't lie to you Daniel. I have a hatred for some women. But I also have a hatred for myself."

"From what you said in our first meeting Will, it would seem that much of both those issues stem from the relationship you've always known with your mother."

I'm unsure whether this is a statement or a question, but I respond anyway. I'm on relatively safe ground talking about my mother as long as I don't get carried away. "I was the runt of the litter in her eyes," I begin. "Still am. Even though I was the second out of the four of us, she's always acted like she doesn't want me around."

Daniel tugs at his beard. "It's more unusual, for a second born to be the *black sheep*, for want of a better term. In my experience, this sort of difficulty is more likely to occur with the first or last child in a family."

"Really? Well, if I had an explanation for how she's treated me over the years, there's a chance I might be able to deal with it."

It's true. I've often wondered what I did so bad as a kid to make her detest me so much. What sort of mother says *it should've been you who died?*

"Have you ever tried talking to her? Telling her how she makes you feel and the damage you think she's done to you."

"The damage I *think* she's done." My voice rises. "You mean the damage she *has* done. And yes, of course I have. Several times. She shuts me down. Won't discuss it. Once, when I brought it up, she said she didn't know what I was going on about. Another of her go-to lines is that *the past is in the past. Dead and buried.*"

"You offered some examples of how things were for you last week." Daniel flicks a page back in his notebook. "Did you bring in some photographs like I asked you to?"

"Yep." I slide them from my jacket. "There weren't many of me though, and what my mum had, she handed to me not long after I'd left home. As far as I know, she's kept no photos of me as a kid."

"OK – tell me about these pictures."

I spread them out on the table between us. Side on, so he can see them too. "This one's my school photo, from when I was seven. This one's of all of us. That's Dean on the left – the one killed by Ingham's wife – that's Mark, and that's Claire on the right. And this other one is me, when I was thirteen."

Daniel peers at them. "OK - take a good look at yourself as a boy, the seven-year-old-one first. Tell me what you see in it that's caused your mother to reject you."

He seems more sympathetic this time. Which is good because his indifference didn't do me any favours in our last meeting. In fact, it's one of the reasons I found myself outside the Yorkshire Arms again. He can take some of the blame for that, along with Eva. If I'm not listened to and supported with all this, I'll be out of here. Perhaps Daniel can sense that in me, which is why he's improved his attitude. It's me who's paying, after all.

I stare at the dark-haired, slightly tubby seven-year-old and see sad eyes and a forced smile. I'm wearing one of Dean's old jumpers and my fringe is lopsided. My dad used to cut it to save money at the barbers.

"What do you see that may have invited your mother to *detest you*, to use your words?"

"I was so bloody miserable in those days." The words seem to stick in my throat. "On that school photo, I'm forcing myself to smile, can you tell?" The picture blurs slightly in front of my eyes. "Most of the time, she didn't even buy my school photos, only if they were of all of us, after Mark and Claire had started school as well."

"You didn't answer the question."

"I can't see any reason why she would detest me. I was only a kid."

"And what about the other picture?" Daniel points at me at thirteen.

"It was much worse by that time," I reply. "She could get away more with sending me from the house. All I ever wanted was to be treated the same as the others – allowed in the house and able to be part of the family."

"Looking again at the picture, can you see why?"

I stare at it. It's not as if I was bad looking. All the girls in my year were after me. "No matter how much I try to deny it," I reply. "I look like her. Maybe that's it. She probably sees herself in me. Most of my negative traits I share with her."

"Such as?" Daniel sits up straighter.

"You know, temper, brooding on things, liking to be in charge – nothing major."

"That said, it's quite unusual for a mother to completely single out one child. A mother would normally have some level of rejection towards *all* her children, after all – everyone has negative traits." He shuffles his feet on the carpet. "There must be more to why only *you* received this treatment."

"Don't you believe me or something?"

I'm aware of the edge my voice has taken on. But it takes guts to admit to my status as an outcast in front of a near-stranger. If he doesn't believe what I'm telling him, there's little point going on with this.

"I'm not saying that – I'm only asking if you've any idea why it was only you. Apart from perhaps taking after her."

"You'd need to ask her that." I continue to stare at the photo. By thirteen, I was putting gel on my hair and saving for clothes with my paper round and dog walking money, but still I wouldn't smile properly. With plenty of girls chasing me, I had more to smile about than I do nowadays. I tell Daniel this.

"How old were you when you started having girlfriends?" he asks.

"Fifteen. I remember the first serious one well. We waited for a couple of months before we slept together. We were inseparable for a whole summer."

"And what happened next?"

"She got pregnant. Then she got rid of it without ever telling me."

"How did that make you feel?"

"Angry. Powerless, I guess. Like I didn't matter." The irony of Eva now snatching back my hopes of fathering a son isn't lost on me. They say history repeats itself. When Tina had done this to me, I'd wanted to kill her. Maybe I should track her down again.

"Not long after that, she dumped me and started going out with someone else in our year at school. Someone she knew I couldn't stand. Because he was a bigger lad, he'd offered me out a few times."

"And were there more girlfriends?"

"Kind of. I never let anyone else get close though. Not after how Tina had treated me. I decided that no woman was ever going to have that level of power over me again. Especially with the mother I had as well. So I started sleeping about." I wonder for a moment whether to tell the truth, then think, *sod it, why not?* He'll probably be impressed. "I must have slept with around a hundred girls between being fifteen and nineteen... and then my brother died and everything changed."

Daniel arches an eyebrow. "A hundred."

He writes this down. I suppose it is a noteworthy number – one I've never disclosed to Eva. She thinks I'm still in single figures. I shrug. "There was something in me that stopped respecting myself, but more to the point, them."

"You mean, women?"

"Yeah - it became a game, a challenge to see how quickly I

was able to lay them, and how many. Sometimes I had two in one night. I'm not saying I'm proud of it now, but... I guess Tina messed me up, and my mother. Plus, in those days, I was drinking a lot."

"Really? You stated on the health questionnaire that you're teetotal."

"I am now." Suddenly, the sense of being drunk creeps over me and I almost sway in my seat. I recall the taste of lager in the back of my throat and feel ill. "Back then, I'd grown up with my parents drinking regularly in the house, so it was normal for me. To be honest, I drank that much in my later teens that I didn't know what day of the week it was half of the time."

"Did you practice safe sex with all these girls?" His voice is still passive. I'm trying not to let it annoy me. He obviously thinks I'm beneath him.

"Only if the girl I was with at the time insisted on it. Like I said, I'm not proud of myself. I could have biological kids running around all over the place that I'm unaware of."

"OK. So how do you think you were changed from this sort of behaviour after the death of your brother?"

Question after question after bloody question. It wouldn't be so bad if he came across more genuinely than he does. And who's *he* to refer to 'this sort of behaviour?' Who does he think he is?

"Dean took some of me with him when he died." Tears stab at the backs of my eyes. It's a peculiar sensation. I *never* cry. Ever. I glare at Daniel Hamer for being able to break me in this way. The last time I cried was the day Mum threw me out of the house at nineteen. She'll never find out about that though.

Daniel slides the tissue box in front of me and crosses his feet, clad in stripy socks, the other way. It's strange how much you notice about another person in a situation like this. Other people probably don't notice his socks, the gingery tint to his beard or the crease down the centre of his trousers.

I shake my head. "I don't need a tissue. I'm good thanks. Dean's dying stopped me from drinking. I haven't touched a drop since. When a drunk driver does that to your brother..." My voice trails off as I wonder whether to be honest about the skunk weed and its effects on me. I guess I'm OK to be partially honest without jeopardising anything. Admitting to a smoke won't harm my work.

"I smoked a bit of weed in my early twenties," I say. "Who didn't?"

The hint of a smirk on his face suggests he did too, but I can't imagine that it shot his head through like it did mine.

"What effect did the weed have on you Will?"

"I guess it calmed me down." If I tell him about the voices, my conspiracy theories, and the Obsessive Compulsive Disorder, he'll be on the phone to police headquarters before I'm out of the building. I'm a serving police sergeant, heading up high-speed chases when all's said and done. "I didn't smoke it for long though," I add quickly. I probably shouldn't have said anything.

"How else did your life change after the death of your brother?" Daniel gestures to Dean in the photo as he asks the question.

I hardly ever look at photos of Dean. He'd have been forty-three now and might have been a copper like me and Mark. I'm sure my life would have been very different if he'd lived. He'd have probably come with me when Mum threw me out.

"Will?"

I keep zoning out. It's a peculiar sensation. As though I'm not here, though I know I am.

"Sorry. I was just so – *angry*. Mainly that the people in the car were never punished." My voice sounds peculiar too. Like it isn't really mine. Like I'm being told what to say.

"Will. Are you OK?"

"Sorry. It's... well... they robbed me of my brother. And I

was angry that Claire and Mark seemed to support each other and not me. It was like they didn't give a toss about what I was going through."

"That must have been tough."

"I still can't believe that my mother didn't even visit me in hospital after the accident. And not long after that she threw me out of the house."

"That must have been a lonely time for you."

I shrug again. "It was pretty shit. I started off in a bedsit. I was working in a factory. Some days, when what I earned only just covered the rent," I don't say skunk weed here, "I'd be literally on baked beans for the rest of the week." I have another flash of anger towards my mother. "I lived like that for months."

"What made you decide to train for the police?"

"My dad was a copper, so I suppose it was in the blood. He died when I was fifteen. My brother Mark's in the force as well, he's up for a promotion." I think of Tyler taking *my* commendation and grit my teeth before continuing. "But most of all, I wanted to rid the streets of drunk drivers who think they can do what they did to my brother."

Daniel nods his head slowly. "So that's why you joined the traffic division, is it?"

I nod.

"Have you caught many drunk drivers in your career Will?"

"Who knows? All I can say is that the streets have been cleared of many drunks because of me."

Daniel takes a deep breath and looks away from me then back to his notepad. He writes something.

"What are you writing?"

"I'm getting a sense of the past really feeding into the present here." He ignores my question.

"Isn't that the case with everyone?"

"Well yes, but the ramifications from person to person can

vary a great deal." He rakes his fingers through his fringe. "What one person can cope with can send another into very dark places."

I stare at him, not really sure what he's getting at, but become distracted anyway as I follow his gaze to the clock.

"In our next session, we'll talk more about the present, so I can get a better overview..." He trails off.

"What then?"

"And then, that's when we can really double down on what needs taking apart for everything to be resolved once and for all."

"That sounds promising." And it does. I get a sense that the money I'm paying Daniel Hamer won't be wasted.

"It will be. Oh, and there's a bit of *homework* I'd like to set you."

"What?"

"I'd like you to watch your thoughts more closely. Make a note of them where you can, in a journal, particularly the darker ones. That's when the real deep work can be undertaken."

He's using words like *deep*, *darker* and *undertake*. What the hell does he know about me?

10

I'VE GOT NEARLY two hours to kill before my shift starts. I head across the road to the café Suzannah's just recommended to me.

Daniel followed me back down to reception and was fiddling with some papers in a tray. So instead of being able to linger for a few minutes, I just paid my bill, made another appointment, and asked Suzannah for the cafe suggestion. If Daniel hadn't been listening in, I'd have turned on the charm, and probably asked her to come with me.

I winked at her as I left, Daniel didn't see that. Hopefully she got the message that she'd be welcome to join me. She looked the business again today in a tight-fitting skirt and a purple bra this time. I wonder if she wears matching underwear. She's doing it on purpose – I'm sure of it. In fact, there's a name for women like her. Try as I might though, I can't shake the sense that I've seen her somewhere before, which is another reason she's got my full attention. Possibly when we were younger? She could have been one of my hundred notches. I'd like to ask her if we've met before, but I probably won't. It sounds too cheesy.

No matter what, Suzannah was a welcome distraction, as that session with Daniel was heavy - and my head is still buzzing. He was certainly right when he said the therapy would get worse before getting better. I hate talking about being a kid. How that bitch of a mother treated me. And I've certainly lived up to all her expectations during my adult life so far. She's as much to blame for what I've done as I am – if not more so.

I order a coffee and slide into a seat next to the window, wishing I'd had the foresight to buy a newspaper to occupy my mind. I glance towards the empty newspaper rack beside the counter and then around the rest of the café. An elderly man has his head stuck in The Times and another man, all suited and booted, has commandeered The Guardian. My eyes fall on The Mail, which I'd normally buy. It's folded into quarters in front of a young woman. She's not even reading it – too busy warbling to the man behind the counter. I rise from my chair and head towards her.

"Have you finished with this?" I rest my hand on the corner of the paper.

"I've not started it yet." She laughs and places her hand squarely in the centre of it.

I tug at it. "Aren't these newspapers meant for everyone? You're not even reading it. I've been watching you."

She gives me a look as if to say *weirdo*. She ought to watch herself.

"Well, I will be, alright?"

"Easy mate." The man looks up from his wiping and frowns at me, possibly sensing the anger in my voice. "If she says she's reading it, you'll have to wait your turn."

Several people are gawping at me. Story of my life. Everywhere I go, I'm stared at and disliked. There literally are only two people in the world who seek me out and enjoy my company. My daughter and my niece. No matter what happens, I owe it to them to be the best dad and uncle I possibly can be and get myself right. If I do that, perhaps other people will behave differently towards me. Starting with my wife. What is wrong with everyone? What do I have to do to be treated with respect?

I'm sweating beneath my jacket and scarf, so drape it over the back of my chair and wipe the steam from the window with my sleeve. I can see across to the office window of The Alder Centre and just about make out Suzannah moving about in the window. Maybe she *will* come over here for her lunch break. I'm convinced that's why she suggested this place, knowing it was close by. Perhaps she's watching me here right now. Something within me stirs. I pull out my phone to occupy myself whilst I wait for her.

I don't normally spend much time on social media, but there's little else to do as I sip my coffee and wait for my sandwich. It does my head in to see all the perfect families, wives, kids, babies, dogs... Suddenly I recall the girls' pleas for a dog when we were travelling to the airport.

Then, as if by fate, my gaze falls on an advert for some Labrador pups. They're a thousand quid each but well worth it to make Heidi and Alysha's day, week and month. It may even melt Eva somewhat – bring back that fleeting maternal urge she had in Florida and distract me from lusting over this Suzannah one.

I really want a son. A mini me, without the flaws of course. So I can say, *this is my son*. A young man who'll carry my name on. But until I persuade Eva, a puppy it will have to be. I hit the hyperlinked telephone number.

~

"Aren't you supposed to be at work?" Eva stands from stuffing laundry into the washing machine.

"I'm on my break, actually." I close the kitchen door behind me to drown out the yelping from the pet carrier.

"You don't normally come home for your break." Distrust is etched across her face. "Is everything alright?"

"Dad," Heidi shrieks from the hallway. "Oh, wow!"

Eva strides past me towards the door. "What have you been up to?"

I search Eva's face as Heidi takes the puppy from the pet carrier. It's a cross between fury and curiosity.

"Is this for us Dad? I don't believe it."

I've never seen an expression on Heidi's face like this one. And I've got to be honest – what I'm experiencing as I watch my daughter is definitely a better buzz than the other kind I've been fixated on over the last couple of years. I'll have to remember this moment in times of temptation.

"Should you not have run this by me first Will?" Eva seems to be trying to frown through a shadow of a smile. At least she's not ordering me to get rid of him. Well, she could try. Heidi might put up a fight though.

"I wanted to surprise you both, that's all."

"This is the best surprise EVER. Can Alysha come round? He's so cute. It is a he, isn't it Dad?"

"Yes." I glance at the appropriate spot just to make sure. "You'll have to decide what you're going to call him."

"Wow. Wow. Wow."

I knew she'd be over the moon. It's good, behaving like a *normal* dad, instead of the man who's inhabited me for as long as I can remember. I really, really, really have to hang onto this moment.

"It's not you who'll be feeding and walking him though, is it Will?" Eva stands, hands on hips, looking as though she'd like to move closer to the puppy but holding back in front of me. She'll be all over him when I go back to work.

"I'll do my bit – don't worry." And I will. I like the idea of training and walking a dog. I'll be its master.

"We're just short of one family member now." I look from the dog and Heidi to Eva.

"What do you mean by that?" She walks to the front door in response to something landing on the mat.

"You know exactly what I mean. Heidi?"

"What Dad?" She can't tear her gaze away from the little dog trembling on her knee. After leaving his mother, facing us lot must be quite something. Even the bloody dog had a mother. This counselling is raking up so much shit. I can see why people refuse to have it. Still – if things are going to change, then I've got to do the work.

"You'd like a baby brother as well as your puppy, wouldn't you Heidi?"

Eyes shining, she looks from me to her mother as though she might explode with excitement.

"Can we? When? *Really?*" Heidi cuddles the puppy closer, her blonde pigtails falling over his fur. I might have got things far from right in life, but I've produced a cute kid.

Eva flounces back towards the kitchen, evidently pissed off with me.

"I'll be back in a minute love. You'd better decide what you're going to call him."

"That's really not fair Will." Eva tugs cups from the dishwasher and slams them into the cupboard. It's a miracle they don't crack. Her face would if she smiled for a change.

"I'll tell you what's not fair." I throw my keys onto the counter, march over to her, blocking her path back to the dishwasher. "It's making a promise of another child to me and then retracting it."

"I've said I'm sorry." She doesn't shrink back as much as she normally would. It's since she got that job – it's changed her. "There's been so much going on this year and it's such a big step. It's not as if things between us have been rock solid either."

"What's that supposed to mean?" I take a step closer, towering above her.

"Mum. Dad." Eva and I turn from where we're squared up to each other, towards our daughter.

"I'm going to call the puppy Biscuit. Because he's the same colour. What are you going to call my baby brother?"

I look from her back to Eva, then step away and grab my car keys. "Ask your mum love. I need to get back to work."

"Where are we at tonight?" I say to Tyler as I slam my locker door. "Is there anything new in?"

"Yeah – we need to get down to Carlton Bridge sharpish, and close off the road, both ends of the bridge. DI Jones has already sent a car – we're in the other. You're late back, aren't you?"

I've seen this irritation on his face too many times towards me. Jumped up prat. Just because he's robbed me of my commendation.

"Yeah. Had to nip home. Anyway, who put you in charge of me all of a sudden?"

He flushes to the roots of his red hair, making his freckles appear to join up. "It's just - we should have been down there by now. Come on. I'll fill you in on the way."

He strides ahead of me towards the exit into the car park, and the thud of our boots echoes around the stone walls.

"Carlton Bridge, you said? How come?" *As if we're getting sent down there.* Of all the places.

"A recovery operation. Reported missing yesterday."

"A body?" I try to keep my voice steady. "From the river?"

"Yeah. Another woman. Saturday night, by the sounds of it."

Another one?" I keep my gaze straight forward and hope my face isn't giving anything away.

"Our orders are to close the west side of the bridge," he continues, "take charge of crowd control and divert the traffic."

"All that's come from Jones, has it?"

"Yep. They're recovering the woman from the river right now."

I head round to the driver's side as we reach the car. "It'll be all over the news shortly."

"There's been nothing official released yet on what's happened, or about who she is. No doubt word will be out soon though." He glances at his watch. "Come on. We need to get there."

To say it's a Monday night, a hefty crowd has gathered. The two designated police constables seem to be struggling to keep people back when we arrive.

"You took your time," the youngest one snaps at Tyler. Even in the darkness, I can see how red-faced he is.

I open my mouth to remind him about respect for more senior ranks but think better of it. We *are* later than we should've been down here so had better get on with it before anyone more senior challenges us.

With only one car – they've been able to block off the west side of the bridge and have so far, managed to direct traffic at this side. But with traffic backing up at both ends, there's angry complaints being fired at them left, right and centre. After all, Carlton Bridge is the only route through the town centre and to go round puts ten minutes on a journey with a clear run, never mind when this sort of thing is going on.

I give the siren a quick belt to allow us to get through and park horizontally across the east side. I switch the blues on and get out of the car. Tyler joins me beside the other constable.

"So what's going on then?" I point upstream to the near bank, which is lit up like a Christmas tree. The scene is uncannily similar to the one last February in which DCI Ingham leapt off this very bridge to evade capture. Then PC Canvey seemed to think he was a hero and jumped in after him. The rest, as they say, is history. It's a shame it was him, having a young family and all that. And as constables go, Chris Canvey was alright – he just ended up in the wrong place at the wrong time that night.

"She's still being examined." He gestures towards the tent, grimacing. The tent is ghostly white against the dark sky, more so with the shapes of people moving around inside it. The PC looks fresh out of training and probably hasn't had to witness the dredging of a body from a river before. "It's looking like she went in further up and has drifted down here." He points as he speaks, his voice wobbling.

The first dead body I ever saw was my brother's. I blink away the image – it's never far away and nothing good comes of it when I allow it to fester.

"I can't believe it's another woman." Tyler shakes his head. "That's three, in less than a fortnight. They'll have to open an investigation after this one."

"But Ingham's dead," the PC replies. "And there's been no word as to whether there's any cause for alarm yet."

Tyler pulls his attention from the scene back to us. "I guess they'll have to be really thorough after last time. We don't need another Police Complaints Commission jobby. We're already lower than low in the public's eyes."

White suits swarm like flies. Then I notice that they have positioned only an inner cordon. I reach back into the car and pull out the tape for the outer cordon. There doesn't seem to be any sign of a commanding DCI yet, but the lack of an outer cordon will see the PCs well in the firing line. Me and Tyler too, with us being the more senior ranked here. And I was late back from my break. It's going to be years until I get a promotion, the way I'm going.

Perhaps Ingham was talking some sense in those moments before I sent him on his merry way earlier this year - perhaps I only got to Sergeant level because of my hold over him. Maybe I'll be stuck here forever.

Even Mark's got a promotion in the offing, which really pisses me off, and he's bloody five years younger than me. I'm shocked Mum hasn't made some sniping reference to it yet. She normally would.

"Stand back please." PC whatever-his-name-is shouts to the surging crowd, his voice jolting me back to what I'm supposed to be doing.

I hope that outwardly, I appear to be surveying what's going on around me and acting in my professional capacity. I usually feel like ten men when I'm in uniform. Inwardly, though, everything is tumbling around.

The woman went in *yesterday.* I was here in the early hours *yesterday.* I can see the bench I was sitting on from where I'm standing now. My gaze shifts from the bench to the entrance of The Yorkshire Arms. I watched that pub door, I'm not sure how long for, but it seemed like a long time. I *know* what I was waiting for, no matter how hard I've tried to fight it. I should have been nowhere near here in the first place.

Sometimes, I go into what I can only describe as a trance. Like I've been taken over. It's happened repeatedly to me since the days of smoking the skunk weed. Things go into slow motion, and I hear my own voice, though it sounds like it's echoing around me, rather than coming from somewhere within me. And I develop a physical strength which surpasses my usual limits. Everything's a blur afterwards – as though I've blacked out. Maybe my mind is trying to protect me from the actions I'm capable of.

I scrunch my eyes closed, trying to bring Saturday night back to mind. I remember the bench. And I'm sure that at some point I was talking to someone. *Or was I just talking to myself?* It could have been the voices. I recollect leaves slippery underfoot along the path of the riverbank. *Where was I walking?* I have a sense of walking beside someone. The full moon of that night has stuck in my mind. I remember thinking, the fuller the moon, the darker the behaviour. And then... nothing.

Once back home, I had a shower in the main bathroom, rather than our en-suite, so I didn't wake Eva. *Why would I have needed a shower at that time of night?* I'd already had one before I'd got into bed the first time.

I recall the time on our alarm clock showing it was after three when I got back in beside Eva. I went to great lengths to ensure my still chilly skin didn't brush onto hers. Luckily, she hadn't moved.

Normally I'm up by seven at the latest every morning – even at the weekend, after a long stretch on days. That's one gift of being a non-drinker. But yesterday, it was pushing towards ten before I even opened my eyes. And still I was exhausted. After all these years, I can't recall how a hangover feels, but I was on edge all day yesterday and ached from head to foot. I can't have been far away from how a hungover person might be. Even Eva was asking what was wrong with me, when normally, she wouldn't notice.

When I've had trance episodes before, or have been taken over by the voices, I usually get flashbacks for several weeks. Sometimes they start straight away, at others they elude me for days, or even weeks. I've learned not to fear what's going on anymore, but to use them to my advantage when they happen. After all, knowledge is power, and it's just my mind drip feeding me the knowledge, one piece at a time, so I don't become overwhelmed.

I feel different this time though. Like I never have before. Normally, I have a stronger sense of what I've done. Something has changed here, and it doesn't feel good. Not at all.

I've got ninety minutes remaining of my shift. "It's my turn to get warm," I say to Tyler as he strides from the car, sliding his hands back into his gloves. "There's not a lot doing here now."

The woman's being moved to the mortuary. Several of them carry her on a stretcher out of the tent and alongside the river to the waiting private ambulance parked beside me. More officers walk alongside, holding sheeting against the stretcher, but they're all so out of sync with one another that they're doing little to protect the body from prying eyes and lenses. I wonder what will happen if one of them loses their footing on the muddy bank. They'll fall like a row of dominoes, the sheeted up woman being the last one to hit the ground. But at least she won't feel anything.

The forensics search is still going on, and we've to keep the road blocked off until the next traffic cops take over from us. At least the crowd has largely dispersed; the November mist that's now rolling in would have that effect on anyone. The constables knocked off at eight, so we've hung around. Actually, I offered to. Being here may throw light on any involvement I may have had this time. Staying around where it happened should bring it back to me. When I see the picture of the dead woman when it's released, I'll know then.

Sometimes, these things come back when I'm sleeping, which is a concern in that I could give something away to Eva. I've lost count of how many times I've heard. *"Will. Wake up. You're having a bad dream,"* as I writhe around our bed, Eva's hands on my arms trying to still the turbulent states I get myself into. Like I keep saying, I want to change. Whether I can is another matter.

Tyler's got the car heated, so I get myself comfortable in the passenger seat and pluck my phone from my pocket, grateful for a few minutes of warmth and a sit down at last. I stare out at the inky black river. It's difficult to see where the sky ends and the water begins. Drizzle falls onto the windscreen – I've been so wired, I didn't even realise it was raining. I rake my fingers through my damp fringe, wanting the dark sanctuary of my bed. I don't want to be here, at Carlton Bridge. It's too soon.

There are three missed calls from Claire. I hit call to ring her back, accidentally pressing Facetime and getting an eyeful of my double chin and dark eyes on the screen. I look like shit at the moment – it's the appointments – I'm not sure they're doing me any good. Quickly I press cancel and go for audio. She answers after one ring.

"You rang?"

"I've been trying to get hold of Mark, but I think he's off with that Sara."

"Really." An image of her lipsticked smirk floods my brain. It's women like her... There's a saying that certain people can make the hairs stand up on the back of your neck, and she is one of those at this moment. "They seem to be spending a lot of time together. She was round there the other night."

"You're not kidding. Have you heard from Mark today by any chance?" Claire sounds really miserable.

"No. I rarely do. Apart from when he's stuck for someone to babysit Alysha."

"I don't think she's too struck on Sara, either. She's much clingier to Mark when Sara's around. Poor little thing."

I resist the urge to tell Claire to sort her own shit out and leave our brother to it, but something tells me I shouldn't. If I come between the two of them, I might become the first port of call for Claire's woes. And anything I say usually gets repeated and turned back on me anyway. The curse of being the black sheep.

"We can take Alysha more if she doesn't want to be around Sara," I say. "I wouldn't want to be around her either."

"Nah. That would just free Mark up more when he's not working, giving Sara more chance to get her claws into him."

"I thought you liked Sara?" The doors of the private ambulance slam at the side of me, though the crowd of ghoulish observers has dwindled even further since I got into the car. Hopefully, we can get out of here soon. Just being here evokes all kinds of unwanted impulses within me.

"I did like her when she was Lauren's friend. We were going to plan the hen party together." Claire sighs, a real guttural sigh. "But it's too soon for Mark, and I can't help wondering what her motives are."

"I'm with you on that one. I can't stand the woman, personally." She's stuck in my head now, her trowelled on make-up, standing in her cloud of throat-clogging perfume. "I reckon she's after helping him spend some of that money they've awarded him."

"It's more than that," Claire says. "I bet she's wanting to pick up where Lauren left off. She's literally there all the time. Brenda says the same as me. She can't bear the possibility of Mark getting involved with someone else so soon after Lauren."

"Are they...? Have they...?"

"I think so. I turned up early yesterday morning with Mum, and Sara was there." Her voice takes on a sharper edge.

"How early?" As if he's having it away with her. Mark's always got more action than me. In fact he's always had more *everything* than me.

"Early enough to know that she'd definitely stayed over - she was wearing Lauren's dressing gown for God's sake."

"I don't know why Mark hasn't got rid of Lauren's stuff yet." I take a swig of water from the bottle in the door pocket. "It's been, what, nine months? When Lauren first snuffed it, Mark was on about moving. Now he's made the house into some sort of shrine and taken to shagging her best mate."

"We don't know that for sure. Anyway Will." Claire's voice changes tone. "Why have you got such a bloody awful way with words? *Snuffed it.*"

"It's just me. Better get used to it, hadn't you?"

"Well, I've had long enough to." There's a trace of amusement in her voice. After Heidi and Alysha, I guess Claire is my next go-to. She's a decent person, she just does my head in because she's always been so close to Mark. *And* she seems to be letting Mum in more. Which could be a problem.

11

My NEXT APPOINTMENT with Daniel Hamer comes around quickly. I've asked to be rostered onto a late on the same day every week so I can continue going. DCI Mills raised an eyebrow when I made the request but didn't delve for more information after I told her it was medical.

Strangely, this week, I've looked forward to coming back here. I expect part of this anticipation is the thought of being in proximity with Suzannah Peterson. I watch her bustling around the reception area whilst I wait for Daniel to call me in. Well, specifically, I watch her arse as she plucks a file from the bottom of the cabinet.

"Do you have access to *my* file?" I ask as she rises and opens the file out on the top of the cabinet.

She appears to startle at my sudden question in the peace of the office. "Of course. I'm the practice manager. I do all the administration."

"Do you read what's in it?"

She turns to face me then, and I notice how blotchy her neck is against the white of her blouse. She's wearing a white bra today. "Read *what?* The notes in your file? Not especially."

"I'd rather you didn't read any of it."

The last thing I want is Suzannah being privy to anything that might be going on in my head, or anything I divulge from my childhood. All I want her to see is my best self.

"Then, I won't." Without looking at me, she sits back behind her desk, leaving the file she was looking at open on top of the cabinet. She fiddles with some papers in a tray.

She seems so uncomfortable that I decide to explain myself. "It's just, I wouldn't want you to know what I say to Daniel. What I think. What I feel." Tone it down Will. I'm going off on one here. I act in some peculiar ways at times. Words leave me before I plan to say them.

She raises her eyes from the sheet of paper she's been staring at. "We have a strict code of confidentiality here, Mr Potts. As Daniel will have explained to you."

"Call me Will, Suzannah. And thanks for recommending that little café to me last week. Perhaps this time, you might like..."

"Will. Hello." Daniel Hamer appears in reception. "Apologies for being a few minutes late." He looks pointedly at Suzannah. "Are you OK?"

She nods and smooths the folds of her blouse with her fingers. I long to do the same. This is a woman who's the polar opposite of the women I want to rid the world of. She has class and control over herself. A woman who wouldn't stagger alone from the Yorkshire Arms on a Saturday night, after drinking her own body weight in wine. Nor is she someone who'd drive a car into two lads, killing one and leaving the other one, well, like I've been left. How I've turned out is not my fault. It's Pat Ingham's. And my mother's. But now Eva's having more of a negative effect on me as well. And I'm not sure what to do about it.

· · ·

Daniel slides his feet from his shoes and leans back in his chair, facing me. "Tell me about your time since I last saw you."

"Why do you do that?" I point to his feet.

"Do what?"

"Take your shoes off." I try to disguise the irritation in my voice. But I do find it irritating. It's as though he's trying to intimidate me. "Don't you think it's a bit..."

"What?" He's staring at me from underneath his heavy eyebrows. I don't like that either. The way he looks at me.

"Unprofessional."

"To be honest Will, I do it with every client I see, not just you. No one else has complained."

"Oh." I'm not sure if I like being called a *client*. I stare at his socks – spots this time. With the beard and the beige clothes, the socks are the most interesting thing about him.

"Taking my shoes off makes me feel more grounded. Perhaps you should try it."

"No. You're alright thanks."

"If it's a problem, I'll wear the shoes."

"No worries. We can't have you not being *grounded*, can we?"

"Anyway, we're not here to talk about my shoes, or lack of them." He clasps his hands behind his head and asks again. "How's everything been since I last saw you?"

I stare at him, fighting the urge to tell him the truth. How my brain won't allow me to recall whether I've ended the life of another woman in the river Alder. How I'm fighting the lust to go back and do it all over again. I want to talk about that power I get from the freeze of a woman paralysed in terror, and the horror in her eyes when she realises where she's going. I jump as the sound of a scream slices through my mind.

"Will?"

I open my eyes and realise I'm clutching the chair arms. I stare at the painting behind Daniel of the river scene. It's as though it's goading me.

"Are you alright?"

"Yeah. Thanks. Sorry." I scrunch my eyes together, then open them again. "It's been a stressful few days?"

"In what way." He tilts his head to one side like a dog waiting expectantly at a door.

I take a moment to steady my breathing. "Home. Work. Family. The usual."

"Have you written any of it down? Do you recall me asking you to make notes about your thoughts at our last appointment?"

I shake my head, becoming slightly calmer. "I'm not really a writer. It's bad enough having to fill in reports at work."

He glances towards his desk in the corner and then back to me. "I wonder Will, would you have any objection to me recording our session?"

"Recording it?"

Bloody hell. *What if I were to speak out of turn?* I've done well so far, but if my guard slips, there'd be evidence. "I don't know. I'm not sure I like the sound of that, to be honest."

"It's so I can go back over it and pull out the aspects I need to prepare for some of the deeper work. There would only be me with access to it."

"Let me think about it." I don't know if it is acceptable for a therapist to record his clients. I need to do some research into it. Plain and simple – I don't trust anyone these days.

"OK, well let me know then, perhaps in time for next time. And remember, our sessions are covered by the confidentiality contract I referred to when we first met."

"Like I said, I'll think about it."

He unbuttons the top of his shirt. "Since you've not done the note making, do you want to tell me about what's been going on for you instead?"

"My wife's gone back on us having another kid." He's the first person I've said anything to about it. It's weird. Very weird.

Like it's giving him power over me. I'm not sure I'm comfortable with it. The man barely knows me and I'm telling him stuff like this. I'm not really sure what I'm doing, but keep talking, regardless. "She'd come off the pill and everything."

"What were her reasons?"

"None that made any sense. She just said she'd changed her mind and wasn't saying *never*, just not now."

My voice is surprisingly even. I could tell Daniel at this point how angry Eva made me, and how it's partly her fault that I'm fighting the urge to return to my old ways, but I can't say a thing. He'll report me, for sure. I notice my hands are balled into fists on top of the chair arms.

Daniel appears to notice them too. I quickly uncurl my fingers, surprised at the ache within them.

"And how has this change of heart made you feel Will?" His voice is so soft, I barely hear it,

Feel. Feel. Feel. I don't want to feel.

"How do you think it's made me feel? How would *you* feel?"

"I don't know. This isn't about me. I can see by the way you're holding yourself so rigid that you're angry. Do you get angry often Will?"

I wish he'd stop saying my name. *Will. Will. Will.* "Sometimes. Doesn't everyone?"

"I guess so. It's a natural human emotion. The difference is in how we allow ourselves to express it, or whether we turn it inwards on ourselves or outwards onto someone else."

"Great, so I'm here for a psychology class today."

"Not at all. I'm just interested to find out how you express your anger?" He strokes his beard, another thing that annoys me about him. Or maybe I'm just that way out with myself today. It's warped now to think I was looking forward to coming here – but that's probably more about Suzannah. I keep looking at her Facebook profile, at the stuff she allows everyone to see. I should send her a friend request, then I can see the lot. How I would like to see *the lot.*

"How do *you* express your anger Daniel?" I slide my own feet from my shoes and plant them on the floor. Granted, I do feel slightly calmer for doing it.

Daniel lifts his gaze from my feet back to my face. "Like I said, we're not here to talk about me."

We sit, facing each other for a moment. Perhaps this is a complete waste of time – this psychotherapy. It's not as though I can go into the complete truth anyway, so what use will any of this be? And without going into the truth, how can I ever change? How can I ever become an everyday husband and father, and stay well away from the river Alder on a Saturday night?

"Why don't you tell me about your work?"

I glance again at the river painting. "Did you hear about the body that was pulled out the other day? From the Alder?"

"I did."

"I was there whilst they recovered it." I think back to the blue lights swirling against the night sky. The white tent illuminated in the police floodlights. The sheeted body being stretchered along the riverbank.

"I thought you were part of the traffic division?"

"We were patrolling the road closure. If it's quiet, we get roped into that sort of work. It's not all high-speed chases up the M1."

"What effect did that have on you?" His voice softens again, and he's no longer holding eye contact with me. It's as though he suspects something.

"I'm a traffic cop, aren't I? I've seen more mangled bodies than you've had hot dinners."

"But considering what your family's been through, it must..."

"Yeah. It's tough, I guess. If she hadn't been so pissed though..."

"What? Who?"

"She might still be alive."

"Are you talking about the woman who died on Saturday?" Daniel sits up straighter in his seat. "The one whose body was recovered?"

"Yeah." I close my eyes. "She could hardly walk."

"Did you see her Will? Were you with her?" That gentle voice. I'm safe in this room. I'm slipping back to who I used to be. I don't want to but...

"Will?"

As I open my eyes, Daniel is writing something down. "Where were you on Saturday night Will?"

I laugh. "I'm the one who's the copper Daniel. I know how pissed she was from the CCTV and the toxicology report, that's all."

"Someone called Suzannah Peterson has rung." Eva rushes around the kitchen, looking in dishes and drawers and under cloths and papers as she speaks. "Apparently you left the Alder Centre without paying your bill or making another appointment. Have you seen my car keys anywhere?"

"Look in your handbag, that's where most things end up." I used to find this endearing. Now it annoys the shit out of me. And she bites my head off if I go anyway near her handbag. Sometimes I wonder what she has to hide.

"She wants you to ring her." Eva points to the block of post-its we use to take messages. "She says you left in a hurry, and they were also wondering if you were OK."

"She shouldn't be saying things like that to you. It's meant to be confidential."

"I'm supposed to be your wife."

"What do you mean, *supposed to be*?" The familiar anger snakes up my spine. "Mind you – yeah. Husbands and wives have families together, don't they? Husbands and wives have sex." I ignore the look on her face – as though I've slapped her. "You've become frigid since we got back off that holiday Eva. Bloody frigid. You should see a doctor."

She swings around from the pot she's searching on the windowsill.

"What did you call me?" There's a fire in her eyes I don't like. She's certainly finding her backbone again. It's time for me to snap it.

"You heard Eva. I work all the hours God sends for this family. I take you on a once in a lifetime holiday and *this* is how you repay me." I stare at her, realising I really, really am not attracted to her anymore. She's certainly no Suzannah Peterson.

"I didn't realise I had to *repay* you Will."

"And can you shut that bloody thing up?" The dog's whining from the utility room. He started shitting everywhere, so now he's in one of those dog cages. It's his own fault.

"You brought him here." Eva steps towards me, her hands on her hips. She even has the audacity to raise her voice. "I didn't want a dog and I certainly don't want another kid. Not with you."

"Then who with? You stupid bitch. No one else would look twice at you anyway. Have you seen the state of yourself."

"If I'm in a state, it's because I'm married to such a nasty piece of work. I want you to leave Will." Her voice wobbles now, which returns my sense of control. "I've had enough. I can't live like this anymore."

"Live like what?" Shit. She means it.

"You're cold, you're controlling and there's something inside you that scares me." Though the way she looks at me suggests she isn't scared right now. She's never stood up to me like this before.

"*There's something inside me that scares you?*" I repeat, the level of sarcasm in my voice surprising me. But I don't like what she's said. Mum's told me repeatedly that there's something nasty within me.

"I'm being serious Will. I want you to leave."

"Give over. It's my house. Who pays the fucking bills? I'm going nowhere." I slide my keys from the kitchen counter and drop them into my pocket in case she gets any ideas about getting hold of them.

"We'll go then. We'll go to my Mum's." She looks around again.

"You bloody won't."

"Try and stop me Will."

"You're my wife and you're not going anywhere – have you got that? And you're certainly not taking my daughter to stay with that demented bitch."

"We're not your property. I've let you control things around here for long enough. And don't *ever* speak about my mother like that. I hope you end up with Alzheimer's one day."

"Well that's a fucking nice thing to say, isn't it?" I kick the door to the utility room. "Shut up." The dog whines even louder.

"If you won't let me go, I'm calling the police." She darts past me and plucks her jacket from the back of the chair.

I throw my head back and roar with laughter. "*Call the police!* I am the police."

"I'll tell them who you really are, what you're *really* like. Even your own mother detests you."

That's it then. Red mist. I lurch forward and grab her by the throat.

"Get off me." She gurgles as I march her backwards across the kitchen, my hands around her neck. There's a crack as her head connects with the fridge door, scattering fridge magnets in all directions. I've always told her they clutter the place up.

Agony shoots through me. The witch has grabbed me by the balls. I sink to my knees, powerless to do anything. She's going to get me locked up. I try to rise from the floor, but I'm winded by the pain. There's nothing I can do to stop her making the call. I listen to her voice above the yelps of the dog.

"Yes. He's just gone for me. I need some help. I want him out of here."

"You fucking liar!" My voice doesn't sound like my own. "You will not get away with this."

12

I LOOK at the officer who's processing me. "I'm supposed to be on shift. I should have started ten minutes ago."

They have driven me to a station on the other side of Alderton. It's procedure for me not to be dealt with at the same station I work at. The officer carries on with whatever he's doing on the computer, without answering me. His ignorance is infuriating, and it's hard to rein my anger in.

"I'm in traffic," I continue. "Can you at least tell them that I won't be in today?"

Though whether I'll have a job after what Eva's engineered is anyone's guess. I must hang onto the reality that it will be my word against hers. No one else was there.

"You're allowed one phone call." He slides the phone across the counter towards me. "And the right to legal representation, as I'm sure you won't need me to tell you."

"Is the number withheld on outbound calls?" I take it from him. "I can't have anyone knowing where I am. And no, I don't need a solicitor. I've done nothing wrong. This is a complete waste of time."

He shrugs and returns to the keyboard tapping.

After telling my station I'm ill, I'm led towards a cell. I shrink back as I'm told to remove my shoes and belt.

"You can't lock me up like this." I tell the officer. "I'm a bloody copper for God's sake."

"We'll come and get you when we're ready to interview." He slams the door after me, and the clunk of the key lets me know I'm truly incarcerated.

Eva is going to pay for this. She's going to wish she'd never met me. And that officer. I'll make sure he ends up with a warning for being so ignorant.

As I sink to the bench, it's as though I've returned to my trance state of earlier. Again, it's like my mind is trying to protect me from what's going on. I bring my legs up and lie down, but the room seems to be slanting to one side. I feel weird, disorientated, just like I do when I'm on the riverbank. There are definitely two William Potts inside me – the one who yearns to be a contented family man, and the other, well – perhaps it's going to take more than a few poxy *let's talk* sessions with Daniel Hamer to sort the other one out.

And he wants to record our meetings. I don't really understand that. And my trust in him has slipped since he suggested it. What if he plays it back and lets Suzannah listen? Or someone else. There's no one I do trust anymore. Even Eva's shown what she's really made of, and she's totally let me down. My chance to punish her for it will come. If she says anything to Heidi about what's happened between us this afternoon, I won't be responsible for my actions. If there's one thing I can't abide, it's women who poison their kids against their fathers. It's child abuse as far as I'm concerned.

I watch as the barred window in the top corner of the cell turns orange then darkens to dusk. The flickering of the fluorescent overhead lighting makes my eyes ache.

"Turn the light off." My voice echoes around the stone walls and suddenly I have the urge to throw my head against them. I squeeze my eyes together, willing myself to find some clarity instead of this fog that's swirling in and around me. Then a memory of throwing my head against my bedroom wall as a child floods my brain. The pain. The giddiness. Then my mother's face. Then Dean's. I scrunch my eyes even tighter.

"William Potts." The voice of an officer I don't recognise cuts into the silence. "We're ready to speak to you now." Great. I've got a woman interviewing me. No prizes for guessing whose side she'll be on.

"I'm DI Moriarty." She gestures to a seat on the other side of the table. "PC Cameron will also sit in on this interview. Shall we?" She nods at her colleague, the jumped up constable who processed me when I first arrived. I glare at him.

The long tone of the recording equipment cuts into the stillness of the interview room. Our station is busier than this on a Thursday afternoon. Getting out of the cell has helped my head fog to clear slightly – I just need to get out of here now. It's surreal being on the wrong side of the interview table. I've never been arrested in my life, which is miraculous, considering what I've done.

"My name is Detective Inspector Susan Moriarty. I'll be conducting this interview with," she nods at me. "Can you confirm your full name, address and date of birth please?"

"William Lee Potts. 42 Riverside Close, Alderton, 27th November 1980." I realise they might not let me go home after this. What will I do? It'll be like being nineteen again when Mum kicked me out.

"And my colleague." She nods at the pillock across the table. He doesn't look old enough to be shaving.

"Police Constable James Cameron."

"Sergeant Potts. We've arrested you on suspicion of assaulting your wife, Eva Jane Potts. The alleged incident took place earlier this afternoon, at your home address, which you've just confirmed, at approximately 12:50 pm. You do not have to say anything. But it may harm your defence if you do not mention when questioned something which you later rely on in court. Anything you do say may be given in evidence." Her robotic tone of voice changes. "As a serving police officer, I assume you won't need any explanation about your rights."

"No. Of course not." The neckline of my t-shirt is baggy from where Eva had hold of it earlier when she was fighting me off, and my groin is still smarting. Some wife.

"Is it alright for me to call you William?" DI Moriarty asks with her Celtic lilt. I've seen her in passing before, at police functions, but this is the first time we've spoken. She can't be far off retirement age. I nearly demand that I'm addressed by my rank, but I don't want to alienate her. If I can get her on side, I'm more likely to get out of here, with minimal damage caused. It's worth a go.

"Call me Will. I hate William." My mother's face enters my thoughts again. God, she's going to have a field day when she finds out about all this. I've played right into her hands here. Everything she's ever known about me...

"Can I clarify that you've declined your right to legal representation?"

"Yes. I've done nothing wrong. I don't need it."

"OK, Will. Let's start with you explaining what happened at home between you and your wife earlier this afternoon."

I take a deep breath. "We've been having a few problems lately. It's been a difficult year – my sister was attacked in February, and my sister-in-law was murdered."

I see sympathy swimming in DI Moriarty's eyes. "Yes Will. We are well aware of Jonathan Ingham."

"It's all taken its toll on my wife Eva, well all of us. She's been taking on more at work and anyway, we were bickering earlier, then she totally lost it and went for me."

I notice PC Cameron writing something down.

"*She* went for *you?*" DI Moriarty clasps her hands together on the table, looking at me from beneath overly plucked eyebrows, her thumbs curling round and round each other. I want to tell her to keep them still.

"It was totally out of character," I continue. "She's normally easy-going. Anyway, she went straight for the jugular, if you know what I mean." I smile as I point downwards. Neither of them smile back. Maybe they're not sure what I mean.

"That's not the story Eva is telling us."

"I don't deny I retaliated and grabbed her." I glance from one to the other. I've got to get them on my side. "But only in self defence to get her off me. What's a bloke to do when his wife's got him by the balls?"

"So, you're insisting that she went for you first?"

"Absolutely." I nod, loading as much sincerity as I can muster into my face and my voice.

"What were you arguing about Will?"

"She's been wanting another kid." It's the first thing that comes into my mind. "And I don't, at least not at the moment – not with everything that's gone on this year. And I'm sure all this baby longing has sent her round the twist. You hear of it with women, don't you?"

The policewoman's expression is passive.

"It's her you should've arrested really, but well," I shrug, "I'm a copper so I came quietly when the police arrived, to diffuse things. It's honestly been blown into something far bigger than it is."

"I see. And were there any witnesses to this altercation between the two of you? Someone who'd be willing to collaborate your story?"

I shake my head. "No, thankfully, Heidi, our eight-year-old, was at school. I'd have hated for her to have seen her mother go for me like that." I pack as much regret and misery as I can into my words.

"The thing is Will..." DI Moriarty pauses and glances at her colleague. "Your wife is adamant that it was, in fact, *you*, that started the violence, and on that basis, we have a duty of care both towards her and to your daughter."

Fear grabs at my throat. Shit. "What are you saying here? I'd never harm a hair on my daughter's head."

"I'm saying that your wife would prefer you not to return to the house." DI Moriarty looks me straight in the eye. Her gaze is unwavering. Bitch. She doesn't believe me.

"But it's my house. How can she stop me going back there?"

Eva can get lost. Why didn't I say she could go to her mother's when she suggested it? I just want to go home, shut the door, and get beyond today.

"Is there somewhere else you could stay, at least until things calm down Will?" DI Moriarty leans back in her chair.

"No! There bloody isn't. I'm going home. To my own home. I just want to sort things out with my wife."

"I'm sorry Will." Though she doesn't sound sorry at all. "I'm afraid that won't be possible. It's your word against hers, so we're going to have to make further enquiries into exactly what happened."

I stare at her. "You mean talk to my neighbours? No! That bitch has dragged my name through the mud enough today." I slap the table with the heel of my hand. "No way. I'm not having this. There must be something I can do."

"Ultimately, it will be up to a court to decide who's telling the truth, that's if your wife decides to testify against you."

"I don't believe this. I don't bloody believe it! I have rights. She can't do this. You can't do this."

The expression DI Moriarty displays tells me plenty as to her opinion of me. No doubt Eva will have presented herself as some sort of pathetic battered wife. She's clearly ensured that everyone takes her side. I'm sick of being screwed over by women. Now I can't even go home.

"She'll have to leave," I say. "She can go to her mother's, like she said she might do earlier. No way is she turfing me out of my house."

"She's said she's staying at home to us," DI Moriarty replies. "There's your daughter's schooling to consider."

This is really happening. "There's no way I can be prevented from going home. On exactly what grounds, anyway?"

"On the grounds that we have arrested you for assaulting your wife." DI Moriarty's voice is infuriatingly even. "We're going to release you on police bail, pending further enquiries."

"Bail? But you haven't even charged me. You've got nothing on me! No evidence. *Nothing.*"

"Will. You can choose your own path here. We can lock you back up whilst we proceed with our enquiries, or we can release you under the conditions of not contacting Eva Potts, directly or indirectly."

"You're taking her side without even having any evidence?" This stinks, this does.

"What's it to be, Will? Back in the cell or police bail?"

"I'll stay at my brother's." I sag further into the chair. "How long will all this take to clear up?"

"We'll take some details from you at the desk," she replies, "and we'll keep you posted whether there'll be any charges once we've concluded our investigations."

"What about my work?" Bollocks. The enormity of what Eva's done weighs on me even more heavily. "I'm in traffic. I'm back on shift tomorrow. I should've been there today."

"I'll have to inform your commanding officer about what's happened," DI Moriarty says. "You'll no doubt be put on desk duty until this is sorted – either way."

"Great. Everyone will find out about my private life?"

She shakes her head, her jowls waggling from side to side with the movement. "Not at all. We will keep this completely confidential. Right. We'll get your bail processed and then you'll be free to leave." She rises from her chair, and I notice her belly protruding between her shirt buttons. "We may need to ask you some further questions. So you might want to ensure you have some legal representation when you return. Interview terminated Thursday 10th November at 16:52."

"*When* I return? What else could you possibly need? My wife and I had an argument. She attacked me. I defended myself. No one else was there. No witnesses. End of."

"You idiot." Mark swings the door open. "What the hell have you done?"

"I take it Eva's been in touch?"

"Of course she has. She's in a right bloody state." He narrows his eyes as he stares at me in the porch light. "I've just got back from her house."

"*My* house."

"Whatever." He folds his arms and for a moment, I'm worried that I'll be finding a park bench tonight. Surely, he doesn't think that little of me?

"Can I come in Mark? I can't go home, can I?"

"I know. The station rang to check you could stay here." He takes a step back into the hall. "I'm not happy about it Will. This is the last thing I need."

"Bloody hell." I step forward and he still doesn't move. "It'll only be for a night or two. Am I really so awful to have around?"

"Why didn't you say you'd go to Claire's? She's got more room."

"Cos she'll be squarely on Eva's side, won't she? I doubt she'll even consider my side of the story."

"I can't imagine what makes you think I will." Mark holds the door wider, and I step into the hallway. "You know what I think about violence towards women."

Alysha is peering around the edge of the door, looking worried. *Surely, she hasn't been told anything about what's happened?* Normally, she'd come flying out to say hello.

"Go in there for a few minutes," Mark says to her. "I need a word with your Uncle Will."

At least he's referring to me as *Uncle Will,* which means he still regards me as family on some level. I follow him to the kitchen and tug a chair from under the table. "Don't tell me you're taking Eva's side as well? Whoever said it was a women's world is bang right."

He flicks the switch on the kettle. "I've just seen her Will. She's got a massive lump on the back of her head and bruising all around her throat. She's in a right state – you must have *really* grabbed her. You've never known your own strength. You were the same as a kid with me and Claire."

"She flew at me first. Right for the nuts as well."

"She grabbed them to get you off her. She's told me."

"And you believe her?" I glance around his kitchen. I shouldn't be here. I should be at home, in my own kitchen. Well, *really,* I should be at work. This is shit.

"Eva wouldn't hurt a fly. She says you've become even more controlling and nasty lately. How do you live with yourself Will? How can you treat your wife like that?"

"Here we go again. You're supposed to be *my* brother. On *my* side. Thanks Mark."

"I can't abide blokes who hurt women. Psychologically as well as physically. From what she's said, you've been giving her a really hard time lately."

"And you trust every word she says, of course." I stare at the back of Mark's head, hatred spewing from my every pore. For Eva, for the family that has always cast me out, including him, and for myself. Eva's really messed it all up. "Are you going to let me stay here, or is it a cardboard box for me tonight?"

He sighs as he drags two cups from the cupboard. "It doesn't sound as if I've got a lot of choice, does it? But Will, I'm telling you, one ounce of trouble and you'll have to go somewhere else. I mean it."

"It'll only be for a couple of nights," I say. "I pay every single bill in that house. If she thinks she can make me homeless, she can think again. She'll have to go and stay with her crazy mother."

"The poor woman's got Alzheimer's. You should watch how you treat people, you should. I'm a big believer in what comes around, goes around."

"Of course you are. Saint Mark."

"You'll probably be on the sofa here." Ignoring my Saint Mark dig at him, he turns to look at me. "I've already got Mum, Brenda and Claire constantly fighting over the spare room."

Bloody Mum. Maybe with me around, she'll make herself scarce.

"Hopefully it will all calm down." Mark slides a cup towards me. "Let's just see what happens."

"I'll be going home. That's what'll be happening. Does Mum know anything about all this?"

"She's round there now."

"With Eva? You're joking, aren't you?"

He shakes his head.

"For fuck's sake. That's all I need. Her getting involved. She'll be loving all this."

"You can watch your language around Alysha whilst you're here as well." Mark frowns at me, then appears to brighten. "Anyway, I'm off out tonight." He sips his tea. "Brenda's coming over to look after Alysha."

"Well, there's no need for that. Not now I'm here." I can't face Brenda's judgement. No doubt someone will have told her by now what's gone on between me and Eva. If my mother knows, Brenda will too, and she'll be treating me like some mad axeman.

"Under the circumstances, you've enough on your plate without babysitting for Alysha. Just get your head back together for now. Work out how you're going to sort yourself out from here."

"Where are you off anyway?" I'm glad to change the subject from my current drama.

Mark seems to be searching for an answer, which tells me all I need to know.

"You're not out with that bloody Sara one, are you? You were saying yourself that Lauren's barely cold in the ground. And you judge *me* for my behaviour?"

"One more reference to Lauren like that, and you can piss off somewhere else." Mark slams his cup on the table, slopping tea everywhere. "Do you hear me?"

I decide not to rise to his anger. I do need to stay here. It's not as if I've got anywhere else to go. "I've no idea what you see in that Sara. Really, I haven't."

"It's not up to you, is it? Besides, we're just friends."

"Yeah. Like hell." The tea burns the back of my throat and misery burns at the back of my eyes. I've had enough.

"Just leave it Will."

We sit in silence for a moment.

"Are you at work in the morning?" The tone of his voice has changed. I suppose I'm lucky I had somewhere to come. Not every bloke has that luxury when their wife kicks them out. I've heard of it time and time again. Women hold all the cards and it's time things changed. It's in moments like this when my previous actions towards women seem more justified than ever.

"Hopefully. The DI who interviewed me said I'll probably be put on desk duty until this mess gets sorted out."

"You'll have to be. They won't allow you to carry out active

duty – not whilst you're on bail. Anyway, I'm off to get ready."
He rises from the table and puts his cup on the draining board.
"Just, I don't know – make yourself at home and make sure you
leave Brenda out of it all when she gets here. She doesn't need
to hear your problems."

13

I NEED COFFEE. I've had an appalling night's sleep on Mark's sofa, mulling over how I'm going to handle all this. But I'm stopped in my tracks as I walk into the kitchen.

"No one told me *you* were here. Surely, you haven't been here all night."

Sara sits at the kitchen table like she owns the place, shovelling cereal into her mouth. Mark and Alysha are banging about upstairs, so I have free rein to say what I want.

"I'll be gone shortly, not that it's any of your business." No longer under the cover of her heavy make-up, she looks as rough as a badger's arse.

"Lauren's dressing gown suits you, Sara. Are you going to be wearing *all* her clothes now she's dead?"

"Keep out of it. Where I stay or what I wear has got nothing to do with you."

"What do you think she'd say if she could see you now, muscling in on her family and her life?" I step towards the table and lean onto the chair facing her.

"That's not what's happening here. God only knows why I'm explaining myself to you though." She points the spoon at me.

"You're aware that Alysha can't stand you, aren't you?" I grin.

"Who told you that?" She shrinks back as I tower over her.

"I'm her uncle – she told me that. And we're close, Alysha and me. Anyway, it's sick if you ask me – what you're up to."

"Nah, I'll tell you what's sick," she drops her spoon into the bowl, "what you've done to your poor wife – that's sick."

"How do you know about that?"

She smiles. "How do you think? Mark tells me everything now."

I open my mouth to take Mark to task as he strides into the kitchen, but am stopped short when Alysha trots in behind him. She probably knows too much as it is.

"Get yourself sat down." Mark nudges Alysha towards Sara. "You've got two minutes to get some breakfast down you or else we'll be late for school."

"I don't want to sit with *her*." Alysha sidles round to my side. It feels nice to have an allegiance, albeit with a six-year-old.

Hopefully, *I told you so* is conveyed in the grin I flash at Sara.

"Don't be like that Alysha." Sara pushes her bowl away and looks at Mark with wide eyes. I want to punch her. I know all the tactics of women. She probably wishes Alysha would disappear completely so she could get her claws fully into Mark.

"Am I always kind to your friends Alysha?" Mark tugs the Rice Krispies box from the cupboard, then turns to her.

She stays silent at my side, but her lip is wobbling. Granted, it's out of character for her to have an attitude like this. And it's rare for Mark to pull her up.

"Yes, I am Alysha. I'll answer the question for you, shall I?" He pours cereal into a bowl. "So what I'm saying is that you should be nice to my friends too."

"But Sara is Mummy's friend, not yours." Alysha's voice is

barely audible, even to me. "And I don't like her wearing Mummy's dressing gown."

How perceptive for a girl her age. I pull her towards me.

Sara strides towards the kitchen door, glaring at us both. "I'm off to get a shower."

"Make yourself at home," I call after her.

Mark glares at me. "Give it a rest Will."

With Mark out of the way taking Alysha to school, and my appointment with DI Mills to discuss my home crap an hour away, I prop the lounge door open. I want to make sure Sara doesn't sneak out after her shower without me having the opportunity to collar her. And this time, she won't have my naïve brother for protection.

I pace around the lounge, noticing how things are still exactly the same as before Lauren died. Mark made noises about moving to a new house at first, but seems to have let go of that idea now. I stare at a photograph of her from when they got engaged. I fancied Lauren something rotten when Mark first introduced us and couldn't understand how she could have preferred him to me. She wasn't even flattered when I made a move on her. She seemed more disgusted. It wasn't the greatest thing for my ego, and I wasn't in a good place when she rejected me, either. Then, as the years went by, it was obvious how she avoided me as much as possible, though she always got on with Eva.

I got the chance once to pull Lauren to one side and challenge her about her hostility - at my and Eva's wedding. I reckoned she'd be more amicable because it was my wedding day. I told her I expected things to change given the fact that we were now officially family. However, I'll never forget the way her eyes bulged at me. It was as though I had a contagious disease. She told me to stay away from her and added that I made her skin crawl. She'd jutted her chin out in a similar way to what Alysha does when she's being asked to do something she doesn't want to. At times, it gets to me how much Lauren lives on inside Alysha, to the point where I find it difficult to be around her. It was an issue for me several times when we took her to Florida.

The wedding was supposed to be a happy day, but I'd had to stop myself from lamping Lauren there and then. I knew there and then she was going to get it. How dare she put such a downer on everything? But there was something about what Lauren said and the way she said it that had an echo of my mother. No matter what shit happens in my life, it always circles back to my mother.

At the creak of Sara at the bottom of the stairs, I bolt towards the lounge door. Here we go.

"Going without saying goodbye, are we?" I lean against the doorway.

"You'd be the last person I'd want to exchange pleasantries with."

I'm pleased to see a hint of fear in her eyes, probably at the realisation that she's alone in the house with me. She'd be extremely afraid if she had any inkling of what I'm really capable of. She's wearing jeans and a jumper that I can't tell are Lauren's or not. Sara dresses so similar to how Lauren did that it's hard to say.

"So what's going on with you and my brother then?"

"I'm not talking to you about it." Her voice drips incredulity as she drops her bag to her feet and slides her feet into boots. She's wearing my brother's socks. What a bloody charity case.

"Doesn't it make you ill, shagging Mark I mean? He was getting married to your best mate?" I want to make her feel as low as I do right now. Why should *she* be happy, taking advantage of my brother?

"I wouldn't expect you to understand feeling something for another person, or caring about anyone other than yourself." There's a shake in her voice now. If Mark knew me, *really* knew me, he'd never have left me alone in the house with his shag piece. He will only have himself to blame if this goes pear-shaped.

"So what is it you're after Sara? Mark's money? Lauren's life? You know for sure now that my niece can't stand you, don't you?"

"She'll come around in time. She's just a kid who's lost her mum."

"Well, I'm going to do everything in my power, *love*, to make sure you disappear."

"What do you mean?"

"Carry on sniffing around my brother and you'll find out."

"Are you threatening me?" There's a hint of a smile as she steps towards the door before turning back to me. "God, Lauren was spot on about you. You're totally warped in the head. I can't believe Mark lets you within spitting distance of his daughter. You're a weirdo."

"What did you fucking say to me?" I step towards her, fists bunched, ready to retaliate. But as I see the anticipation on her face, I realise that's what she wants. For me to go for her. And I'm on police bail.

"Do one, you slapper. And remember what I said."

"I'll take you on Will. You don't frighten me. Get out of my way."

I'm shocked at myself as I allow her to push past me towards the door. Nobody gets away with speaking to me like she has. But for now, she'll keep.

~

"Come in." DI Mills continues staring at her computer as I stride into her office.

I pull a chair backwards, ready to sit down.

"Remain standing," she snaps. "This won't take long."

The resemblance she has to my mother is eerie, right down to the haircut at the jawline and the condescending tone of voice. I can barely stand being in the same room as DI Mills. But she and DI Jones are my line management, so I have to keep my loathing for her under wraps. She was alright to start with – when I first qualified and we were equals, but she's become so far up her own arse that she can probably see the inside of her ribs. Jones is OK, and from what I can gather, he barely doubted me when I was being investigated for any part in the river deaths. I bet Mills was trying to put her oar in and guide things in the opposite direction.

"I expect you've heard about my marital problems ma'am." I stand with my legs astride, my hands behind my back – a supposed stance of respect in front of a more senior officer. Really, I should be doing her job. The word ma'am almost lodges in my throat. She became a sergeant well after me. Being a woman, she's probably shagged her way behind that desk.

"If that's what you're calling things." She looks at me straight on, her steely grey eyes meeting mine. "Obviously, until the situation is resolved, you'll be on desk duty, and then if you're charged, you'll be looking at a suspension until it gets to court."

"I won't be charged, and nothing will get to court." My jaw throbs. I can't relax any more. I'm holding myself so tightly all the time with all that's going on. If only I could turn the clock back by two weeks. Return to Disneyworld – be a father, husband and uncle looking forward to another kid and getting a dog. Normal. Though what is normal? Maybe I'll never know. Maybe I've never known.

"You must report all developments in your case to myself or

DI Jones immediately so we can take the appropriate measures."

"The only development is that this nonsense against me will be dropped."

"I'm watching you Sergeant Potts." Her feelings towards me are evident in the sneer on her lips. "Very closely indeed." She drops her gaze back to the papers she was shuffling on her desk as I walked in. "That will be all."

What is it with women? What is it they see in me? I need to bring my next appointment forward with Daniel Hamer, or book an extra one. If I don't, I'm going to do something. I can't take much more of this – someone is going to have to pay.

14

I DON'T NORMALLY GO inside pubs, but the four walls of Mark's house were suffocating me. He and Claire haven't moved all evening and have been sitting like a pair of old folk, glued to some crap on the TV.

Eva still won't answer the phone to me. Not that I'm supposed to be ringing her. My bail conditions specify no direct or indirect contact. But they can't expect me to not communicate with my wife. Where are my rights?

I've still got two weeks before I have to return to the station to answer my bail, and I can't get my head around not being able to go home for all that time. What about being able to see my daughter? It worries me what she'll have been told as well.

How I'm being treated is wrong on every level. With no firm evidence, I don't understand how anyone can prevent me from going home? I'm growing angrier with every hour that passes, and this hasn't been helped by the last two days stuck on desk duty with DI Mills walking past my desk every five minutes. I'm certain word has got out about me being on bail – DI Mills won't have been able to keep her fat mouth shut. The other officers seem to be even more unfriendly than normal, barely speaking to me or meeting my eyes. How will I ever forgive Eva for putting me in this situation?

And now it's Saturday. I should've been on a late, which would have removed some of the usual temptation until I go for the extra therapy appointment I've made with Daniel Hamer for Monday.

Instead, I've found myself drawn back to the Yorkshire Arms. The place has become like my drug of choice again, and tonight I can't do without another hit. What else have I got in my life?

I sit with my hands wrapped around a pint of orange as the dickheads around me get drunker and drunker. Their attempts at trying to cop off with the bimbos in short skirts on the dance floor are pathetic. If you can call a patch of uncarpeted floor in front of an ageing DJ a dance floor. It's probably the only place in the pub where your feet don't stick to the floor as you walk.

A couple of women are nudging each other as their eyes bore into me. It's an empowering feeling. I'm not the average punter admittedly, sitting with my back to the wall - alone, watching, choosing, waiting. I've known from a young age that women like someone with an edge and I've certainly got that. I'm the sort of man I will warn Heidi about when she gets older.

Heidi. I picture her sleeping in the princess bedroom I decorated last summer, and rage prickles at my skin. How dare Eva keep me away from my daughter?

The ratio of women to men is two to one easily. It always is in here. They flock to the cheesy nineties music and special offers on cheap wine. Judging by the state of some of them, it's going to be easy pickings this evening. So long as there's some separation in their groups. There usually is later on when drink has obliterated all faculties.

My ears are buzzing as it ticks around to one in the morning, and the DJ finally stops playing the thudding crap. The noise in here is a nightmare and I wonder whether I should have waited on my bench like normal. But there were a couple of patrolling officers when I arrived. Coming in here meant I wouldn't be seen or challenged by anyone. Hopefully, they'll have gone when it's time to leave.

I can't understand what the attraction is with spending hours in these places. As I continue to watch and wait, I slide my phone towards me. Eva still won't answer. She'll be lying in the bed I paid for, in the house I'm paying for - suddenly I wonder if she's even on her own in the bed I paid for. Maybe that's why she's seeing this through. Perhaps that's why she put the brakes on having another kid. There's no other reason there could be.

I decide to text her as I don't want her thinking I've gone quietly. Instead, she should be looking over her shoulder, wondering what I'm going to do next.

> Hasn't this gone far enough? You're living in my house, with my daughter, driving my motor around and using furniture I've paid for. If you want out of our relationship, you'd better get your shit sorted as I will not let you leech off me.

She couldn't afford to keep that house on her own anyway. Not on what she earns from her poxy fitness classes. She'll have to take me back eventually. And she can't continue to prevent me from seeing Heidi. I'll get the best solicitor money can buy if she tries. What Eva has no idea about is how much I've made, and got put away in stocks and investments.

The shrieking of drunk women from the next table cuts into my thoughts and sets my teeth on edge. Two of them stagger towards the toilets and I am again brutally reminded of Dean. I always am when I'm around women as drunk as some of these are. Which reminds me, Mark still hasn't mentioned the date of his visit to Pat Ingham – another situation I need to get to grips with. There's no way I can allow that to go ahead. She's another woman who needs disposing of, permanently. She can still do me a lot of damage if she comes up with any concrete evidence. And where she is right now, there will be plenty of time for her to consider how to get it.

I get a notification that Eva's read my message. She's not replying though. There's only a handful of men left in here – still probably fancying their chances with the pissed-up remaining pickings. You'd have to be desperate. The women from across the pub have sidled over to the now-vacant table beside me.

"Is that orange juice?" The darker-haired one of the two can barely get her words out. She looks to be around the same age as Lauren was, and Sara, so around ten years my junior.

I nod and glance at her friend who's speaking into her phone, trying to get a taxi by the sounds of it. She's in a similar state.

"You driving or summat? Why would you want to drink *orange* on a Saturday night? I wouldn't have bothered coming out."

"Because I like to stay in control of what I'm saying and doing." I cock my head to one side. She's after me. It's written all over her face.

"Ooooh. And I'm not in control. Is that what you're saying?"

"You tell me."

"How come you're on your own?"

"Because I like my own company."

Her eyes widen. "Would you like us to go away?"

"The only taxi we can get is in forty minutes." The blonde one slams her phone onto the table. "I want my bed. I've had enough for tonight."

"Me too. I'm not waiting that long Carly. I can be home in less than ten minutes if I cut along the river. Why don't you stay at mine tonight so we're not walking on our own?"

This is it. Easy pickings. What's meant to be will always find a way.

"I can't. I've got to be somewhere in the morning."

Their conversation pings back and forth for a few moments. It's extremely interesting.

"Ten minutes away down the river," I eventually repeat, dropping my phone into my top pocket. "I can walk with you, if you like, and then get back in time to see your friend into her taxi safely." Hopefully, my expression is passive enough for them not to sense my true motives.

I glance around the pub, double checking the CCTV. I'm positioned out of range of the main camera, but the one over the door will pick me up as I leave. Though, when I pull my hood up, as I have before, I could be anyone.

"But you could be anyone." I'm startled as the blonde one echoes my thoughts. How does she know what I'm thinking? I've often suspected my thoughts can be read. She throws her head back with laughter. Here we go, another woman is laughing at me. I only offered to see them safely out of here.

"Actually, I'm a police officer. A sergeant."

"Yeah right." She laughs even harder. "So show us your truncheon."

At this, her friend laughs too. I slide my ID card from my wallet. It isn't until I place it onto their table that it hits me what a huge risk I'm taking, letting them see what my name is. However, it doesn't matter. It's not as if they'll be around for much longer.

"You can't be too careful out there." I lower my voice. Women cackling from the corner of the pub lounge is grating into every fibre of my being. "Especially after the last couple of winters."

"True." Carly looks thoughtful. "Anyway, since you're a police officer..."

They both laugh as she struggles to say the word *officer*.

"I'm safe, waiting in here, for now," she continues. "There's still loads of people about. Why don't you walk Lucy here home and come back for me, like you said?" She points from her friend, then back to herself. "You play your cards right and I might even give you a lift in my taxi." She winks at me. "I've always liked a man in uniform."

"Eh, you." Lucy nudges her. "I saw him first."

"I'll pay a call." I get to my feet. "And I'll see you outside the main door Lucy." I wink back at her friend. "Then I'll be back for you."

15

MARK SETS a tray of mugs on the coffee table with a rattle. "You will not bloody believe this. Another two women have been pulled from the Alder." He hoists his jeans up. Skinny git. "Flick the news on Claire. I need to see what's going on."

"Oh my God." She tucks her hair behind one ear and reaches for the remote. "Are you sure? *Two*? Are they...?"

"Cheers bro." I reach forwards for my coffee, then settle back on the sofa to enjoy the after-effects of my handiwork. The national news is still on, then we have to sit through the weather and a round of adverts.

By the time the local news begins, the anticipation's killing me. The river Alder is the first item. I've always loved it when it's the top headline.

I recognise the reporter, huddled under an umbrella. The scene behind her looks to have been cordoned off exactly like it was a week ago. I'm glad it's not me on patrol this time. That was a long evening.

More cameras and emergency vehicles are around this time. I guess there would be with two of them being dead. But only one tent is visible – the other one, as I very well know, will probably be along the west bank of the river. This does, of course, depend on where Lucy washed up.

We bring you the early report of the discovery of the bodies of two women, thought to be twenty-nine-year-old Lucy Wilkins and twenty-eight-year-old Carly Sherwood. Formal identification has yet to be made, but their families have been informed.

Both women were seen leaving the Yorkshire Arms by the main entrance separately in the early hours of this morning. Lucy is believed to have left the pub alone on foot at 1:10 am. However, she has been captured on CCTV, walking near to a hooded male, of medium build and approximately six feet tall. Police are working to reproduce images in relation to this person of interest and ask that if he is watching, that he comes forward to be eliminated from this inquiry.

Carly Sherwood had booked a taxi, but CCTV shows her walking alone in the opposite direction to the main road. Both women were reported missing by their families yesterday.

It is too early to say whether these latest deaths add to the accidental death toll on this stretch of river, or whether this will become a murder inquiry. We will bring you more on this story as we get it.

"Here we bloody go again." Claire curls her hands around her mug and looks from Mark to me as she seems to nestle deeper into the huge jumper she's wearing. She looks like Mum with the expression she's got on her face. The older she gets, the more like Mum she becomes, right down to the beady eyes and the pointed cheekbones.

"At least this time, they're keeping an open mind about it being a murder inquiry." Mark's staring at the photo of him and Lauren.

"We all know what was going on last time Mark." Claire sips

from her cup. "It was nothing to do with anybody keeping an open mind, was it?"

"Jones is keeping me out of the inquiry, but I'm watching what's going on closely."

"How can you, if you're being kept out of it?" I don't want Mark anywhere near it. Especially with me having to stay at his house for the next couple of weeks.

"I've got a couple of colleagues keeping me in the loop, don't you worry."

"Leave it with the dramatics – the silly cows were pissed, that's all. Everyone knows what it's like down there. You go on that riverbank with a few drinks inside you in winter and you take your chances."

"But they're all women, *again*. A drunk bloke could just as easily slip and fall in." Claire tucks her legs under her. "It's too much of a coincidence, if you ask me. What's that now, *five*, in the last couple of weeks?"

Mark nods. "I'm trying to stay calm about it. But I swear to God, if there's some nutter on the prowl, some copycat of Ingham, I'm going to get him myself."

My attention's diverted to the driving rain against the window, then back to Mark. "I've seen more fight in a worn out dishcloth mate." I laugh.

"Do you reckon?" He puts his cup on the table and looks me straight in the eye, making me wonder if he knows something.

It's been another sleepless night which I've spent cursing Eva for forcing me to sleep on my brother's sofa. After my shower, I pad along the landing to the spare room. Mark picked up some of my clothes when he was round at my house, having tea and sympathy with Eva. He's on shift today and Claire's gone home, so it's a relief that the house is in silence for a change.

It's four days since all that shit at home and I'm feeling a real sense of displacement. I don't love Eva in the slightest. In fact, I'd go as far as saying I despise her. I don't really care about anyone apart from Heidi, and Alysha to a lesser extent.

I've been wrenched out of my life, and I'm certain Eva planned what she was doing all along. She engineered the whole thing to get rid of me. I'm totally pissed off at this situation that I've lost all control over.

She's ignored my calls and texts apart from sending me one back earlier, threatening to report me for breaching my bail if I don't leave her alone. I never knew she had threats like that in her.

I've still got ten days to wait before the bail's either extended or dropped. And then, she's going to wish she'd never got on the wrong side of me. And as for threatening me...

"It's only me love."

The front door bangs and I realise I've got Mum for company. That's all I need in the mood I'm in. I pull on jeans and a jumper, and head downstairs, braced for her warm welcome.

"Oh, it's you." She steps away from the coat rack and looks me up and down as though inspecting me. "I thought it was Mark."

"Well you thought wrong." That's why she said *love*. She's never called me that in my life.

"How long are you staying here, anyway? Haven't you sorted things out with your wife yet?"

I sit on the bottom step and reach for my shoes. "What would you care?"

"I'm only making conversation. There's no need to bite my head off."

"No you're not. You're sticking your nose in."

She leaves a cloud of perfume behind as she makes for the lounge door. "Where's Mark, anyway?"

"I didn't realise he'd given you a key to his house." I follow her in. "You've got your feet well and truly under the table here, haven't you?"

"Why shouldn't I? Mark's my son and Alysha's my granddaughter." She sniffs as she collects the mugs we left on the coffee table last night. "I want to be around for them more, especially after what they've been through."

What she means is that she doesn't want Brenda being their go-to. She'll be wanting to keep up appearances. That's one of Mum's main traits. How others view her is a big deal.

"And what about *me*, Mum?" I get the door for her as she stands before it with her tray. I know what she's doing – she's trying to rub my nose in how much she cares about Mark, like she always has.

"What do you mean?"

"You *never* ask how I am, what I'm doing, or anything. If it wasn't for Eva and Heidi, you'd cut me off completely."

"And do you blame me, the way you carry on?" She heads through the kitchen door with the tray without looking at me.

"The way I carry on, as you put it, is a product of my upbringing."

"I'm not responsible for how you've turned out. The misery you inflict on that wife of yours. If I've anything to do with it, she'll be dropping you like a ton of bricks. She might not be the sharpest knife in the drawer, but she can do better than you. And then, perhaps, I *can* get you out of my life as well."

I push in front of her at the kitchen sink and stand facing her. It's been a long time since I've been in such close proximity to my mother alone. "Why do you have to be such a cow?"

"You're in no position to judge me. I know *who* and *what* you are, remember?"

I stand, staring into her face, knowing what she knows, but being aware that she'll never have the guts to do anything about it. She can't. It's too late.

149

"Get out of my way." She laughs. "You don't scare me, *son.*"

The way she says *son* makes me want to rip her head off. "I'm no son of yours." I thump the top of the tray, sending the lot hurtling to the tiled floor.

"You..." The crash vibrates in my ears as I dart from the room. "Get back here and clear this up."

"Fuck off."

I don't even smile at Suzannah Peterson as she answers the door to me. I can't be arsed with small talk today, not even with Suzannah. Besides, I've still got Mum's vitriolic voice buzzing in my ears.

Suzannah's staring at the portable TV which faces me on the wall of the waiting room. As I slump in my seat, I read the headlines which are rolling along the bottom of the screen. *Police are treating the latest two drownings in the river Alder as suspicious. They are appealing for help to trace a man they wish to speak to in connection with the deaths of five women in the last two weeks.*

They keep saying five. Well I was away in Florida when two of them happened. Three, yes, five, no. Though where this will end up now, I've no idea. Perhaps I'll be blamed for all five. My urges are in full throttle again. They are intensifying year by year. It all starts with the thrill of watching and waiting, and is followed by amusement when I gain trust from revealing my position as a police sergeant. This swiftly turns to power when they realise my intentions aren't entirely honourable and ends with the control I have as I become God – ridding the world of these drunken idiots once and for all. Women like my mother. And Pat Ingham. And Lauren Holmes. And Sara.

Some are too shocked to scream as they slap into the water. I'm always careful to get them far away enough from the road and the pub where nothing will be heard if they do. I've taken bets on it inside my head. *Will she scream or won't she?* I never hurt them first. I don't need to. I just end them. There's only been one occasion when the woman got away. I agonised for days whether there would be any comeback from that. There never was. She probably crawled back under whatever stone she'd emerged from.

"Mr Hamer will be with you in a few minutes." Suzannah's voice is cold, similar to the day when I booked my first appointment on the phone. "He apologises for keeping you waiting."

"It's alright. It's my day off today, anyway." I wonder whether she could have found anything out about me being on police bail, but quickly decide she couldn't have. *Who would have told her?* Nobody knows exactly where I come for my appointments anyway. Not even Eva.

Her eyes flit from me up towards the TV screen as they're flashing a CCTV still of yours truly up. Well, I can see it's me, but really, it could be anyone. It's a man in a hood. Yes, they're right. I'm of medium build, slightly shorter than six feet tall and aged late thirties to early forties. Yes, I was wearing jeans and dark shoes. But because of the darkness, they can't make out any colours. Because of the hood, there's no distinguishing features. I've outsmarted them again. And they're aware of this only too well.

"Will." Daniel curls his head around the doorway, and I dutifully stand.

"Catch you later." I wink at Suzannah whose face appears to redden. For all her aloofness, I've always sensed that I'm in there.

"Does it bother you if I take my shoes off today?"

I let Daniel's note of sarcasm pass as I shake my head, my eyes instinctively drawn to the fact that today he's wearing *odd* socks, and not even slightly odd. One has a zig-zag pattern, and one is spotted.

"They're my sister's idea of a joke." He looks at his feet. "She bought me a box of odd socks last Christmas."

"How nice."

"So why the extra appointment Will? I wasn't expecting you until Thursday."

"I'm on bail to stay away from my wife." The dead tone I hear in my own voice takes me aback.

Daniel seems to lurch in his seat, as though he's remembered something. "Before we get into that Will, do you remember I mentioned recording our sessions the last time you were here? Have you had any further thoughts about it?"

"Yes, and I want the truth about why you want to record me."

"It's only so I can go over it afterwards. I don't always pick up nuances in what my clients say until later."

Once again, I bristle at being called a client. It makes me sound like a rent boy.

"Recordings help me write everything up as well." He waves his notebook in the air as he speaks. "There can be a lot to remember, and I prefer just to listen as you speak, rather than having to make copious amounts of notes."

"Fair enough." I shrug. "Do what you've got to do." I totally can't be arsed anymore. My life's a pile of shit.

"Bear with me one second." He strides across the carpet to his desk.

With him out of the way, the river painting is in full view. I remember the last time I was sitting in this chair. I was going back home afterwards to Eva and Heidi; I was due on shift on active duty, and I didn't have two more women chalked up.

When I was younger, I had notches on my bedpost – now in my early forties, it's names on a mortuary list. Still, if this is my purpose in life, I have to go where I'm sent.

Daniel pushes the tissue box to the side of the table and places his dictaphone between us.

"Right, Will." He presses a button. "Our voices are being recorded. The usual confidentiality applies – I will only repeat anything to anyone if you disclose information where I deem you, or someone else to be at risk, or, of course, where a crime has been committed or is going to be committed."

Where a crime has been committed. I smile to myself. If only you knew Daniel. I could make it into a game, all this.

"So... you were telling me about your wife. Did you say you're on *bail*?" He slides his brown 'Mr Bean' style jacket off and folds it at the side of his chair. I wonder for a moment how old Daniel is. Thirty going on seventy, by the look of him.

"We had a fight. I was raw after being here last week and she kept goading me. She's good at that."

"Goading you? In what way? What about?"

"She was spoiling for a row from the moment I walked into the house. She knows exactly which buttons to push with me." My fury is rising merely from talking about this. "I'm believing more and more that she engineered the whole thing – it's the sort of thing she'd do to get me into trouble and to get me out of the house."

"Why the police bail Will?"

"I acted in self-defence when she went for me." I look down at my fists tightly bunched in my lap. "Though it's a women's world isn't it? They're allowed to do what the hell they want to you, and afterwards, they can say whatever they want, even if it's a load of lies."

"Was she actually hitting you?" I can see the scepticism in his face which further infuriates me.

"She had me by the balls. Literally." I wince as the memory of the agony and the look on her twisted face revisits me.

"How did it all start?"

"It was all the usual stuff. The prospect of having another kid, my mother, my work, her work, money, our daughter."

"Your mother?"

It's interesting how Daniel singles out *her* from the list I've just given him. But it brings something back to my mind that I'd totally buried. "It was when Eva said *even your own mother hates you*, or words to that effect, that I completely lost it."

"It sounds like she hit an exposed nerve."

"Several nerves." I grin, despite my anger at reliving what Eva said to me. "She said it to rile me, knowing how much my mother's attitude has messed me up over the years."

"From what I'm hearing from you." Daniel leans over the dictaphone and tilts it towards him. "Sorry – it looked as though it had stopped recording. From what I'm hearing – it sounds as though your mother is at the root of many of your difficulties, as we've alluded to before."

"I hate the woman. We even had a run in before I came here today. I used to want to please her. Basically, I've gone beyond caring what she thinks about me now."

"And what does she think about you? What might be her over-riding opinion?"

"That I should have died in that hit and run, not my brother. And nothing I've done since that day to atone for it, is ever going to be good enough in her eyes."

"To *atone* for it. What do you mean by that?"

"You know."

"I don't. I want you to explain it to me."

"What atone means? Surely not." Didn't the pillock go to university? Probably not, looking at him.

"I mean that there's part of me that *would've* gone in my brother's place," I begin. "But if that had happened, nothing would have ever been done to bring his killers to justice. Or others like her. I've made the world a better place. A safer place."

"In what way?" He leans towards me, his eyes not leaving my face.

"I rid the world of drunken women."

"How – Will?"

"I've told you what I do for a job, haven't I? I'm a traffic cop."

"Yes, but surely..."

"Anyway – I'm on desk duty whilst they're poncing around with this bail crap. I can't see how they'll make anything stick though. It's her word against mine and when all is said and done, I'm the one who's a pol..."

"Did you actually hurt your wife?"

"No, I only held her off me. If I was going to batter her, I'd have done it long before today."

"Why don't you like women, Will?" He leans even further forwards, and I don't like the way he's looking at me.

Not for the first time, I'm not keen on his tone of voice. "There's one I really do like, actually."

He ignores my last point. "Your dislike of women comes out in everything you say."

"Does it? I guess it's because they've so much influence over me, so much power. The ones I've known have totally wrecked my life."

"How do you get on with your sister?"

"She's OK, in small doses. Probably because she doesn't drink herself stupid, like my wife's started to."

"I see. And what about your mother? Does she drink?"

"She used to. A hell of a lot. Especially after Dean died." I think back to one occasion when she was literally frothing at the mouth in drink, when she had a go at me. "She seems to have sorted herself out now though. She still drinks but not as much."

"It's understandable why you feel so strongly about excess drinking in women. After what happened to your brother – anyone would."

I look at him. I can trust him. He's said he understands. Besides, I can't help what I'm about to say. The voices are back. They're telling me to tell him. And they're even louder than his voice today. Maybe they're being recorded as well. I raise my voice above them. "I keep being told to get rid of them." I grip the arms of the chair.

"Rid of *who*?"

"All of them." I stare at the painting.

"Women, you mean?"

I nod.

"Who's telling you to do this? To get rid of them?"

"I can't stand them anymore. I want to go back home and do my job, but everywhere I go, I've got women or voices inside me calling the shots. I've had enough. Sometimes I want to die."

"Do you hear voices Will?"

"Don't we all?"

"I suppose so. We all have an inner voice. Tell me about yours."

"Voices. Lots of them. I want them to stop. I want to be normal. What I've done at the river isn't my fault – it's theirs. I can hear them now – I'm struggling to hear you at the same time."

"Whose?"

"Stop asking me so many bloody questions, will you?"

The voices are getting louder – they're trying to drown out the drone of Daniel Hamer. I need to get out of here. Work out my next steps on my own.

And all I know is that her downstairs, in that office is in for it next – that's what the voices are telling me to do. Suzannah Peterson. *Everything* about her is a front. I can't believe that I've only just worked out why she looks so familiar. It's only now that it's come back to me.

PART II

EVA

16

EACH OF WILL'S words hits me like a thump. "Open this door right now! I mean it."

"Heidi. Get to your room." The door is literally busting at its seams with every boot. If he gets through it before the police get here, God only knows what he'll do to me. With shaking hands, I slide the top and bottom bolts across the already locked door, then turn to Heidi who hasn't moved a muscle. "It's OK." I try to keep my voice calm, as though everything is alright. Though it's far from alright.

"Why can't he come in Mum?" She sinks to the bottom step with tears in her eyes. "It's not fair. I want you to let him in."

I guess she would take his side. Will gives Heidi everything she wants - she only ever sees the best in him, even when he's treating me like rubbish. I guess she's too young to make sense of who he really is. The longer I stay with Will, the more I'm portraying to Heidi that living like this is acceptable, therefore the more likely she'll be to repeat my horrendous mistakes and errors of judgement when she gets older.

Thankfully, something's snapping in me at last. I don't think I can have him back here. Not least because of the worrying computer history I stumbled across earlier. I suspected he wasn't wired right, but what I've found has totally confirmed that.

Heidi scowls at me and stomps upstairs. Will's banging on the back window now. *Come on,* I hiss in between bangs as I cower in the hallway. The police should be here by now. That's what the operator said anyway. She wanted to keep me talking, but I hung up on her, preferring to keep my wits about me to deal with the situation here, and to keep track of exactly where Will is in the garden. The dog's yapping in the utility room. Bloody dog. I never wanted it here in the first place. Now I'm going to have to either train him or get someone else to take him. Someone who isn't trying to escape their marriage from a violent maniac. Shit. He's booting the back door now. Any moment now, he'll be in here. After all, as a cop, he'll be no stranger to kicking a door in.

I take the stairs two at a time to check on Heidi.

"Open the back door for me," Will's telling her from the garden. "Then we'll take Biscuit out. You'd like that, wouldn't you?"

"The police will be here any minute," I yell before slamming the window. Heidi sinks to her bed, tears streaming down her face.

"I'm sorry sweetheart. I really am." I pull her towards me. She shouldn't be witnessing all this. I've got to get it sorted, once and for all. I feel so guilty.

The doorbell makes me jump again. Then more thumping. "Police!" I expect all the neighbours will be nosying at what's going on here.

Thank God. "Wait here," I say to Heidi. "And don't touch that window, I mean it."

"I'm coming!" I shout as I race down the stairs and slide the bolts back. I turn left and right from the porch. There's no sign of him.

"Eva Potts?"

"Yes. It's me that rang you." Now that they're here, tears are burning at the back of my eyes. For the moment, I'm safe.

"Are you OK Eva?" Jade from next door calls over the fence. "I've taken photos of him trying to get in, if that helps."

"Thanks Jade. I'll pop round later," I call back, tears of relief rolling down my face. "I'm sorry," I say to the policewoman before me. "I'm just so stressed with it all."

"There's no need for apologies. You're alright now." She tucks her gloves into the pocket of her jacket. "My colleague's just checking around the back, but it appears your husband's made a run for it."

"Thanks for getting here so quickly." I wipe tears away with the back of my hand. "It's going from bad to worse. I can't take any more."

"I'm Detective Inspector Susan Moriarty," she says, jerking her head upward as if telling her colleague to get over here, "and this is Police Constable James Cameron. Can we come in Eva?"

I hold the door wider to invite their entry, glimpsing Heidi peeking around the banister.

"Is that your daughter?" DI Moriarty looks up the stairs.

I nod. "Heidi love. If you could just put the TV on in your room for a few minutes. Then I'll phone Uncle Mark and see if Alysha wants to come over and keep you company." Really, I've no intention of bringing Alysha into this snake pit. But I can't have Heidi eavesdropping whilst I speak to the police. She's seen and heard enough already.

"OK." With a sniff, she heads towards her room. Somehow, I'll make it up to her.

"She hasn't seen much of what's gone on." I beckon towards the kitchen. The last thing I need is them involving Social Services and telling them that Heidi's at risk here.

"Someone wants to be out of there." The policewoman

points towards the utility room where Biscuit is still carrying on.

Poor dog. He should have gone to a more loving home than this one. "I'll sort him out shortly. In fact, let's go through to the lounge, where we can hear ourselves think."

They follow me into the lounge and sit side-by-side on the sofa. I sit facing them in what's normally Will's chair. If he was here, he'd tell me to shift.

"Are *you* alright Eva?" Concern is still etched across PC Cameron's face. "We're the officers who bailed your husband last week. It must be a really difficult time for you."

I'd composed myself a minute ago, but now blink back the fresh tears that fill my eyes. Everyone's been so nice since I spoke out about last Thursday. However, I don't want to be seen as a victim. Not anyone's victim, and certainly not *Will's*.

"He's been hounding me since you released him."

"Has he? You really should have reported that to us earlier." DI Moriarty takes her hat off and holds it in her lap. "We could have rearrested him - we can't do anything if we're not aware of him breaching."

"That's what I was afraid of – him being arrested again I mean."

I reach towards the coffee table and pull a tissue from the box. Of course it's stupid, but I'm feeling terrible about it all. He's Heidi's dad and still my husband when all's said and done. And he'll make me pay, I know he will.

"I didn't want to make things worse. It's awful enough as it is."

"We're here to help you, Eva. And there's a unit on the way round to your brother-in-law's. They'll be taking Will in for breaching his bail conditions and for the threatening behaviour you reported when you rang."

"Mark's house?" Alysha's going to get dragged in after all. "Then what?"

"Well, now that we've been able to get your neighbour's witness statement from last week, we'll be charging Will with the assault on you. As well as for his threatening behaviour towards you this evening, and, as we're now aware of, he's also in breach of his bail conditions."

"What's going to happen?" This is like a bad dream. How did it all get this far?

"That'll be up to the Crown Prosecution Service to decide. Then, most likely, the magistrate's court. That you've had to call us out tonight will go very much against him."

"He's going to kill me for this."

"I gather this is the first time you've called us here?"

"Yes."

"Then I'm not sure what the CPS will decide. Is there a history of domestic violence Eva?"

"Nothing as serious as what happened between us last week. He's grabbed me and shoved me the odd time." I stare down at the grey carpet Will chose. He's picked everything in this house. "It's more the way he tries to control me that I can't cope with anymore."

"What do you mean, *control you?*"

"He's such a bully. It's always his way or the highway." I smile at the irony of saying that about a traffic cop. Then it hits me. "What about his job? Will he get suspended after this?" It then dawns on me that no way will I be able to afford this house on my own. It's all such a mess. I can't take him back though. Having seen his true colours more and more lately, I'd rather live in a cardboard box than continue to live with him. Which brings me to my other worry. I'm going to have to say something. "You should look at the search history on our computer whilst you're here."

The two officers glance at each other.

"Why do you say that?" DI Moriarty glances at the desktop in the corner of the lounge. She's somewhat older than me, which is reassuring. I expect she'll know exactly how to handle this.

"I've been agonising over what to do," I reply. "Who to tell. I only came across it earlier today when I was searching for a solicitor. Usually Will wipes his search history, but he hasn't this time."

"Do you mind showing it to us?" DI Moriarty rises from her seat and makes her way over to the computer, tugging a spectacles case from her pocket as she goes.

I nod and follow her over. My stomach is churning, and I need a glass of wine. I don't normally drink on a Monday, but I think I can be excused after Will's performance tonight. I can hardly believe I'm turning my husband over to the police, but what choice have I got with this? One search he's typed in has given me particular cause for concern.

I log into the computer and she watches over my shoulder as I scroll through the recent search history. PC Cameron joins us and watches over my other shoulder. Then, glancing out of the window, I realise Will could still be out there, observing all this. I lurch to the window and drag the curtains across.

"We're going to have to seize this," DI Moriarty says eventually, pushing her glasses back up her nose. "I can see why you're concerned." She turns to her colleague, her bun wobbling on the top of her head with the movement. "These are all Google searches," she says, "which means he could delete them from another device. We need to make a pocketbook record of them and then take the computer. See what else is on here."

"Read them out to me." PC Cameron slides his pocketbook from his jacket. "What about all the sites he's visited?"

"Can you click on the history tab please Eva?"

I do as she asks. There's only the searches I've done lately.

"Most have been deleted from the history," she says.

"The tech team will be able to get access to all that, won't they?"

"I should think so, right James, are you ready? Eva? Can you read the searches out please?"

I start down the list of what's possibly only a fraction of what's going on in my husband's warped and chaotic mind.

"Can a therapist give evidence in court? Puppies in Alderton... How long before a body surfaces... Suzannah Peterson Alderton... How to find out if wife's had an abortion..." I glance at DI Moriarty. "The Alder Centre... Can a counselling session be recorded without knowledge?"

I pause for a moment. I'm evidently going too fast. "Wife drinking too much... Stop wife taking daughter away... Center Parcs holidays... Death in river Alder... How long to renew passport... Why men kill women... Finlay's solicitors... Hearing voices."

I have to re-read a couple that PC Cameron has missed, then DI Moriarty turns to me. "You were right to flag this. There's certainly some cause for concern here."

"I know." My hands are shaking on the keyboard.

The puppy's settled down now and I can hear music from Heidi's TV. I'll have to take Biscuit for a walk with Heidi soon. But I dare not go anywhere until I'm told for certain that Will's not hanging about. I wonder about getting someone here to be with me, but I don't really want to bring anyone else into this. I'm firmly of the belief that anyone who Will perceives as 'crossing' him will be at risk from him.

"It's this, *why men kill women* that concerns me the most." DI Moriarty looks back at the computer. "Have you any idea why he might have searched for this?"

"I've never suspected him of being out to kill me." I laugh, though it's a laugh full of nerves. "It could be some sort of research for work. How long will it take you to get the results of the sites he's visited?"

"It's strange how he's wiped those but not his searches," she replies. "Though they'll all be on the hard drive. I'll check with my line manager to see if we can expedite things. And I'm sorry to say this, but we're going to need to check any other devices he uses. Any laptops, tablets and suchlike."

I nod. "He's got a tablet and a phone. His tablet's in the bedroom. I'll get it for you, but he'll have his phone with him."

PC Cameron's radio bleeps. He brings it to his chin, and I notice how clean-shaven he is. Will's chin is normally in shadow by this time of day. "Five one zero zero two," he says. "Have we any updates on the search for Sergeant William Potts?"

"We've visited the bail address. The property's empty."

"Can you keep it under surveillance?"

"We are doing. And a warrant's gone out for breach."

"Right you are. We're just with his wife, Eva Potts." He gives me a weak smile. "Keep surveillance on her house too."

"I'll pass that through."

"That's partly to keep a watch for him if he comes back here," DI Moriarty explains, "and also to keep an eye on you and your daughter." She pulls the curtain to the side and looks out into the darkness. "Unless... is there anyone you'd like to stay with tonight? We can take you if it's close by."

"He's not driving me out of my own home," I reply. "No way."

Though I won't get any sleep tonight. I want him to be arrested and don't want him to be arrested. It's a peculiar conflict, wanting him to account for his actions whilst trying to protect him at the same time. I twist the wedding and engagement rings around on my finger. I'm going to take them off when they police have gone. I don't want to be Will's wife anymore. It's going to be weird not wearing them after eight years. I don't want him anymore, but this sense of aloneness and displacement feels akin to losing an arm.

"I understand that – I really do. I suppose you'll also want to keep your daughter in her routine. She'll be at school tomorrow?"

I glance at DI Moriarty's hand. She's married too. I nod.

"Perhaps there's someone who could come and stay with you Eva?"

I do a mental reckoning of people close by. They're mainly all related to Will. There's my mother, but she's got enough on her plate, having recently being diagnosed with Alzheimer's. Besides, as soon as I tell her the truth there'll really be no going back. Plus, if she's having a more lucid day, I'll have to contend with the *I told you so's.*

Perhaps I shouldn't write Will completely off yet. Maybe the counselling he's having is forcing him to bubble over and carry on like this. What if there's a chance we can get through this? I echo my thoughts to DI Moriarty, cringing at the desperation she must sense from me.

"I think it's commendable that you're showing concern for your husband after his behaviour," she tells me. "But for now, you'd be as well to focus on yourself and your daughter. We can put you in touch with some help if you decide you need it."

And in this moment, something cements within me, and I reconcile myself to the fact that there's definitely no going back.

17

I DRAIN my glass and head for the foot of the stairs for what feels like the millionth time this evening. "You should be asleep by now love. It's nearly ten o'clock."

"Can I sleep with you Mum?"

"I wasn't coming to bed just yet?" I reach the top of the stairs and notice that Heidi's bottom lip is trembling. How can I say no?

"I'm really worried about Dad. It's making my tummy hurt. Is he at Uncle Mark's house with Alysha?"

I pull her towards me. "He'll be fine Heidi."

"What if he's having to sleep outside? That's what he said would happen if I didn't let him in." She looks like she's been crying. This is awful. Somehow, I must stay strong.

"He won't be sleeping outside, Heidi. And he's a grown-up. You don't need to worry about anything. He shouldn't be saying things like that to you."

"He told me he wanted to come in and get something to eat. What if he's hungry?"

"He's got plenty of money in the bank to buy anything he wants." I stroke my hand down the length of her hair.

"But I can't stop worrying about it."

"He has lots of places to go sweetheart. Your Uncle Mark's, your Auntie Claire's, your Grandma's house."

"He won't go to scary Grandma's house." She lets go of me.

"All I'm saying is there's no need for you to worry." Fancy Will heaping this sort of emotional guilt on an eight-year-old. It shows exactly what he's made of.

"So can I?" She swings herself around on the banister.

"What?"

"Sleep in your bed."

"I suppose so. I'll come up and read a book at the side of you, after I've made a cup of tea and let Biscuit out for a wee. Go and get yourself comfy."

By the time I get upstairs, she's dropped off to sleep. I let out a thankful sigh, hoping she stays that way. I perch at the end of the bed and stare at her for a few moments. *What are we doing to her?* We haven't been getting on for ages and I'm only just seeing the effect it's all having on Heidi.

Will's treatment of me has got worse since Lauren died, and Claire was attacked. Even Mark's handled everything ten times better than Will has, and he's the one whose fiancée was murdered by Ingham.

I sip my tea and stare at the same page in my book, trying to focus. Then I re-read it. Finally, I give up, turn out the light and snuggle into Heidi's warmth. Tears stab at my eyes at the prospect of life being like this from now on. Me and my daughter, clinging together. Me, fearing what Will could be capable of. But those internet searches. They're seriously weird.

It's not long before I accept that I will not sleep tonight and reach for my phone instead. I've had a text from Brenda saying the police have been around looking for Will. Mark's out apparently, but she says she'll get him to ring me in the morning, and has told me to call her if I need anything. The morning seems like an eternity away. She'll be worrying her head off if I know Brenda correctly. She goes to pieces with all the family politics and fall-outs.

I stare into the darkness, wondering where Will might be now. He'd be arrested if he were to show up here again, so from that point of view, I'm reasonably safe. I'm sure Jade from next door will keep an ear out, and the police said they would keep us under surveillance as well. That probably just means driving past the house every so often.

But it doesn't stop me from hearing things and imagining noises. Eventually I flick the TV on and find Love Actually. It's what I need right now. A happy, mindless film to fall asleep with. But I don't. Instead, the tears roll down the sides of my head as I watch the happiness unfolding. Happiness, I fear, that will never belong to me.

"Find your PE kit Heidi. We need to get a move on." I've already decided to cancel the classes I should be teaching today. No way can I fake the enthusiasm and energy that's required of me to stand in front of the groups of women I teach. I'm normally so bubbly, so they'll sense something's wrong with me straight away. And if anyone's nice to me, I'll bawl my eyes out. The gym has got two hours to cover my first class if I tell them now that I'm not going.

The receptionist sounds puzzled when I tell her I'm not well. "As far as I can see, all three of your classes today have been covered already."

"They can't have been. I'm only just ringing to say that I'm not coming in."

"We got your email last week. Hang on a moment." Computer keys tap in the background. "Here it is."

"What email?"

"The one you sent last Wednesday."

"But I haven't sent any emails."

"Kirsty, the operations manager replied to you. Saying she was sorry you were leaving, but understood your reasons. I've got the email here, in front of me."

"*Leaving!* I honestly have no idea what you're talking about."

Then I realise. It's the only explanation. Will must have emailed from my account. *Oh my God.* I was aware that he didn't like the new-found freedom my job's been giving me, but bloody hell.

"I really haven't sent an email," I blurt. "I'm going to come in and explain what might have happened. Can you tell Kirsty I'd like to see her this morning? This is a huge mistake."

Heidi and I usually walk to school, but today I'm safer in the car. There's been no update yet whether the police have caught up with Will or not, but I'm certain they'd keep me informed if they had. I can feel it in my bones that he's still out there somewhere. He could be watching me now.

As we cross the playground, it occurs to me to let Heidi's teacher know about the drama at home in case she's not herself today. Then I decide against it. I should speak to her, but after only a couple of hours' sleep, a migraine is buzzing behind my left eye. I rummage in my bag for my tablets. Damn – I'm out of them. Thank goodness I've got a prescription ordered at the chemist. The sooner I get a tablet into me, the more chance I can stave it off. I can't let anything stop me from calling to speak to Kirsty at the gym. I'm going to need my job more than ever by the looks of it.

. . .

"I'd like to collect a prescription. Eva Potts." The pain's really taking hold. It's no wonder with everything that's going on.

"Just a minute."

After a moment, the pharmacist returns with a paper bag. "There's just your Naratriptan migraine medication in there. We received your request for the cancellation of the Desogestral."

"Really?" I squint under the shop's lighting. I haven't cancelled the contraceptive I've been on since I had Heidi.

She looks as though she wants to move to the next customer, but I stand firm.

"But I haven't requested any cancellation. When? How?"

"Through the online repeat service."

"Not that I need that medication right now..." Despite the pain in my head, I almost laugh at the irony, "but that wasn't me."

"Oh!" She frowns. "Does someone else know your login for the prescription service?"

As I wander in a daze back to the car, I wonder what Will hoped to achieve by causing another disruption to my contraception. I still can't believe he threw away what I had in the bathroom cabinet. But it isn't as if I've gone anywhere near him since we returned from Florida. And I'd have been even less likely to without protection from pregnancy. We might have got on OK whilst we were away, but when we got back, normality resurfaced and I realised what an idiot I'd been, agreeing to his whimsical idea of another baby. It would be nothing but a sticking plaster. I've enough to worry about with Heidi, and Biscuit now.

As our life together goes on, and especially with the events of this year, I'm seeing that there are two Wills within my husband. And I wonder whether the dark Will might have been trying to force the baby issue through controlling me. This more shadowy side of him certainly seems to be winning the fight for existence.

I nearly turn the car around when I see the figure on my drive, hopping from one foot to another, evidently trying to keep warm. At first glance, it could be Will, then I realise it's Mark. Though neither of them will ever admit it, they have a look of each other, apart from the hair colour. Mark's is darker than Will's.

"I've only just found out what's happened Eva." Mark stretches his arm towards me, and I accept a brief hug. It's virtually unheard of for Mark and I to hug – well, for anyone in Will's family to. It's not how they were brought up. The last time anyone did was at Lauren's funeral. That's a day I could never relive.

"Thanks for coming round." I point the key towards the car to lock it and check down the side of the house, before heading towards the porch. "Have you been waiting long?"

"A little while. I chanced it that you might come straight back after taking Heidi to school."

"I had to call in at the gym and save my job." I open the door.

"*Save your job*. How come?"

"Long story. I'll tell you over a cuppa if you've got time." I shrug my coat off and hang it over the banister.

"Of course I have. How are you doing anyway?" He follows me into the kitchen. "I hear my dear brother's been making a nuisance of himself."

"That's putting it mildly." I glance out of the window, checking the garden.

"You're OK whilst I'm here – are things really so bad between you?" I see similar concern in his eyes to what I saw in PC Cameron's last night. I hope I hear from the police with an update soon.

"You've no idea how he's been with us lately." My old friends, the tears, stab at my eyes. "Where is he anyway?"

"I was out with Sara last night." Mark walks over to the kettle. "You sit down Eva, you look done in. I'll make us a drink. Brenda told me what was going on this morning. That's why I got round here."

"You haven't answered my question." I wearily tug my scarf from my neck as I sink to a chair at the kitchen table. "I need to find out where he is. I can't rest until I find out."

"We don't know either." Mark sits facing me. "I've asked both stations, ours, and the other one in Alderton to keep me up to date. He might get remanded after this, anyway. He's broken his bail conditions and after how he's behaved against you, I'll be surprised if they let him back out."

"Yeah, but he's still a police sergeant isn't he?"

"Which makes it even worse."

"I wish I didn't feel so guilty." A tear rolls down my face. Mark tears off a piece of kitchen roll and passes it to me.

"You've got absolutely nothing to be guilty about. We all know how difficult he is. Insensitive, miserable, irritable..."

"You don't know the half of it."

"So tell me. Let me pour these drinks out and I'll be right with you."

It's a relief to spill everything, even if it is to Will's brother. I've always got on with Mark though. I haven't really talked to anyone about how things have been, especially in the last couple of weeks. The friends that used to be around for me have drifted away over the years. Will never made anyone welcome here. Jade from next door sometimes calls in when Will's out on shift, but lately he's taken to randomly appearing back here when he's on breaks.

Our marriage was bad enough before we left for Florida, but I refused to admit it to myself. It was easier to keep the peace. But since we've got back, I've been forced to accept how isolated I've become.

"There's always been something dark inside him Eva, especially with him being with Dean when he died. He definitely went downhill after that." Mark sets a cup of tea in front of me.

"Your mother hasn't helped though, has she?" I blow my nose and wrap my hands around the mug, comforted by its warmth.

"Well, she got worse too." Mark's expression suggests he's remembering something. "It would be best if they had nothing to do with each other. I can't recall them ever getting along."

"I just don't know what to do. I'm scared he'll turn up here again. All this is having an awful effect on Heidi." I stare into my tea.

"I'm going to have to go home soon, unfortunately." Mark glances at the clock on the oven. "I've got a few calls to make and I'm on shift this afternoon, but I'll send Claire a message to come up as soon as she finishes work." He looks thoughtful for a moment. "You and Heidi could stay at ours, but everyone's already fighting over the spare room."

I shake my head. "I'm staying here. He's not forcing us out. I've already told the police that."

"Like I say, the way he's going, he'll be lucky not to be locked up before too long. Which reminds me... Damn."

"What?"

"Oh nothing. I've just remembered something." He puts his cup down.

"Tell me,"

"It's nothing to do with Will. It's just, well, I'm visiting Pat Ingham tomorrow, and I've got to get in touch with the prison – I've misplaced the booking reference I need to get in."

"*Booking reference.* You make it sound like you're going on holiday." I smile for the first time today, not that there's anything to smile about. "Anyway, I'm sure it won't matter, you being in the police."

"At least you're not having a go at me for wanting to see her. Everyone else has gone ape."

"That doesn't mean I understand it. I don't get why you'd want to see *her* of all people. After everything that's happened."

"It's for closure, if anything. And she reckons there's stuff she needs to clarify. She wants to talk to me face to face, apparently."

"About what?"

"Well, that's what I intend to find out."

We sit in silence for a moment. The only sound in the kitchen is the ticking of the clock. Biscuit must be sleeping in his cage.

"Do you reckon any of it might involve Will?"

"I shouldn't think so. They cleared him of all involvement."

I suddenly recall the internet searches. "Mark. There's something I should tell you about. Something I've had to pass onto the police."

"I'm listening." He grips the edge of the table. Poor bloke. He's had enough of a rough ride this year, without having to contend with whatever psychological problems his brother might be hiding.

"The police took our computer and Will's tablet."

"Why?" His voice rises and his face drops.

"Will's deleted whatever sites he's been on, but not his searches."

"And?" Mark peers at me from beneath his long eyelashes,

the same as Will's. It's not often I look closely at Mark but extra lines on his face and grey flecks around his hairline have emerged this year. And I'm about to give him a few more.

"Well, the technical forensic team, or whatever they're called, are going to find whatever sites he's visited from the hard drive," I begin.

"And what about the searches? What were they?"

They should be imprinted on my mind, but suddenly, I'm struggling to recall them. "I can't remember word for word, but there were some really dodgy ones. The worst was something along the lines of *why men kill women.*

"Bloody hell. Why would he be searching for something like that?"

"Then there were one or two relating to the river Alder deaths, and one was a question about how long it takes for a body to surface."

Mark stands without saying anything and rinses his cup under the tap.

"What are you thinking Mark?"

"I don't know what to think."

The speed at which he replies fills me with even more doubt as to how well I know my husband. Mark is seemingly having similar misgivings.

"Could the investigation have got things wrong Mark?"

"I can't imagine that. Not after getting it so badly wrong the first time. It's already cost the police millions in compensation, not to mention our reputation."

"I've got a horrible feeling."

"I know what you mean. And maybe Pat Ingham's got something to say that might offer some clues, who knows. That might be why she's wanting to see me." He dries the cups then turns to face me, his face dark. "God, I can't believe I'm even thinking this way about my brother."

"When did you say you're visiting her?"

"Tomorrow." He folds the tea towel into quarters. "I'm dreading it to be honest."

"Is anyone going with you?" I do a mental check. Kirsty at the gym has covered my classes for the rest of the week. I'm taking it as annual leave, then going back next week. I could do with keeping busy.

"Claire was supposed to be, but she's bottled it. I can't say I blame her. Why?"

I can tell by his face that he already knows what I'm about to ask. "Can I come instead?"

"Is that a good idea?"

"If there's anything to find out about Will, I want to hear it from the horse's mouth." Suddenly I really *do* want to go. And to eyeball the woman who's partially responsible for so much misery in our family. Along with her dead husband.

"It depends whether she agrees for you to come in with me. And also whether they'll swap the visiting order from Claire to you at such short notice."

"I'd like you to try if that's OK. Surely you can pull some strings?"

"OK, but I'll warn you now. They're really not the nicest of places."

"I'm not expecting the Hilton."

"And it's probably easier to get into Buckingham Palace. When I've been involved in prison interviews, it's a right rigmarole to get in. And that's even when I've queue jumped as a police officer. Tomorrow I'm going in as a civvy."

"What time do you have to be there?"

"The visiting order says one till three. You'll need to get Heidi collected, or booked into after-school club. I'm booking Alysha in."

"I'll sort it. I actually want to come with you."

There must be a reason Pat Ingham wants to see Mark, and Claire of course. I'm certain Will's going to be a big part of what she wants to talk about. With the internet searches and the recent violence towards me, I need to find out anything I can, to try to understand what's going on in my husband's head.

18

I FLICK from channel to channel, looking for some news. Not that Will's going to feature just yet. He's still under investigation. And I've no idea if they've even found him. My channel hopping leads me to the recording of the reconstruction from earlier this year, and for some reason I couldn't possibly explain, I press play.

I only watched it once after doing it. I'll never forget pretending to be Lauren in her final moments, having to swallow the terror that must have consumed her. Tears slide down my face as I watch myself cycling along that path beside the stream, my hair billowing out behind me as I draw closer to the animal who killed her. Of course, this is all acting, but tomorrow I'm going to face her killer's wife across a table. What on earth am I doing?

I spend the next couple of hours catching up on housework. If my home is in some sort of order, maybe my scrambled mind will find some order too. I can do nothing apart from put one foot in front of the other and wait to see what comes out of this mess. Really, I need to know now. Once they get to the bottom of exactly what sites Will's been visiting online, I might get some idea of what I'm dealing with. Or it might all amount to nothing. The not knowing, however, is horrendous.

I'm about to sit down to eat a sandwich, when the doorbell echoes through the house.

"Who is it?" I shout from behind the door. I hate living like this. I can imagine how life is for Pat Ingham behind lock and key. Biscuit yaps at my feet.

"It's DI Moriarty and PC Cameron again. Can we come in Eva?"

I slide back the bolts I put on after Mark left and shut the puppy in the lounge. "Come through." I lead them to the kitchen. "Take a seat. Apologies for the tuna smell."

"We've just come on shift – well, an hour ago," DI Moriarty begins. "We wanted to make you our first port of call. Oh - sorry to interrupt your lunch."

"No worries. I'm not that hungry." I slide the plate from the table and put it in the fridge. "Have you found him yet? Will, I mean?"

"I'm afraid not." PC Cameron shakes his head. He's a good-looking man. Without meaning to, I glance at his ring finger. Married. Shucks. I can consider these things now. The way things are looking, Will and I are over forever. Though at the moment, I'm more scared of where he is, and what he might do to me next, than the prospect of being single again.

"Given that he breached his bail conditions," DI Moriarty says, "we've circulated his description across the Yorkshire forces and we're regularly checking in with his family."

"Mark, his brother, was here earlier." I take a seat at the table with them, squinting against the sunlight facing me. My migraine will be back if I'm not careful. "He hasn't seen him. But you're probably wasting your time with his mother. He wouldn't go to her in a million years. They don't get on at all."

"What about his sister?"

"Claire? She practically lives at Mark's. But she's going to come here when she finishes work."

"I'm pleased to hear that you're being looked after."

There's a short pause. "Have you found anything out about the computer yet?"

PC Cameron shakes his head. "It can take time, depending on what backlog the department has. It's gone to the lab. However," he pauses, "there's another reason we've come to see you."

I look from him to DI Moriarty. "What's that?"

"What has Will said about the counselling he's been having?" DI Moriarty nods at her colleague who pulls his pocketbook out again.

"It was me who suggested in the first place that he needed to speak to someone. Like I mentioned before, he has an awful relationship with his mum, which I think is at the root of a lot of things." I rub at my head. It looks like another migraine tablet might be in order. "As well as his brother being killed when he was younger."

"Go on."

"In my opinion, it's what happened earlier this year with Lauren and Claire that has really made things worse in his head, but... anyway." I notice they're both watching me intently. "What he's been having is something more than counselling... Psychotherapy apparently."

"Why didn't he go through Police Care?"

"I got the impression that he was concerned they might report whatever he talked about back to his management. Not that he particularly said much to me about it all."

"They wouldn't have been allowed to - it's all totally confidential – well, it is to a point, depending on certain circumstances." DI Moriarty is doing all the talking now.

"Plus," I say, "he probably needed something deeper than

just counselling, to unravel whatever's going on in his head. It's obviously deep shit."

The kitchen is silent apart from the hum of the fridge and the tick of the clock. My face flushes. "Sorry I didn't mean to swear."

"There's absolutely no need to apologise - we hear far worse. Did he tell you how he came about it? The therapy, I mean?"

I recall the attractive woman who slipped Will her card after the public inquiry. I'd been able to tell he fancied her, and to watch him shamelessly flirting under my nose had really needled me. Now... only a few weeks on, I'd be grateful if another woman took him off my hands.

"A woman approached *him*, after the inquest," I tell them. "Literally straight after. She made out like the offer was open for any of the family who might benefit, but she only spoke to Will. As far as I'm aware, he's paying privately for it."

"OK. We're asking because the therapist has come forward." She clasps her hands in front of her on the table. I notice the pale pink she's painted her nails.

"Really? Has he or she said anything about what Will's been talking about?"

"It's a he. We can't tell you word-for-word what he's said. We've only been authorised to speak to you about the gist of things at this stage, but what I can tell you is that his therapist has got some viable concerns."

"What sort of concerns?"

"Things that might be collaborative with his internet activity. I'm sorry to ask this Eva, but are you aware of *anything*, anything at all that might suggest his involvement with the deaths in the River Alder?"

"Oh my God. You mean there might have been a mistake? You mean he's been let loose to do..." A queasy feeling steals over me. *Two more were thrown in on Saturday night!* And another one the week before. What if...?

"We don't know yet. The therapist apparently recorded their last session together, with Will's consent, that is. It sounds as though he lost the tight grip he usually has on himself and let a few things slip."

"He certainly doesn't have a tight grip on his temper." My stomach is whirring like a cement mixer at the prospect of what my husband may be implicated in. Those last two women were only a few years younger than me. What if it *really* was him? What the hell would I do? "Have you listened to the recording?"

"He's bringing it in to us this afternoon. Whilst we're waiting, we wanted to talk to you – to see if you've had any suspicions yourself, now or in the past, about where he's going, or what he might be doing?"

"Will's a lot of things, a misogynist for one, but I can't get my head around him being a murderer." I shake my head. "He's perhaps been overly interested in what's been going on with the river deaths, but he's a copper, isn't he? We've been married for eight years. I'd have known *something* if I was married to a serial killer, surely?"

An uncomfortable silence hangs over us for a few seconds. It's broken by the washing machine entering its rinse cycle in the utility room. He was supposed to be staying at Mark's on Saturday night, so I, at least, won't be asked to verify his whereabouts this time. I can't even kill a spider – how could my husband be capable of what seems to be emerging?

"Throughout the course of the investigation," DI Moriarty sounds more business-like now, "on three of the occasions when women died in the river, you said Will was at home with you?"

"Yes." Why are they on about this again? My breath becomes shallower. I had an inkling this might come back to haunt me.

"Sleeping in bed, you said?"

I remember my sandwich in the fridge. Twenty minutes ago, my stomach was rumbling, but now my appetite has completely gone. *What the hell are they accusing me of here?*

"Yes."

"Are you a heavy sleeper Eva?"

"Sometimes. Not always."

"We've been wondering if it's possible on these occasions that Will may have got up and left the house whilst you were sleeping. Without you knowing."

"Possibly, I was asleep, wasn't I?" At least she added *without you knowing* to the end of her sentence. As if anyone could think I'm capable of colluding in what they seem to be suggesting. My mind is jumping all over the place. "Surely CCTV would've picked him up somewhere if he'd sneaked out after I'd gone to sleep."

"He'll be informed of exactly where the cameras are. And more importantly, where they aren't."

I stare miserably at the table. I'm seriously doubting myself now. Since coming back off holiday and seeing this change for the worse in him, followed by stumbling across that internet search the other day... God – who the hell am I married to? We've got a bloody daughter together. *And two more women died only three nights ago.* Possibly at the hands of my husband. This really can't be happening.

"Eva, would you be willing to change your statement?"

"How do you mean?"

"That you can't be completely certain of his whereabouts on the nights you've provided alibis for the last two winters?"

What's transpiring here is like a bad dream. As far as I was concerned, this was over. "I'm not in any trouble, am I?"

"No. Not at all. But depending on what's about to come to light from the computer, and from the therapist, we'll need you to officially verify that because you were asleep the whole time, there is a *possibility* that Will may have left the house, done what he had to do, and returned without your knowledge?" The cut of the glass in her earrings refracts the light from the window, making rainbows.

"Surely that's clear from my original statement. I'd always said I was asleep." Although I can recall that DI Jones's exact wording of the statement relied on my *conscious* knowledge of Will's presence in our bed and I did nothing to correct it.

When Heidi was tiny, I'd be more likely to have a *conscious knowledge* of Will being in or out of bed, but from the time when she started sleeping through the night, I've slept soundly again, unless I've had a glass of wine too many. The whole time DI Jones was here earlier this year, he kept apologising for putting me through having to make a statement, when our family had been through so much already.

"Having read your statement earlier, I'm not sure it's obvious that you've said you were asleep, actually." DI Moriarty looks apologetic. "If it was to go to court as it is, it would be ripped apart."

I guess they don't need me to tell them how damaging an additional statement will be to the already fragile reputation amongst the police force, if they find Will to have been involved after all. But that's the least of my worries. I'm married to the man. He's the father of my little girl.

But surely they'll need something more cast iron than me being sound asleep on three of the nights in question. And if I was able to give them more evidence than that, I really would.

"Can you tell me anything about what he's said to the therapist? Surely I've got the right to be kept informed. After all, it's probably me who's in the most danger from him, and indirectly, Heidi too."

"We don't know much yet Eva, but even when I've listened to the recording, I'm not sure exactly what I'll be allowed to tell you. Not whilst it's part of an ongoing investigation."

"Alright, I understand."

I nearly tell them about my potential visit tomorrow with Mark to visit Pat Ingham - if it actually goes ahead, that is. It could be relevant to things, with her being the wife of the man who was originally convicted of the river killings. But something stops me saying anything. With me being Will's wife, perhaps I'd be prevented from going to see her, with all that's going on.

There's no denying, in my opinion, that Will's been overly interested in the deaths at the river Alder. He was always asking Mark tons of questions, and would be glued to Facebook and the news when it was all happening last winter, and the winter before. I thought his interest stemmed from it all being so close to home, not the fact that.... I flick the thought from my mind. These thoughts will pull me under so I've got to keep fighting them. But when I discovered he was attending some of the funerals, I pointed out how odd this was. I must mention this in my statement. And he shrugged me off when I spoke to him. Will has always done what Will wants to do. But what if it is something far worse than I could ever have imagined?

From the news reports flying around since yesterday, it appears the nightmare is continuing. I suspected they wouldn't be accidents. Not after last time. As soon as I heard about the mother and daughter drowning whilst we were away, I just knew. But for the mother and daughter, I can definitely provide Will with an alibi. After all, we were in Florida.

I decide to wait in the car until the bell goes. Normally I'd chat with some of the other mums, but I can't face it today. Whilst Will was being investigated, I had total faith he'd be cleared. *Total* faith. Of course, the police were duty bound to take Pat Ingham's claims seriously, but I *knew* my husband. At least I thought I did. Yes, he'd had his issues, but he also had a strong moral compass. That was one thing that first attracted me to him. He was occasionally derogatory where women were concerned, but I was working on changing that.

A sick emptiness has been spreading through my gut since I found the search history the other day. And with each new piece of information that's coming to light, I know, I really know what he's capable of. I've nothing concrete yet but that shadow of doubt is looming over me. A man who can treat his wife like Will has treated me lately is capable of *anything*. And who'll believe that I had no idea what was going on? They'll accuse me of lying to protect him. And supposedly giving him an alibi. I'll be guilty by association.

Although nobody knows anything yet, I can't bring myself to get out of this car and hold my head up in public. There's only Mark I can discuss this with. I suspect even he doesn't truly believe that his brother might be warped enough to be behind the river deaths. Once the results of the hard drive come back and we find out what conversation the therapist has recorded, who knows. If Will turns out to have been wrongly cleared and is as guilty as I'm starting to fear he is, I'll be forced to move away with Heidi and start again.

The school bell interrupts my thoughts and I watch as one by one, the children are united with their parents. I wait until there are three left with the teacher, one of them Heidi, before I slip from the car and across the playground.

"Mrs Potts. I need a word," the teacher says as I reach them. The school secretary also appears at the cloakroom door. "Oh - hang on."

"Telephone call Mrs Braithwaite. It's urgent."

"I'm sorry. We'll have to speak tomorrow instead Mrs Potts."

"Sure." I catch Heidi's hand and head back to the car. Her pigtails are dishevelled compared to when I dropped her off, and she looks exhausted. It's no wonder, really. "What did Mrs Braithwaite want, did she say?"

Heidi looks sheepish. "I got upset about Dad not being at home."

"What do you mean, *upset?*" Remorse tugs at me.

"I was crying. I need him to come home."

"Oh sweetie. I'm really sorry you're so sad." But a voice is screaming inside me that we've got absolutely no idea what he's done yet. I must protect Heidi from him. And myself. If the police don't find him soon, maybe I *should* stay at Mum's. But how can I put all this on *her*, especially with what she's facing herself? It's not that the Alzheimer's is debilitating her too much yet, but she's been devastated at her diagnosis. No, I can't burden her more than that – besides, Mum's would be the first place he'd look for me if I wasn't at home. Plus, I risk him moving back in whilst we're not there, and maybe me and Heidi losing our home. No – I absolutely must fight this out.

The landline is ringing as I unlock the door. I snatch it up just in time.

"Is that Eva Potts?"

"It is." My heart thuds at the official sounding voice. *What now?*

"It's Suzannah Peterson here, from The Alder Centre. Your husband's been coming here for sessions with Daniel Hamer. We spoke briefly last week, if you remember."

"Yes. I do. Can you bear with me one moment please?"

"Heidi. Go and play with Biscuit for a few minutes. When I've finished on the phone, we'll put him in the car and take him out somewhere." *Miles away from here,* I say to myself.

"OK Mum." Her expression is brighter than when I first picked her up.

I dart to the front door and pull the bolts across before returning to the lounge.

"Sorry about that. I needed to sort my daughter."

"It's fine. Look, I'm sorry to bother you, but I gather your husband is on bail to stay away from you at the moment."

My heart beats faster. "Did *he* tell you that? When did you see him?" I can picture this woman now with her dark-haired perfection. Glancing at my reflection in the lounge mirror, I drag my fingers through my hair. I can't even remember whether I've brushed it today.

"No – we..."

"Look it's really important. If you've seen him..."

"Not since yesterday – he was in a bit of a state when he left here. I wanted to warn you about it before now, but Daniel, his therapist, said not to – he wanted to see what the police suggested first."

"What do you mean, *in a state?*"

"Angry. Agitated. As though he might do something. I'm really sorry for not contacting you earlier, but I was acting on Daniel's instructions."

"Well, I wish you had. Will turned up here last night. Things are even worse than they were before, especially for my daughter. She's only eight and wouldn't even sleep in her own bed last night."

"I wanted to tell you, really I did. I've agonised ever since he left here. Anyway, I've made contact with you now, despite what Daniel told me."

"So what happened exactly?"

"I really can't say too much – obviously I don't want to get our business into trouble, and myself. But now I've found out what's been going on for you, I wanted to say – woman to woman – for God's sake, don't let him back into your house."

"Why are you saying that? What have you found out?"

"Look Eva. I promise that you'll hear about *everything* soon enough, but he's dangerous. You must be able to see that for yourself."

"I've been with the man for nine years. Are you saying you know more about my husband than I do?"

"No. But you need to be warned that everything is about to blow up. Daniel has taken some evidence to the police. I wanted to tell you, so it doesn't come as too much of a shock. Like I said, I wish I'd been in touch earlier, but..."

"Warn me about what exactly?" I'm not going to tell her that the police have already spoken to me. I want to hear what she's got to say first. "What evidence?"

"All I can say at the moment is that we've got him recorded, admitting to something."

"Such as?"

"I'm really sorry Eva. I've probably said too much already. Daniel's going to kill me for getting in touch with you. Only, if Will were to hurt you – I wouldn't be able to live with myself. I feel bad enough as it is."

"What did you say your name was?"

"Suzannah."

"You're not really telling me anything new Suzannah. Can't you be more specific about what Will's said to you.? Is this about the women who've been killed in the river?"

"I'm not totally sure at the moment. But Eva. Until they find your husband. Be careful. Please. Sorry, I've got to go. Daniel's coming."

19

As Heidi heads into the cloakroom, her teacher comes dashing out. "Mrs Potts..."

"I've got an appointment. I'm sorry. Really, I've got to go." It's a total lie. Mark's not even due to collect me until eleven. But I've lain awake half the night turning everything over, as well as listening for signs of Will outside, and I can't face being grilled by Heidi's teacher. Until I find out exactly what's going on, I'm not sure I could hold a coherent conversation.

The prison is on the outskirts of Yorkshire and it can take up to an hour to get through security, according to Mark. He rang earlier to say he'd got me onto the visiting order and Pat Ingham has agreed to see me. Mark also said he's found something out and he'll tell me during the drive there. I begged him to tell me over the phone, but he wasn't shifting. I can't imagine it's going to be anything positive.

I pace the house, awaiting his arrival. It's as clean as a hospital ward, so I can't even occupy myself with housework. I open and close drawers and wardrobe doors, wondering how empty it will be once I get rid of Will's things.

There's a whiff of his Hugo Boss aftershave when I open the bathroom cabinet. It catches my breath - not the smell, but the memories it evokes. When things were different. That he swept me off my feet sounds cliché now, but there's no other way to describe it. Throughout our first few months together, we had a ball. I got flowers, compliments, kept promises, and his undivided attention. He couldn't do enough for me. I did, however, witness flashes of his jealousy. He ruined a couple of what should have been wonderful nights out – one where he accused me of flirting with the waiter, and another when a man at the theatre had struck up a conversation with me during the interval. Will had gone to the loo and had made his presence very much known when he returned. On both occasions, I'd been beyond embarrassed at his behaviour, not to mention baffled by it. I only ever had eyes for Will.

He was probably judging me by his own standards, as once he'd got beyond that initial jealousy, he'd ping-ponged between me and his ex for a few months, which had broken my heart at the time.

It was only when I decided enough was enough and I was going to move on from Will, that he suddenly pursued me to the ends of the earth. At first, I suspected that he didn't want anyone else to have me. These days, I dare not speak to other men. There's only Mark, and even with him, Will's made the odd barbed comment over the years about me supposedly flirting with him. To say Mark and Will have been brought up in the same family, I'm amazed at how different they are. I've never considered Mark in any other way than as a lovely brother-in-law, but I've often wished Will had more of his brother's caring and easygoing temperament.

Will, at one time, had me convinced of his desire to deal with his fears of commitment and his trust issues. He wanted to be with me more than anything, he had promised, and was going to spend the rest of his life proving it. And I'm going to spend the rest of mine watching over my shoulder and waiting for him, the way things are turning out.

"Any sign of him yet?" I swing the door open after checking it's definitely Mark on the other side.

"Not a thing. He's completely gone to ground." Mark looks knackered too as he steps into the hallway. "I keep checking with Mum and Claire. I've obviously had to tell them what's going on. They've a right to be kept involved."

"Everything?" I lock the door after him.

"Well, not quite everything. What I'm going to tell you though, you have to keep to yourself Eva. Even Mum and Claire haven't heard this. Hell - even I shouldn't have been told, and to be honest, I wish I hadn't."

"OK." I take a deep breath, bracing myself for whatever might be coming. I stand facing him with my arms folded, as though trying to protect myself. One part of me is saying 'bring it on' and the other wants to jump on a flight out of here. I'm not sure how much more I can take at the moment.

"Eva. You've got to promise me, for now, that you can keep this to yourself. You've got to. It's really bad shit."

Oh God. "Tell me Mark."

"DI Jones, my line manager, called me in last night. I've been sworn to absolute secrecy. He trusts me, even if it's my own brother we're hunting down."

"Hunting down?" My hand flies to my mouth. Everything I've feared is about to be confirmed.

Grim-faced, Mark gestures towards the door. "Come on, we'd better be hitting the road. I'll tell you on the way. Have you got some photo ID for the prison?"

I grab my bag from the bottom step. "I've got my driving licence."

I lock up and crunch across the gravel to Mark's car, my thoughts swirling. *What's he going to tell me?* Judging by the look on his face, I'm not sure I want to hear it.

"Right. Out with it."

He turns the car in the cul-de-sac and glances at me. "Remember, this is for your ears only. And we can't mention it in front of Pat Ingham either. We'll listen to what she's got to say and leave."

"That sounds like a plan. And of course I won't say anything in front of her."

"Right firstly." He blows a long breath out. His face is riddled with anxiety. "DI Moriarty jumped the queue for the hard drive analysis on your computer."

"She said she might be able to. Go on." I grip each side of the passenger seat. Here we go.

"It's serious shit Eva. He's been on all kinds of sites."

"Such as?"

"The *tamer* ones, if they can be described as that, are the anti-women sites, kind of white male supremacy ones. There's quite a few of them."

"That doesn't surprise me one bit." It really doesn't. He's always tried to rule the roost at home, seeming to be of the opinion that my only place in life is within the house, serving him.

"And there's all the research he's been doing around killing in water and drowning people."

"What kind of research?" I dig my nails into my other hand. If I'm having some kind of nightmare here, hopefully the sting of my nails will wake me.

"It's detailed stuff, such as how to avoid leaving evidence and how a body might surface after drowning." He pauses at a roundabout and looks at me. "He's been on some really graphic sites according to DI Jones."

Mark hasn't looked this haunted since Lauren died.

"We were aware about his warped interest in the River Alder cases, weren't we?" My heart is hammering. "Perhaps that's all it is. A warped interest." I'm still trying to hang onto this denial.

"There's quite a few searches of that sort of thing. But I'd say the most worrying thing is the images he's downloaded."

"Images?"

"Yeah. They were in a locked folder inside another encrypted folder."

"Images of what?" I close my eyes and the question enters my head about what on earth I'll tell Heidi about her father when she gets older. I brace myself. What bloody images has he been looking at?

'I haven't seen them, Nor do I want to. DI Jones said they were grim, so I took his word for it."

"What of Mark?"

He takes a deep breath. I look sideways at him, noticing his dark expression and the clench of his jaw.

"Dead and mutilated women. But it gets even worse than that. Some are pictures of the river victims."

"The river victims? But he's a traffic cop. How's he got hold of pictures of them?" Images of Will sneaking around the mortuary fill my head. I can't imagine he'd be able to get in there, unsupervised. He's more deranged than I ever imagined, but at least the 'images' are not of what first entered my head when Mark mentioned it. I had all sorts going through my mind. But this is nearly as horrendous.

"He'll get access to things through the police server, I suppose." I notice there's a grey tinge to Mark's face. If he found all this out last night, he'll have barely slept. "They're in the process now of going through everything he's accessed through work and going as far back as they can, so it might take time."

"How did he imagine he wouldn't get caught?"

"We see this time and time again when we arrest people for downloading images. Logic must tell them they'll get caught sooner or later, but the addiction for what they're looking at overrules that."

"This is going to kill Claire when she finds out." I don't ask Mark whether there were any images of Lauren. If there were, that would be beyond depraved.

"I can't take it in Eva. I had an inkling something big was coming, but I really can't take it in. Shit." He slams on the brakes just in time at a junction.

"Focus on the road, Mark. It's going to be OK." I reach across the seat and squeeze his arm. "Do you want me to drive?"

What am I on about? *It's going to be OK.* How can things ever be OK after what's being uncovered about my husband.

"Sorry. I'll be alright." He sets off again.

There's a few moments of silence as Mark gets himself back together.

"The pictures are that bad." Mark's voice breaks into the tension already hanging in the air. "That DI Jones isn't sure if they could even be in category A or B."

"Oh my God." I've heard this term before, in the news and in the crime dramas I watch. If they're categorising them like that, this is even more serious. "Right, so I've got a husband who gets off on looking at photographs of dead and mutilated women. Sick bastard. "Are any of them..." I hardly dare ask, but I've got to know, "are any of them sexually motivated?"

"DI Jones didn't say. What he did say was quite enough for me." Mark's knuckles whiten as he grips the wheel. "I guess, in time, we'll find out the specifics. I just can't believe I'm related to the man."

I'm probably not the only one panicking at being seen to be guilty by association. "What about the therapist?" Again I need to know. Even though this conversation feels as though it's happening outside of me. It's almost like it's taking place in slow motion. "Someone rang me from there yesterday – a woman, and said I was in danger."

"Really? Have you told anyone about this?"

"No – I haven't spoken to the police since. I was going to."

"Why didn't you say anything to me? You shouldn't have kept something like this to yourself."

Suddenly I feel stupid. "It's one more thing, isn't it? In amongst the quagmire of all the rest of it. The woman said her therapist colleague was reporting everything they knew about Will to the police. She wanted to make sure I wasn't having second thoughts about taking him back."

"But she wouldn't tell you any more than that?"

"She said she wasn't allowed to – but that I'd find out what had been reported within the next day or two."

"That might be the rest of what I've found out."

"Go on." As if there's more.

"There are two things on record apparently," Mark begins as he eases around another roundabout. "Will's been voice recorded. And the therapist is willing to testify of things Will said during previous sessions."

"Like what?"

"I've only been told about what's been recorded, so far anyway."

"I'm surprised at Will for allowing that. Do you know whether he gave his consent? He's either been tripped up, or he's slipped up."

"I thought that. If he hasn't given permission, they might not be able to use it as evidence. Anyway, he's been speaking about wanting to cleanse the world of drunk women who can't control themselves, as an atonement for what happened to Dean."

"Atonement. Bloody hell. He actually used that word? And *cleanse the world of drunk women.*"

"Yeah, apparently. I should have seen this coming. Will needed serious help a long time ago. I just hoped he was a bigoted pillock. Why didn't I see it Eva? I'm his brother for God's sake."

It's as though Mark's really saying *why didn't I see it as well?* After all, I've lived in the same house as him all these years. "What else?"

"He told the therapist that he hears voices."

"Hears voices?" This is getting worse. "What sorts of voices?"

"Ones that aren't really there." Mark indicates then swaps lanes. "In this case, they've been telling him to get rid of the women. Telling him when, where and how, that's what DI Jones has told me anyway."

I stare at Mark. How he can concentrate on the road whilst we're having this sort of conversation is beyond me. How come I've never known that Will *hears voices?* I wonder how long it's being going on for, and what they might have been telling him to do to me. I shudder. I've been married to a complete maniac, and I had absolutely no idea. We've just been on holiday together. I nearly agreed to have a second baby with him. What if I hadn't got him out of the house? *And where is he?* He could come back at any time. I'm terrified now that I'm getting an idea of how unhinged he really is.

"What do you reckon your mum and Claire will say?"

"Claire won't believe any of it without proof," Mark replies. "Even then, she still won't believe it. Will gets on her nerves but she's always looked up to him in a strange sort of way. She'll be absolutely gutted."

"I know."

"And Mum – well, who knows what she'll say? I'm really dreading it coming out to everyone else. What others will make of it all. What they'll make of us as a family."

"At least we've got some idea of what we're dealing with now. But I know what you mean. I'll have the other mums whispering about me in the playground." I can picture them now and my heart plummets. Things really are dreadful enough without that. "We're going to have to keep as much of it as quiet as we can, for as long as we can."

"But we don't really know what we're dealing with." Mark crunches the gears as he tries to move from fourth to fifth. "Not for sure. DI Jones has told me they're going back through all the CCTV even more meticulously now. Not just from the last few weeks, but where available, over the last two winters."

"Let's see what Pat Ingham has to add to all this. Part of me can't take anymore, but this much has come out. If there is anything else to find out, then I need to know. God knows how Heidi and I are going to go on from this."

"All we can do," Mark peers at me through eyes that are like his brothers, only with warmth in them, "is take it all as it comes. I only hope they find him soon."

"He needs help. What if they don't catch him?"

"You're coming to stay with us Eva. You and Heidi. And I'm not taking no for an answer."

By the time we get to Newgate Prison, I'm wrung out. I've had enough, but something is driving me on. I won't allow myself to become another of Will's victims. Somehow, I'll get through this.

The prison isn't quite what I envisaged. "I was expecting a Victorian sort of building," I say to Mark. "With barbed wire around high walls. This place looks like it could be a day centre for the elderly from the outside."

"Yeah, that's the sort of prison in all the dramas and on the news. This is a Cat C – it's only one up from being an open prison."

Mark announces us at the door, and we're buzzed in. Perhaps this won't be too bad.

"Pat Ingham was lucky – clearly they don't deem her to be much of a risk. It's not as if she's a spring chicken anymore, is it?"

Despite it being a 'Cat C,' as Mark called it, we're still treated almost as though we're criminals ourselves from the moment we step inside. Like I'm not feeling wretched enough already.

"Don't you get special treatment from them?" I whisper to Mark as we pile our stuff in lockers. "For being a copper?"

"Sshh, for God's sakes Eva, don't broadcast that around here. I'll get lynched. I'll have people waiting outside for me."

"Sorry." I colour up. "That was stupid." *Let's add that worry to the list,* I nearly say.

We stand in line as our shoes go over a conveyor belt, airport style. If only I was getting on a plane, far away from my reality. It might be my only option when all this is over.

I definitely feel like a criminal as I'm patted down and heavily sniffed by a German Shepherd. It has a face that reminds me of Biscuit. I suddenly hope Jade from next door remembers to walk him and doesn't let him off the lead. At the moment, when he's taken for a walk, it's a case of who's walking who? And if Mark's so insistent on us staying, I wonder if he's factored the puppy in. A puppy that has frequent accidents and likes to chew.

"Why did they have to look in my mouth?" I ask as we're held in a space between two sets of doors.

"Drugs."

"Of course. And I obviously look like such a druggie." I laugh, despite the awfulness of life right now.

We wait in a second holding area for what seems like an eternity. Mark was right about what it would be like in here. I've had to leave my watch in the locker, but we've definitely been here for well over an hour already. By the time we get in to see her, it'll be time to leave. I look around at the other visitors. There's evidently an unspoken dress code of grey saggy tracksuit bottoms, hooded tops and trainers. These are the husbands, brothers and sons of the women in here. Some of them will have travelled for miles and from what Mark said, they only get one visit every fortnight.

"I should write to the authorities." I prod Mark. "It's not fair that it takes this long to get in. It eats all the visiting time away. Which isn't so bad for us, but imagine what it's like for those who are family."

"You'd be wasting your ink and your energy," he replies. "Prison visitors have even less of a voice than the inmates."

I want to get into the visiting room but am as nervous as hell that we're going to hear even more revelations. I've been increasingly aware lately of the man Will really is, especially after he went for me last week. As soon as I came across his search history, I knew reporting it would not bring anything good. But what else could I do?

The photos of dead women have come as a terrible shock and I can't shake the image of Will prowling around a mortuary. That Will hears voices in his head, evidently ordering him to do evil things has also really shaken me. How evil these voices are, we might well be about to find out.

CHAPTER 20

MARK NUDGES ME.

"Laycock, Anderson, Tayler, Ingham, Khan."

It's unreal that we're answering to the name of *Ingham*. We follow the others into a larger room with no windows. Sunlight seeps through a crack of what might be perspex along the tops of the magnolia brick walls.

Straight away, my gaze falls on Pat Ingham, who's staring back at me. She was thin before, but now she looks skeletal, and her hair is slicked back into a ponytail. It's so thin, it reminds me of my former Maths teacher's comb over. I can't imagine what it must be like serving a sentence at Pat Ingham's age. Well, at any age.

"Place your finger on the screen. We need a fingerprint." There's no please or thank you in this place. Mark's right, if your name's on a visiting order, evidently you're in the same category of scum as the person inviting you to visit. I do as instructed, then follow Mark as we weave through tables, all fastened to the floor, towards the corner of the room.

Pat smiles weakly as we reach her and beckons for us to sit.

She's dressed identically to the others, royal blue trousers and a striped shirt which hangs off her.

"Hello again Pat. Would you like a drink?" Mark's voice is amicable considering the circumstances. He really is a nice man. No wonder that Sara one is after him. "They let us bring some change in with us."

"A cup of tea and a biscuit would be really good, thanks." She looks as though she could do with it.

"Do you want anything Eva?"

I want to implore him not to leave me on my own here but say, "tea for me as well please." Whilst Mark isn't here, I hope Pat doesn't tell me anything. I'm out of my depth as it is.

I sit facing her. "I'm Eva Potts. Mark's sister-in-law. Thanks for adding me to the visiting order at such short notice."

"No problem. I hardly get any visitors so I'm hardly going to turn extra ones down."

I laugh, though it's the most forced sound I've ever made. Nothing right now is funny in the slightest. I study Pat's watery eyes and bony shoulders. They never had children, her and Ingham, and after what they convicted her of, and after what he's done, I can't imagine visitors would queue up to see her. Us being here is probably the highlight of her week.

"You'll be as interested in what I've got to say as Mark, anyway. In hindsight, I should have asked you in the first place."

Her comment pulls me up short. As if I haven't already heard enough from Mark on the journey over. It's surreal that I'm sitting so close to the woman who killed Dean - the man who'd have been my brother-in-law, had he lived. I've heard so much about him.

There is, if I'm honest, a part of me that's always thought that sentencing Pat Ingham to a prison sentence at her age was harsh. She's lived with the guilt for all these years as it is, and the abuse she suffered from her husband seems like punishment enough. In the week before he died, Ingham had her locked in her cellar – she was lucky to get out of there alive by the sounds of it.

"So how are you doing in here Pat?" I'll make small talk until Mark returns. I glance around the room. Officers parade up and down the aisles, full of their own self importance, whilst happy conversations flow over cups of tea. It's as though we're in The Pink Teapot café in town. All we're missing is the hiss of the coffee steamer and the low drone of Radio Two.

"Surviving. It's not too bad. Better than I feared, to be honest."

I glance around the barren walls, wondering how on earth she can say that. "Are you keeping yourself busy?"

"I guess so. I read a lot. And I'm taking a couple of courses."

I sense Mark coming up behind me. He's balancing three polystyrene cups, and some wrapped biscuits which he lowers to the table.

"Thanks." I've not had a cuppa since first thing, so I'm grateful for it. Until I notice that it looks like yesterday's dishwater.

"Leave the lid on." Pat's gaze flicks to the officers.

"How come?"

"In case you throw it at someone." Mark shakes his head as he bites into a biscuit. "Not that it would do that much damage to anyone. It's stone cold."

He looks back towards the serving hatch as though he's contemplating returning the 'tea,' but then must decide otherwise. "Right Pat," he begins. "We're really pushed for time. It's taken an eternity to get in here. So let's get on with it, shall we?"

Pat has a likeness of Biscuit when I put him in his cage at night. This is not a woman who should be caged. She's hardly a danger to society.

"I want to start by saying sorry for how I was when you

came to see me in hospital that time." Pat lowers her gaze and stares at the table. "I hadn't realised before you came whose brother you were."

"Who do you mean? Will's, Dean's or Claire's?"

I'm reminded at this point just how much damage the Inghams have managed to wreak on this family. Dean and Will were mown down by Pat Ingham. Claire was badly beaten by Jonathan Ingham, and Lauren was killed by him. It's quite a list.

"Any of them," she replies, smoothing her hand over her hair. "All of them. Though I freaked because you were Dean's brother. Obviously, I'd already lived with what I did for a long time."

"Well, that's something at least. That you're remorseful for what you did."

"I've done a lot of soul searching in here about the effect of my actions all those years ago. The fact that my drunken actions killed Dean. And what it did to all of you."

To be fair, her tone of voice and facial expression mirrors her words. I really do find myself feeling sorry for her. Everyone who truly regrets something they've done deserves forgiveness and a second chance, *surely?* Well, nearly everyone.

Mark clearly doesn't agree. "And what difference does *doing some soul searching* make? It's not going to bring Dean back, is it?"

"I know. It won't make *any* difference to what I did. But at least I've started to make some peace with myself."

"Is that why you've asked me here?" Mark's voice sharpens some more. "For my forgiveness?"

I pick at the edges of my cup, wondering how Mark's going to deal with this. He's inches away from the woman who killed his brother. He's been in this proximity to her before, but didn't know then what he knows now.

"Not forgiveness specifically. Just the chance to say sorry. I truly am. Keeping what I'd done secret has torn away at me for many years. But I was so terrified of my husband that I was never able to tell the truth."

"I can identify with that." My words come as a surprise, even to me. Who'd have thought I'd have so much in common with Pat Ingham?

"I want to talk about Will in a minute, if that's OK." Fear clouds in Pat's eyes now and I worry again what she's going to tell us about him.

"What I want to know, is why did you drive off and leave Dean and Will like you did?" There's even more of an edge to Mark's voice now. Clearly he's planned what he wants to ask her.

"I've gone over it so many times. I'd do *anything* to get that time over again. Never in a million years would the person I am now have ever driven off."

"Why did you drink and drive in the first place?"

I shuffle in my seat and glance at the large clock above the officer's main station. It's quarter past two already. Hopefully they run the time allowance to the wire, or perhaps they'll make us leave earlier than the visiting end time. But I sense that we're in danger of running out of time here. And I need to find out what Pat Ingham wants to say about Will. But Mark also needs his answers, so I'll give him a few more minutes on this.

"I had such a problem with drink Mark. It's no excuse, but it well and truly had me in its grip. That's what alcohol can do to a person."

"But what compelled you to drive that day? You were so pissed you mounted the entire pavement."

"The moments before I got in the car that day are totally blurred. All I remember is that there was an argument. I recall Jonathan not being too well and demanding that I drive him to an appointment. But the responsibility was mine. I got behind the wheel. It was me who put the key in the ignition. I drove the car."

"And you left one of my brothers dead and the other unconscious. How could you have done that? Then driven away from them? And what's even worse is carrying it for so many years."

"I totally agree with what you're saying. And it's no defence, but back then, Jonathan made threats about what he'd do to me if I jeopardised his position in the police." She sighs a jagged breath out. "He was a sergeant in those days, and he'd knowingly let me drive in that state. In fact, he'd *forced* me to drive."

"I still can't get my head around how you left the scene of the accident you'd caused."

"Your brother had seen exactly who was behind the wheel and so had a man who was passing by. So, the logic was that there was no way we could hang around and pretend Jonathan had been driving instead of me." She seems to sink into herself more as she speaks. "And I was that drunk, all reason had gone out of the window."

"So you kept quiet to save your husband's career in the police. As well as your own arse."

"Mark. I don't expect you to understand this, but I was terrified of Jonathan. He bullied me more than I can describe in those days. He was controlling and violent." Pat's voice is trembling with emotion, and I hope that Mark will ease up. "It took years for him to let me go. And even then, he never completely left me alone."

"Will's never forgiven you. You've no idea of the effect you've had on his life."

That's an understatement. I squint in the glare of the overhead fluorescent light, the familiar buzz of a migraine behind my eye again. It's because I'm stressed. And my bloody pills are locked away in my handbag in the locker.

"What do you mean?" Pat fiddles with her biscuit wrapper. She's not eaten any, nor drunk any of the tea. It seems that none of us can stomach eating biscuits right now.

"Will despises drunks – anyone who drinks alcohol makes his skin crawl."

"He makes out like I'm some sort of a demon for having a glass of wine," I say, remembering the last time Will had a go at me in front of Heidi.

"And he hates women," Mark continues. "Even his own mother."

"And wife," I add.

"He hates the combination of the two even more." Pat sips her tea. "Blimey, call that a cuppa."

"The combination of what?"

"Women being drunks." Her voice is barely audible, but it's clear from her expression what she's getting at.

"They cleared him of that." Mark's clearly playing devil's advocate here. Pat has no idea what we've found out.

"Not that my opinion counts for anything Mark, but the reputation of the police had suffered enough with the botched river enquiry at the time of Jonathan's death." She straightens up in her seat. "It was too easy for the blame to be pinned on him. After all, he was no longer able to defend himself."

"That bastard killed my fiancée in the stream." Mark's voice cracks. "The mother of my daughter."

One of the prison officers glances towards our table.

"I know. That I definitely know. And the other two attacks he carried out after Lauren."

"One of them was my sister."

This is all too much. There's not enough time to go over everything properly. The back of my throat is dry and the pain in my head is intensifying. I sip the disgusting tea. Perhaps I'm dehydrated.

"Jonathan wasn't responsible for the river deaths, not from last winter or the winter before, I absolutely promise you that." Pat leans forward in her seat.

"One metre at all times," barks a passing officer.

"I was there, Mark. I listened to every word they said. They had no idea I was in the house. Jonathan and I had split up, but he'd kept a key as he still had belongings there." She fiddles with a shirt button as she speaks. "Even after we'd split up, I was never allowed to truly shake him off. Normally I'd have been at work, but I wasn't too good that day, so was having a lie down."

"Listened to who?"

"My husband and your brother."

"Will?" I say, rubbing at my head.

She nods.

"When was this?"

"January time. I listened at the top of the stairs. Jonathan must have decided that it was a safe place for them to meet. It quickly became clear that Will was blackmailing Jonathan." Pat looks from Mark to me. "That they were blackmailing each other."

"How?"

"Jonathan knew what Will had been doing to those women. But he was covering for him because of what Will had over him. It was like they'd reached a stalemate." She fiddles with her shirt sleeve now. "By that time, I reckon that Jonathan would have been past caring about *me* going to prison for being the driver, as we'd separated by then, but he'd have certainly been in enough trouble himself." She takes a deep breath. "Perverting the course of justice. Leaving the scene of an accident. Possibly manslaughter. He knew how seriously injured your brother was. He'd have been turfed out of the police on his ear, no question."

"You're saying they were in it together the whole way along?" Mark asks. "Will and Jonathan."

"Will was throwing women to their deaths in the Alder. Lauren had suspected someone was behind it, and had alluded to this in the press. And Ingham was allowing Will to get away with it."

"But you've already told the police all this. None of this is anything new."

"I didn't have a shred of evidence, did I? And neither did the police. Will's too clever for that. But since I've found out he's doing it again, I had to do something, and that's why I invited you here."

There are tears in her eyes. I've no reason to doubt her and I can't understand why the police were so quick to dismiss her.

"I hoped Will might stop killing after getting away with what he's already done, but it seems to me as though he might have some sort of sick addiction to what he's doing. He's got to be stopped."

Mark and I glance at each other knowingly.

"As soon as I knew for certain what the truth was," Pat goes on, "I got in touch with Lauren."

I steal another look at Mark. It must be hard for him when Lauren's name is used in a conversation like this.

"We arranged to meet," Pat explains. "I was going to tell her everything, as I've already said, but unbeknown to me, Jonathan had sneaked into the house, overheard me on the phone to her, then intercepted Lauren whilst she was on her way to meet me."

"*Intercepted.*" Mark spits the word out. "Is that what you call it?"

"I've tried everything to be believed by the police."

She ignores Mark's comment. I have to admit; it was an

insensitive one. *Murdered* or *beaten to death* would be more appropriate.

"Because I'm an alcoholic, albeit a recovering one, and the ex-wife of a bent copper, no one, absolutely no one, will listen to me. They'd rather believe some lunatic like your husband." She looks at me coldly now. "I understand you've provided him with an alibi on some of the occasions that he's killed."

Pat Ingham will be the first of many people who'll point the finger like I've somehow covered for Will. "Actually," I reply, "until a few days ago, I thought I really knew him. And as for alibis, on the nights you're talking about, he came to bed with me. Who would suspect their husband of getting back out of bed to go and murder someone? Tell me that."

"I still say that this is nothing new Pat." Mark folds his arms. "The police have investigated your claims already, and Will was cleared."

"But now that the deaths in that river are happening again, surely you're duty bound to take what I said before seriously. To reopen the investigation." Pat sits up straighter in her chair. "I hoped that here, given the opportunity to face each other in the cold light of day, I could tell you the truth of what I know. Eyeball to eyeball – you've got to trust me." Her voice rises. "What have I got to gain by telling you this, if it isn't true?"

Mark glances at the clock. "I've no idea what's true anymore."

"I found out what Will had been doing the day before your Lauren was killed. I've done all I can to be listened to. Your brother is a serial killer, and he's still out there, isn't he? Free to do it to someone else?"

I study her face, wondering if she knows anything about the developments since the end of last week. Does she mean, *still out there* in general, *still out there* after attacking me, or *still out there* after the evidence from his counsellor and the website history. Though, really, she can't possibly be aware of anything – not from where she is.

"Yes. He's still out there."

"I'm really grateful you've come to see me." Pat's voice softens, then hardens again. "Jonathan was a dreadful man and what he did to Lauren and tried to do to the other two, well – he deserves to rot..."

Both Mark and I watch her as she flails her arms around as she speaks.

"I can't sit in that cell watching the news circle round and round as they dredge more and more women from that river. Your brother, your husband," she points from Mark to me, "needs to be taken off the streets. You're probably in danger as well Eva. You've got to listen to me. He's killed so many women, he's probably lost count. I've no idea how he's got away with it. Especially now that he's not got Jonathan to cover for him." Her voice trails off at the end as though she's run out of breath.

This is happening. It's really happening. She has little to gain from *looking us in the eye,* as she puts it, and making sure we believe her. Will is a convincing liar. He always has been. And his narcissistic edge means he can be charm personified when he wants to be. He certainly convinced me of his innocence in all this and never, ever, would I have suspected the mental health issues, such as the hearing voices, which have now come to light.

"Do you both understand what he's capable of now?"

I nod. Mark rubs at his head.

"Good. Because there's something else. Which is the main reason I asked you here. But you've got to promise me that you'll be careful with what I'm about to tell you." She tugs at her neck as if trying to relieve pressure from herself.

"How do you mean?" Mark frowns.

"I'm putting myself at risk by repeating what I'm about to say. But you need to be told this."

"Of course I'll be *careful.*" He leans forward. "But I can't make you any promises – I'm a police officer. It all depends on what you're going to say."

"The woman I'm padded up with..." Pat lowers her voice. "Her *partner,* or whatever the term is, he's paid to take people out."

"What, like an escort?"

Mark gives me a withering look as if to say, *get with it Eva.*

"No. I mean, like take people out... permanently."

"Are you saying Will...?"

"This man, my padmate's partner, was paid by someone for the two women. That mother and daughter from last month."

"Will was away on holiday in the States when that happened. He wasn't even here," Mark says. "Are you suggesting it was Will who paid for it whilst he was out of the country?"

"Surely not." I shake my head. "I would imagine that kind of thing would run into thousands of pounds."

"It could have been Will who arranged it," she replies, "but I doubt it. My pad mate has been told it was someone trying to goad Will by *stealing his thunder.* So she says."

"What would anyone gain by that?" I'm bewildered.

"Possibly," Mark clears his throat, "to reawaken Will's lust for killing and his need to *reclaim* his territory. It sounds 'out there,' but we studied a scenario like this when I was training."

"Time. Ladies and gentlemen." The prison officer struts alongside our table. "Say your goodbyes now."

"We're going to need to speak to your cellmate." Mark stands. "We'll be very discreet, don't worry. However, we might need to transfer you to keep you safe."

It's only quarter to three. We've had less than forty minutes of our two hours. But I'm glad to get out of here. Pat affirmed what we already suspected. And some. And we nearly didn't get to that last thing she told us about the hitman.

I'm convinced that it was Will who hired this person. I wouldn't put anything past him. I'll let the police get to the truth of it. At least we know Pat isn't just defending her dead husband.

Meanwhile, my husband is prowling around that river at night, watching and waiting for drunk women, responding to orders inside his own head that compel him to throw them, when their only crime has been to get drunk, to horrendous deaths.

Why did I ever cover for him *for certain* when I'd been asleep? Shame snakes around me as I realise I might have done something sooner to stop him, but then I don't know what. It also dawns on me he's possibly been sneaking away to the river when he's been on shift. But who would have suspected *Will* of being involved?

"If you could make your way to the exit please."

"What are you going to do about it? Quickly tell me. Please." Pat looks from the officer to Mark with panic in her eyes.

"I'll have to speak to my line manager," Mark says. "I'll let him know that the investigation needs reopening."

"And I'll back Mark up," I add.

"And we'll deal with the other information. Like I said, we'll be discreet. No one will tell your cellmate that it's come from you."

"Thank you. You really can't. It's hard enough being in here as it is. My padmate doesn't deserve any trouble either. Her partner might be a contract killer, but she's OK."

I stand. My life has become some kind of horror film. I can hardly believe it. A couple of weeks ago, I was an ordinary mum and housewife.

"I'm truly, truly sorry about what I did to Dean." Pat rises from her chair in response to the approaching officer.

"I know," Mark mutters. From his expression, I can tell it's probably the closest he's ever come to forgiveness.

"And I'm also sorry that you've married someone like Will Potts," Pat says to me. "I can tell from the few minutes I've had with you, that you deserve so much better. At least you didn't get to my age before escaping from him."

CHAPTER 21

WE SPEND OVER HALF the journey back in near silence. What's left to say? We have to accept Will is a killer. Especially after what's surfaced in the past few days. The question is, where is he now? Will they catch him before he kills again? Whether it's me or someone else? I can't ever forgive myself for not seeing what was right in front of me.

"At least it was easier to get out of there than it was to get in." Mark glances at me then back at the motorway, which is filling up.

I nod. "I hope I never have to set foot inside one of those places again."

The silence is heavy with the realisation that one, or both of us might soon have to visit Will in *one of those places*. Well, I certainly won't be.

"How are you feeling?" I'm sitting here, wallowing in shame, but it must be as bad, if not worse for Mark. He's Will's flesh and blood. It will be easier for me to change my name and eventually disassociate from Will completely. Apart from the fact that there will always be Heidi who binds us together.

"Right now, if Will appeared on this road in front of us, I'd drive the car at him." Mark shifts into the outside lane. "He didn't kill Lauren himself, but he had a hand in it, didn't he?"

"I've thought that too."

"How about you? How are you coping?" He glances at me as he overtakes a van.

"My head's spinning with it all to be honest. All those women. He's acted no differently. Day-to-day, I mean. How could he just return home after slinging a woman to her death and slide back into bed beside me. How could I not have known who he really is? It's driving me insane."

"You've found out now. You've got the chance to protect yourself and Heidi. And I'm here for you both – we all are. We've got to stick together."

"If the police hadn't dismissed Pat Ingham's testimony, there'd still be five women living their lives in Alderton, instead of being laid out on slabs in the mortuary." My mind flits to the images Will's been found in possession of.

"I'm not sure I even want to stay in the police after this." Mark looks in his mirror, and changes lanes again. Despite the fraught prison meeting, his driving is smoother on the return journey. "They were supposed to have thoroughly investigated Will after Pat Ingham's allegation. It appears they only dotted a few i's and crossed the occasional t, and that was that."

"You can't let your brother ruin your life Mark. You've done nothing wrong and you must keep hold of that."

"I could say the same thing to you. Yet I suspect others won't see it like that. I see it time and time again with people I work with. The families of the perpetrators of these sorts of crimes are often as much the victim as the victims themselves."

The wipers squeak back and forth, ridding the windscreen

of drizzle. I hate this time of year after the clocks go back. It's not long after four in the afternoon and it's nearly dark.

"What the hell's going to happen next?"

"I wish I could tell you, but for now... we'll pick the girls up. We'll drive to yours to get a few things, then you're both coming back with us. No argument. We'll make room." He glances at me before moving his eyes back to the road.

"I'm not going to argue. I'm relieved if I'm honest. The thought of going back to that empty house and being like a waiting target for Will isn't filling me with much glee."

"You're not safe at home." Mark shakes his head. "Not until he's found."

"He's not going to be found though, is he?" My voice rises. After visiting the prison, I've been squashing my frustration about this. "They've only circulated information around the police forces so far and not even to the media yet. I mean, what are they playing at?"

"I was thinking that as well. I might make a call to Lindy at the Press Association when we get back. No one needs to find out it was me who enlightened her." His mouth is set in a hard, straight line. He means business, that much is obvious.

"Are you sure about that?"

"The decision whether I stay in the police might be taken out of my hands if anyone finds out. But she'll certainly get the story out there." He smiles, despite the hellish predicament we're in. "I can't say I didn't struggle with Lauren and Lindy's close professional association, but Lindy taught Lauren everything she knew."

"It might be better if it's me that rings her Mark, not you. Will needs to be caught by whatever means possible. And soon. What day are we on now?" I glance at my phone. "I'm so stressed, I can't think straight."

"Wednesday."

"Three days." I close my eyes.

"What?"

"Three more days until he could strike again. Kill another woman."

"There'll be so many police on that riverbank this weekend, he won't stand a chance." Mark pulls back into the inside lane which I'm pleased about. The rain's getting heavier.

"We can hope. But look how slow they were to do what they should have done last winter. I know you were part of it, but..."

"That was only because Ingham was in charge of the inquiry. I can't believe he knew all along what Will was doing. The term *bent coppers* doesn't scratch the surface of what they've done." Mark rakes his fingers through his hair. "To say they give the rest of us a bad name is an understatement."

"Are you going to tell DI Jones we visited Pat Ingham today?"

"I'll have to. In fact, I might be hauled up for not getting permission from him first. But I couldn't risk them stopping us and now we've been, it will all add weight to the reopening of charges against Will." His voice dies as he reaches the end of his sentence.

"This must be really hard for you Mark. I know how I'm feeling about all this as his wife, so it must be equally as horrendous being his brother."

"I'm trying not to overthink it." He lets a long breath out. "But I can't lie. I'm worried people will think I'm the same as him. We grew up together, we're in the same police force, and obviously we have the same bloody surname. I feel like doing a runner."

"But why should you? No matter what he's done. He needs help. Hopefully, those who matter will see that. If he's hearing voices telling him to do what he's done, surely they'll diagnose him with something?" It's true. If he's doing what he's doing because he's ill, then he needs treatment. I probably sound soft, but something has triggered this for him to have turned into this monster only within the last couple of years.

"Unless that's all a smokescreen. But we'll find out more soon. Mental illness would certainly strengthen his defence. And he'll be better off in a secure hospital than a vulnerable prisoner's wing. I doubt he'd be safe in prison."

We sit in silence for several moments, the weight of his words pressing down on me. I'm in a trance, watching as lights from the other side of the carriageway rush towards us.

"I'm thinking..." Mark's voice makes me jump. "I'll get in touch with DI Jones before I call Lindy."

I nod. "That would be more sensible. Like you said, you might be in enough trouble for visiting Pat Ingham in the first place. Going back to what she said. What do you make of the hitman thing? It's all crazy, isn't it?"

Mark indicates as we approach our exit. "Who knows? It seems I know nothing about my brother." His weariness is clear in his voice. "He's either hired someone himself to throw the investigation completely off track, or there's someone out there having a good laugh at the police for suspecting one of our own."

It's completely dark as we approach the school. The girls will be taken aback when Mark and I arrive together. It will be a novelty for Heidi to have been picked up by school club, as she's rarely attended it, but she'll have been over the moon to find Alysha there as well. The thought of seeing Heidi and Alysha lifts my spirits slightly.

Mark parks up and stretches his arms as he grips the wheel. "Well, what a bloody day. I'm going to call DI Jones when we get back, then it's a brandy for me."

"When are you going to speak to your mum and Claire about Will?"

"Post brandy."

We both laugh as we get out of the car. It feels strange to laugh amidst the awfulness of it all. But if I don't laugh, I may crack up instead.

"Mark Potts and Eva Potts." Mark says into the intercom. "We're here to collect Alysha and Heidi."

The voice on the intercom sounds surprised. "Erm OK. Come in."

I'm aware that Mark's made us sound almost like a married couple as he's announced our arrival. I've never, ever looked at him in that way though and no matter how single I'm about to become, I can't imagine I ever will. How that Sara could zone in on her best friend's husband-to-be is beyond me. I can't imagine how that relationship could ever be a success in the long term. I'm reminded of the friend request Sara sent me through Facebook last week. Probably trying to get me on side. Claire's told me she's been trying to befriend her. Really, it's too soon after Lauren. Sara needs to take a big step back.

"Hi Mark. Eva."

I smile at Katy. She's one of the teaching assistants in Heidi's class, and helps run the school club too.

"Are you here to collect Alysha, Mr Potts?" She's frowning through her smile.

"And Heidi." I glance around the cloakroom for her princess coat. It's so vibrantly pink that it stands out amongst everyone else's.

Katy looks even more puzzled. "Heidi's already gone. She was collected earlier."

"But she can't have been. I booked her in *here*. Yesterday. I rang up and was told there was definitely space." A chill creeps over me. "Who's picked her up?" Please, please let it be Will's mum, or Claire. But I know, deep down that it won't be.

"Her dad came for her. In fact, he was early. At least twenty minutes before the bell. He said he was taking her to the dentist."

"Her dad?" I look at Mark, whose panicked face probably mirrors mine. How could I have been so stupid? I should have suspected Will might do this. That's why he arrived early – he knows I normally come dashing through the gates at the last minute. Heidi's often one of the last children to be waiting at her teacher's side for me.

"Is there a problem Mrs Potts?"

"You could say that. Heidi's dad's wanted by the police." My voice is a squeak. "Yes, there is a huge bloody problem. I booked her into school club, not to be collected by him."

"Wanted by the police! Whatever for?" Her eyes widen. "He's in the police, isn't he?"

"I'm sorry. We can't go into that right now." Mark turns to me. "Did you tell school anything about what was going on?"

"I seem to recall Mrs Braithewaite wanting to speak to you this morning," Katy says. "But you had to rush off."

Shit. SHIT. This is all my fault. Of course, they're going to let Will collect Heidi. I haven't given them any reason not to. He's on her file as the second contact.

"Stay calm Eva." Mark squeezes my shoulder. "I'll go in and get Alysha, then we'll go straight to your house. They'll be there. You'll see."

Alysha comes racing out and launches herself at me. "Auntie Eva." Then her smile turns to puzzlement. "Where's Heidi?"

"We're going to see her now." I reach for Alysha's hand, wishing more than anything in the world it was Heidi's hand at this moment. Please let them be at home.

"I'll go in when we get there." Mark presses his key fob to open the car doors. "He won't dare do anything to me."

"Who won't?" Alysha pokes her head between the seats as we all get in. "Can I play with Heidi soon?"

"You get your seat belt on Miss." Mark turns back out onto the main road. "We're calling in to pick Heidi up, and she's coming to our house for tea."

"Yay."

God, I hope Mark's right. He shouldn't be making promises like that to Alysha. Will's the last person I want to face right now, but if they're not at the house, I've no idea what I'll do.

As we turn the final corners towards home, my heart rate becomes faster and faster. As we turn the last one, I hold my breath. I close my eyes and gather all my courage to open them again. The house is in complete darkness as we pull up under the streetlight. Fear squeezes me in its grip. I turn to Mark. "Now what do we do?"

"Give me the keys." His voice is calm. "I'll see if there's any sign they've been back. And you need to ring him. You stay here with Auntie Eva, Alysha."

"Have you had a good day sweetie?" I twist in my seat to look at Alysha as she watches her dad head towards our porch. How can I make normal conversation with all this going on? Will would never hurt Heidi, but this is the first time he's ever collected her from school. And it's four years since she started. However, I can hardly take issue with the school when I haven't done or said anything to prevent Will from picking her up. Officially, he's her next of kin, and no doubt she'll have been delighted to see him. I've no one to blame but myself.

"It was OK," Alysha replies. "Where's Heidi?"

"That's what we're trying to find out." I watch as lights illuminate the windows, before going out again, one at a time, downstairs first, then upstairs. *Where are they?*

Mark emerges from the front door, shaking his head and carrying the puppy.

"Yay! Biscuit." Alysha unclips her seatbelt at the sight of

him. "Is he coming to our house too? But where's Heidi?" She flops back against her seat.

"I don't think anyone's been back here." Mark slides back behind the wheel. "Let's get to mine and get everything sorted. You'll keep the dog entertained won't you love?" He turns to Alysha. "I grabbed a can of food for him."

"I wanted Heidi to come and play too." Alysha's voice is a whine.

"Me too. She'll be back with us soon." I say the words with a conviction I don't feel. Will's gone for the jugular here. The thing he knows will hurt me the most. I raise my phone to my ear. I'm trying to get my breath in, unable to fathom where he might have taken her. He's not exactly got any family or friends. They've hopefully gone out for tea somewhere. It'll be fine. I've got to stay calm. My earlier migraine will be back if I'm not careful, and I'll be no use to Heidi, or anyone. Straight to voicemail.

It's a good job Mark and Alysha don't live far from us with the dog bouncing around the back seat like he is. At least he's keeping Alysha's mind off Heidi and preventing her from asking too many questions. They bound into the house together and into the lounge.

"Is Biscuit alright in there?" I ask. "He's not the most house-trained of dogs yet."

"Laminate floor. Don't worry. A doggy accident is the least of our problems right now."

"Lauren wouldn't have said that."

He grins. "Biscuit would have been lucky to have been allowed into the garden."

I try Will again as we get into the kitchen. Still nothing. I steel myself to leave a message this time. One where I make my voice sound ordinary and not full of fear. On that basis, he's more likely to bring her back. "Will, it's Eva. I'm round at Mark's. Please drop Heidi here as soon as you can."

"Right." Mark paces around the kitchen and looks out the window.

Since it overlooks his garden, which is also in darkness, I'm not sure what he's expecting to see.

"I'm calling Mum, Brenda and Claire and getting them all here. They need to be told what's going on now." He fills a glass with water. "And they need to hear it from us. I'll call DI Jones after that."

"Do we *really* need *Janet* here?" I can't imagine my mother-in-law offering much support with the situation.

"I know what you're saying, but I'll have to let her know."

"And what am I supposed to do about Heidi? Will's not answering. I've no idea what I should be doing."

"Let's see what DI Jones says. There's also a chance that Will could've contacted one of my lot today."

"You mean Claire or Brenda? I doubt he'd have got in touch with Janet."

"We need to speak to them as soon as possible. They might have some idea where he's taken Heidi."

"And what about Lindy? Are you still wanting to let her in on all this?"

I'm so grateful to Mark. He's helping me keep it all together. Without him, I'd have fallen apart by now.

"I think so. I reckon that if Will doesn't return Heidi soon, it'll be circulated in the media, anyway. We should sit tight for a few minutes." He points to a bottle on top of the fridge. "Pour us both a brandy whilst I make these calls. We're going to find out soon exactly what to do."

"Claire. It's me. Can you get round here as soon as you can?" Mark looks at me as he's speaking. "Something's going on – I need to talk to you... No, not over the phone. Do you reckon you could pick Mum and Brenda up en route? I'll let them both know you're setting off now."

I listen as he calls them, and then his line manager. He's always short and to the point when he's on the phone.

"Mark Potts here," he says. "I take it there's still no news of Will's whereabouts?"

I slosh brandy into two glasses as I wait for the reply.

Mark shakes his head at me. "Right, well, we've now got a complication, sir." For all his attempts to stay calm, there's a wobble in his voice. "Will collected his daughter, Heidi, from school. Nearly two hours ago. Eva, his wife, thought she was in school club, so we've only recently found this out."

Pause.

"No. He's not picking up."

Pause.

"She's eight. I've got my sister-in-law, Heidi's mum, with me now."

Pause.

"You're coming straight round, are you? Good. Right. I've got my sister, mother, and mother-in-law on their way here too." He glances towards the clock on his oven. At least we can talk to them all together and bring them up to date with the rest of what's going on. "See you shortly."

Mark takes the brandy from me. "Blimey, do I need this. I'd better only have the one."

"Me too. In case I need to go looking for them." My voice trembles. "I don't think he's going to bring her back Mark."

"He's got to. He's in enough trouble as it is without taking Heidi on the run." Mark snatches for his phone as it rings. "Oh, yeah. Hi Sara. No, sorry. I was expecting... oh it doesn't matter."

I can hear her high-pitched voice chirping from where I'm sitting, at the other side of the table from Mark.

"No can do tonight. I've got some family stuff to sort out."

Stuff. Is that what he calls what's going on? Judging from her tone as she replies, Sara doesn't sound happy. I can't hear exactly what she's saying, but her voice has gone up a level.

"Yes. Look I'm sorry. Another time maybe. I've got to go."

"Lauren's friend?" The brandy burns the back of my throat. His use of the word *maybe* didn't sound promising. I'm sure Sara will have picked up on that. Perhaps Mark realises how weird it is for him to be dating his dead fiancée's best friend. I'm keeping well out of it anyway.

He nods. "I kind of like her, but... anyway, this isn't the time to be thinking about all that now. I'll pick your brains when we've got that niece of mine back here, and when Will's been dealt with."

"When Will's been dealt with," I echo. "You make it all sound so simple."

CHAPTER 22

THE PEACE of the kitchen is broken by what sounds like a dozen voices bursting into the hallway at once. I drain my glass and dart towards the door. Maybe Heidi's back. Perhaps Will has dropped her off with one of them.

"Alysha, you stay in there with Biscuit," Mark tells her. "Just pop something on the TV, and I'll come and see you soon."

Alysha sulkily lets go of Brenda and heads back into the lounge. "I haven't had any dinner yet Dad."

"Get some fruit from the bowl for now," Mark calls after her.

Everyone troops towards the kitchen after Mark - Brenda, Claire, then Janet. DI Jones has appeared whilst the front door was ajar. There's still no sign of Heidi, or Will. My breath pumps out in shallow gasps as my anxiety levels rise some more. And when we tell them all what's happened, that will make things even more real.

"Right everyone, have a seat." Mark points at the table. He looks as knackered as I feel. It's been quite a day and shows no sign of abating. Will's got to bring Heidi back soon.

"Is anyone putting the kettle on?" Janet tugs a chair from

beneath the table and looks towards it. Why she can't put it on herself, I can't imagine.

"Shortly," I reply. "Everyone needs to hear this. It's important." I'll let Mark tell them about Heidi - I don't trust myself not to fall apart. They probably think she's in the lounge with Alysha.

Janet raises one eyebrow as if to say, *who do you think you're talking to?*

Mark looks at DI Jones. "Shall I start Sir?"

He nods. "I'll chip in afterwards with the official line."

"The suspense is killing me." Claire pushes her glasses up her nose. She's still in her work clothes. "I take it this is about Will breaking his bail conditions?"

Mark nods. "Partly. Right first off, you *do* all know he's broken his bail conditions, don't you?" He looks from Brenda to Janet.

"After his tiff with Eva last week, you mean?"

I glare at Janet. "It was actually somewhat more than a tiff."

Mark continues. "But you all know, don't you, that the police are looking for Will and will arrest him as soon as they find him?"

Brenda, Claire and Janet echo their acknowledgment. Janet gives me a look I can't read. She's normally fairly civil with me, but something appears to have changed.

"Has anyone been in touch with Will today?" I look at them in turn as they tell me they haven't.

"Right. Well, unfortunately, we, that is, the police, are now looking for Will for more than just breaking his bail conditions." Mark looks at DI Jones.

"Sir. Can you give them the official line – I'm struggling with how to put all this into words. Then when you've finished, I've something to add."

"No problem." DI Jones stands and looks at us all over his glasses. It's a very formal address to be taking place in Mark's kitchen. "You're all aware that Will was the subject of an inquiry into the river deaths recently?"

"Of course we are." Janet's voice bears a trace of sarcasm. "We'd have had to have been on another planet not to have known. But they dropped all that. He should get an official apology for that if you ask me." It's the first time Janet's spoken up for Will in my earshot. I wonder if my mouth is hanging open. Will's would be if he was here.

"Unfortunately, evidence has come to light which has confirmed we made a mistake by dropping the allegations." DI Jones's voice contains no emotion. He's firmly in official mode.

"Again?" Brenda's voice is a shriek. "After what that maniac Inspector of yours, Ingham, did to my daughter, you've got the nerve to stand there and say you've made another mistake!" She wrings her hands in her lap.

"How do you mean?" Claire's voice is much more even. She and Mark are so alike.

"We've looked closer into the alibis Will gave us," DI Jones replies, "at the times when the drownings over the last two winters took place. It seems the explanations of his whereabouts haven't been as reliable as they should have been."

My face is on fire. This is all my fault. People are going to blame me. I blame myself. I'm never going to be able to walk tall again. God, I'm so selfish. I drop my head into my hands. All those women have died, have been murdered, and here I am – thinking about myself. Whilst Heidi is God knows where with Will. I can't take much more at the moment. They're all digesting this new revelation first, instead of the most important thing, which is that Heidi's missing. I suppose that I'll get my chance to steer the conversation there in a moment.

Claire speaks again. "So, why are you only looking closer now? Why not before? What's changed?" She's much calmer than I would expect her to be. After all, for the second time this year, she's having to deal with the suggestion that her brother is a serial killer.

"We've received information that Will has partially admitted to his actions." DI Jones drops his gaze. "Indirectly anyway. We've obtained a voice recording from his counsellor."

I watch as the colour drains from Claire's face. "You're joking."

"He wouldn't be that stupid," says Janet. "He's a lot of things but certainly not stupid."

"What? To admit to who he really is, or to be a killer in the first place?" I stare at her.

Janet doesn't reply, but looks thoughtful as DI Jones asks his next question.

"Were any of you aware of voices that Will claims to have been hearing in his head?"

"Voices?" Everyone looks at me then, as though I have the answers.

"Like a mental health thing, you mean?" asks Brenda, still wringing her hands. Her hair is wavy from the plaits she always wears.

"I'd absolutely no idea about any of this," I say. "Apparently, he's had them for years – they tell him to do things. Bad things."

"What do you mean?" Brenda's not looking so good either. I know how she feels.

"Will's got a problem with women," DI Jones continues. "Particularly women who drink."

"We know that. And no prizes for where the problem's come from." Janet sniffs. "After what that bitch, Pat Ingham, did to Dean, and nearly Will."

Who knows what she's going to make of Mark and me visiting 'that bitch' earlier today. I want to say out loud that Janet should look closer at herself as to why Will hates women so much. After all, she was his first and main female influence in the most important years of his life. And all she ever did was reject him. She should take some responsibility for what's happened. I stare at her, seeing Will more in her hard face than I ever have before. He's turned out like he has because of her. I'm going to do everything in my power to make sure Heidi is subject to as little of her influence as possible from now on.

"The voices Will's hearing appear to be instructing him to dispose of the women at the river Alder." DI Jones looks around at us all. "At least that is what he's indicated to his therapist."

"How do you know this for certain?" There are tears in Claire's eyes. "I'm sorry. I need more proof than this before I'll believe my brother could be remotely capable of killing those women. He can be a chauvinist but he's no killer."

"Like I said, his therapist has come forward with a voice recording." DI Jones removes his glasses and rubs at the bridge of his nose. "And we've also captured some CCTV for the most recent killings last Saturday."

"The two women?"

"Yes," DI Jones replies.

"And it's Will?"

I notice Brenda's holding Claire's hand. It should be her own mother holding her hand. Janet's got to be one of the coldest people I've ever met.

DI Jones nods as I blurt, "And now he's got Heidi." It's such a relief to get these words out. They've had enough time to get their heads around what we're facing with Will. We need to find Heidi.

"How do you mean?" Brenda raises her gaze from the table towards me. "Will's got Heidi? Why didn't you say something sooner? I assumed she was in there with Alysha." She points towards the door.

"Will's on bail to stay away from us both, but he came to the house the other night, making all sorts of threats, and then today, he turned up early at school, saying he was taking her to the dentist. He's never even picked her up before."

"What time did he pick her up?" DI Jones makes the occurrence sound commonplace as he tugs his pocketbook out. Really, Heidi should have been the first issue we dealt with here, rather than going on about Will's bail and Will's voices. With every minute that passes, Will could get further and further away with her.

"They finish school at five past three." I glance at the clock. "So, nearly three hours ago."

"Have you tried ringing him?" Janet's voice is impassive. Clearly, she doesn't think we have cause for concern. Hopefully she's right.

"Of course I have." I'm aware that my voice is loaded with sarcasm, so I tone it down. "It's going straight to voicemail."

"At this stage," DI Jones says. "Will believes he's wanted by us simply for breaking his bail conditions."

"He probably just wanted to spend time with Heidi." Claire reaches for my hand. "Try not to worry Eva. He'll bring her back safely. Despite everything else, he loves her."

"I also have to make you all aware," DI Jones continues, "that according to the therapist, Will may suspect that the confidentiality code between them would have to be broken after his recent disclosures."

"What does that mean?" Claire squeezes my hand, then lets it go.

"It means we've got to tread carefully here." DI Jones's face darkens and every line in his brow deepens. "He possibly suspects we're looking for him for more than just breaching his bail. To put all this out in the media straight away might cause him to panic, which is the last thing we want when he's got Heidi with him."

"He wouldn't hurt his own daughter."

"With all due respect Janet," I snap, "you don't know him properly. You've no idea what he's capable of."

"Actually, I know him better than anyone, love. Which is why I keep my distance from him."

There really isn't an answer to that. I glance at Mark, willing him to step in. He looks away. I expect his mother's abrasiveness is the least of his worries right now.

"I think, Sir," Mark turns to DI Jones. "Take the fact that Will's my brother, and that he's got Heidi out of this for a moment." He takes a deep breath. "We know, almost for certain now, that he's got fifteen killings under his belt, so he's going to feel as though his life and everything about it is slipping away."

"We know nothing of the sort yet." Claire's voice hardens. "Not until I see this so-called evidence with my own eyes."

Mark continues. "So, if Will gets the sense that he's losing it all anyway, he's going to be angry and potentially even more dangerous. He's been on the police radar since last night and we haven't managed to bring him in."

"You're right in what you're saying, but..."

"The public need to be looking out for him as well. And he'll be easier to spot with Heidi in tow."

"I agree," says Brenda. "You should circulate pictures of them on the national news. What are you waiting for?"

"This is my daughter we're talking about here. What if Will hurts her?" Some really dark thoughts are creeping over me. Thoughts of him never bringing her back. Thoughts of him ending both their lives in some sick pact. He's capable of anything. I've kept a lid on myself up to now, but since we've started to discuss it, I'm really panicking.

Brenda grabs my hand from across the table where she's facing me. "You've got to believe she'll be alright love. My Lauren will watch over her, you'll see. Heidi will be back safe and sound."

A subdued atmosphere hangs over the kitchen for a moment as everyone is forced to take in the information of what Will stands accused of again. Then the front door bangs and we all peer at each other. I hold my breath and listen for Heidi's voice.

As I jump to my feet, the kitchen door swings open and Sara looms in the doorway bringing a cloud of perfume with her. She shrinks in the glare she's met with.

"Oh, it's you." I sink back to my seat. "Mark told you he was busy, didn't he?"

"I did Sara, did you not believe me?" Mark asks.

"I didn't like your tone of voice on the phone earlier." She's got a ton of makeup on. Lauren hardly wore it – she didn't need to. I wonder again what Mark sees in this woman. "I wanted to come and see you face to face. You were completely off with me. So, what's going on?"

Her eyes fall on DI Jones as she lets the door close behind her. She's clearly got no shame, turning up like this and ranting at Mark in front of us all.

"I'm sorry Sara, but this is family business." Claire rakes her hand through her hair. "It's not a good time for you to be here."

"Well, I'm sorry too Claire, but as I'm seeing Mark, that makes me part of things."

At least she didn't suggest she's Mark's *partner* or something. Even so, she's got some nerve showing up like this. I don't particularly want her here, either.

"Claire's right, actually Sara. We're discussing my husband. And it's all confidential at this stage."

Sara's face twists with what looks like dislike towards me. "Well, your husband has always been an absolute weirdo, if you ask me. What's he done now?"

"Sara." Mark gets to his feet and steps towards her. "Just go home, will you? I'll call you later."

"Are you OK Mark? You look dreadful." She steps closer to him, and he flinches slightly as she touches the side of his face. "I was Lauren's best friend. I've got a right to be involved if this is to do with what happened to her..."

"Lauren's best friend!" I'm aware of how hysterical the laugh which escapes me sounds, especially amid the situation we're dealing with. "Yet here you are, sniffing around the man she was getting married to." I jump to my feet again. "Just go please Sara. This is none of your business. I'm asking you politely. In a minute, I won't."

She pouts at Mark. "Are you going to let her speak to me like that?"

Brenda gets to her feet now and takes her by the arm. "Come on Sara. Like Mark said, he'll ring you later."

"I'll see myself out thank you. I know where I'm not wanted."

We sit in silence for a moment, then collectively jump again as the door bangs.

"None of this is finding my daughter, is it?" I look at DI Jones. "Surely that's the priority."

"Right. This is what I propose we do." He loosens his tie and sits up straighter in his seat.

"I'll need a picture of Heidi, one of her with Will, if that's OK. And a description of her appearance and what she was wearing."

Something inside me plummets. This is really happening. It's the stuff of nightmares. "She has fair hair, which was in bunches today, and blue eyes." I picture the last time I saw her this morning and tears fill my eyes. "She was wearing a navy uniform - a skirt and jumper with the school logo."

"Did she have her princess coat on?" Claire's eyes are full of tears.

"Yes. And woolly tights, and black strappy shoes."

"Great." As he scribbles onto his notepad, DI Jones looks up at me. "If you can sort that photograph out for me quickly, Eva, I'll get it circulated around the force. What time would you normally put Heidi to bed?"

"Half past seven. She's normally in the bath for seven. Will knows her routine."

He checks his watch. "Her bedtime's an hour away. OK, Eva, for now, I want you to go home and try to keep calm. Mark – can you go with her please?"

"Sure. Brenda, can you stay with Alysha and get her something to eat?"

"Of course I can. I'm not going anywhere."

"Me neither." Claire looks at the top of the fridge. "A glass of that brandy has got my name on it. This is horrendous. As if Will's in the frame for all this again."

"Why are you asking *her* to take care of Alysha." Distaste is written all over Janet's face. "I'm your bloody mother, not Brenda." She points at her.

"I'm Alysha's grandmother as much as you are," Brenda retorts. "More so, in fact."

"What's that supposed to mean?"

"Enough you two." Mark raises his palm towards them. "Right Sir, I'll go back to the house with Eva. Then what?"

DI Jones rises from his chair. "We'll give Will until seven thirty. If he's planning on dropping Heidi off in time for her bedtime, we don't want to spook him. The best outcome here is that he brings her back, and we'll have some officers ready to intercept him as he leaves."

Nausea is whirring within me. "What if he doesn't bring her back? What then? I don't think I can stand waiting for another hour. We should do something now."

"In that time, I'll get a press release ready. And I'll get the Child Rescue Alert sorted and ready to go. It's less than an hour away now. I'm going to head back to the station and get everything in place."

"I've found a photograph." I hold my phone up. "Though at first glance, they appear to be a happy father and daughter. This won't cause anyone to be concerned." I peer back at the photo and realise that I've got to hang on to the certainty that he'll be looking after her.

"Is it a recent one?"

I nod.

"I'll give you the number to send it to me."

"Three weeks ago, in Disneyworld. Is it too happy looking? There aren't many recent ones of them together, to be honest – he's barely around these days." I place the phone back on the table, hardly able to bear looking at the happy faces smiling out at me.

"No, it's fine." DI Jones scribbles a number onto his notepad. "There'll be an accompanying report with the photograph, so we can convey everything else that people will need to be aware of – the photo is simply to get their likenesses out into the public domain."

We all watch as Janet gets up and heads towards the kettle. She's such a selfish cow. After news of this magnitude, she acts like nothing's going on.

"Like I said," DI Jones raises his voice above the hiss of Janet filling the kettle. "I won't hit the button, as it were, until we've given him the chance to bring her home voluntarily. I'll run it past my superintendent when I get back to the station, but I'm certain this is the best way to approach this."

"But I really don't think he will." I want them to get the report out now. "Bring her back, I mean. He's not even answering his phone. I want the picture and the report circulating earlier than that."

"Just listen to the policeman Eva." Janet speaks to me in the most patronising tone she can probably muster, as she sits back down.

"I wouldn't expect you to understand anything maternal Janet."

"Eva." Claire puts her hand on my arm, as though to placate

me. "Things are bad enough without you falling out with your mother-in-law."

"She's been around that infrequently that I find it difficult to think of her as a mother-in-law." I switch my glare from Janet to Claire.

"Come on Eva." Mark swipes his car keys from the kitchen counter. "Let's see if they've turned up." He clearly wants me out of here. It's just as well with the resentment I have bubbling towards his mother right now.

"Will my brother definitely be arrested?" Claire turns to DI Jones.

"Yes." There's a hint of apology in his voice, which irritates me. I can't imagine there's anyone in this town who needs locking up more urgently, husband or not. "We've got the CCTV from last Saturday, and the testimony of his therapist, which is backed up with the voice recording. That's enough to charge him."

"As well as Pat Ingham's account," I add. "We haven't told them we visited her yet." I nudge Mark.

"Yes." He slides his arms into his jacket. "I meant to mention this to you all. Eva and I went to see her today. That's why Eva had booked Heidi into after-school club."

"You went to see Pat bloody Ingham?" Janet throws her chair back with a scrape. "I told you what I thought about that. How could you?"

"Sit down Mum. Hear us out."

"Did he tell *you* he was going?" She points at Claire who nods, a sheepish expression on her face.

"Pat Ingham should have been taken seriously in the first place Mum," Mark says gently, clearly not rising to his mother's ire. "She overheard Will and Ingham talking in her house the day before Lauren was killed. It was all coming to a head, with both of them threatening to pull the plug on each other. I just wish Pat had done something straight away, instead of waiting until the next day."

"That's rubbish," says Janet. "They split up, didn't they?"

"Ingham still had a key to the house and thought Pat would be out when he met Will there. But she was upstairs and listened to every word."

"If only she'd told someone else, like the police, instead of dragging Lauren in," Claire adds.

"Lauren wouldn't have taken much dragging." Brenda smiles as she recalls her daughter, but it's a smile that doesn't reach her eyes.

"Will had the drink drive incident involving Dean to hold over Ingham. That's why he'd turned a blind eye to Will's killing spree. We've got all that on record now," DI Jones says.

"Ingham agreed with what Will was doing, anyway." I add.

"I totally believe Pat Ingham." Mark sweeps his gaze over everyone. "She has no reason to lie, and nobody to protect."

"She's talking claptrap if you ask me," Janet sticks her chin out, looking like a defiant child. "Trying to get herself an early release."

"No one asked you," I say. "Anyway, she looked us squarely in the eye earlier. She said she can't sit back and do nothing whilst Will's targeting more women. She said that she had to make us listen. Then there's the other thing."

"Go on." DI Jones flips his notepad back open.

Mark looks around at everyone. "I'm sorry. On second thoughts, I'll have to tell this to DI Jones in confidence," he says.

"If it involves my son, then I've a right to be part of your conversation," Janet shouts from the other side of the kitchen, her voice echoing around the walls.

"So, he's your son suddenly, is he?" I can't help it. I truly can't help blaming her for this. "It's a shame you didn't act like his mother a few years ago. He might not have been so messed up then."

"How dare..."

"It involves someone other than Pat Ingham." Mark raises his voice to talk over us. "I've promised complete discretion. Sorry – I shouldn't have said anything yet."

"That should go out of the window, given the circumstances. *Discretion!*"

"Shut up Janet." I really don't care about keeping cordial relations with her anymore. "In fact, why don't you do us all a favour and go home. You're not helping, in fact, you never have."

"We'll take another statement from Pat Ingham." DI Jones ignores our altercation. "That, combined with the voice recording and the CCTV will be enough for a conviction. I'm as certain as I can be of it. And I'll come to see you shortly about this other matter."

"This isn't my brother we're talking about, surely." Claire looks shattered. "How are we going to get through this?"

"But in the meantime, he's still got Heidi." Mark rattles his car keys. "We need to get going and see if he's turned up yet."

CHAPTER 23

I TURN to Mark as I put my key in the front door. "I knew he wouldn't be here."

He glances at his watch. "We've got less than half an hour to wait before the press release goes out. Then they'll find him."

"Where do you think they are Mark? You must have some idea. He's your brother – you know him better than I do in a lot of ways." The house smells so familiar, yet alien. I can't stand it here without Heidi.

"You must be joking. After today, I wonder if I ever knew my brother at all."

I dart from room to room. It's impossible to believe that only a couple of weeks ago, this was a mostly happy family home. The way I'm feeling now, I doubt I can go on living here after this.

There's no sign of Will and Heidi having been back since he collected her from school. Suddenly, an awful scenario occurs to me. I wrench the sideboard drawer open. "Well, thank God for that." I let a long breath out. "Her passport's still here."

"I'm not sure if Will would have been told to surrender his as part of the bail conditions." Mark strides into the lounge. "I'll ask when we speak to DI Jones. He'll be here as soon as he's sorted the press stuff. Then we can tell him they also need to be looking for this 'partner' of Pat Ingham's cellmate."

I stare at the recent school photo of Heidi on the mantelpiece, with her hair in plaits, threaded with pink ribbon, and two teeth missing. It was taken just after she went back to school in September. "God, I hope he's looking after her." I walk to the window and peer out. "I can't go on like this Mark. If he doesn't bring her back, what will I do?"

"It's time." I glance again through the window, then at the clock, before turning to Mark. "It's half past seven. They need to be getting the press thing out." My voice is even, but inside it's as though spidery nerves are crawling around my body.

"I'll call DI Jones now." Mark tugs his phone from his pocket and paces up and down in front of the fireplace as he waits to be connected.

"Sergeant Potts here. There's no sign Sir. They've not been back here at all."

I step closer to Mark so I can listen to DI Jones's reply. Mark puts him on speaker phone.

"OK, I'm sorry to hear that. I've got the press release and photo ready to go. It'll be circulated everywhere within the next few minutes."

"Where's everywhere?" My heart is hammering inside my chest as I continue to stare at the photograph of Heidi. It's mid-November and she should be tucked up in her bed, with me reading her a story, not being dragged round who knows where, by her deranged father. I can't shake the fear that once this is out in the news, he might do something stupid to both of them.

"Social media," DI Jones replies. "Texts to everyone who's

signed up for alerts. Ports. Airports. Police forces and local and national news."

"But he's her dad. Will people even take it seriously? They might just see it as some kind of custody battle."

DI Jones pauses. "We're going to have to say something about him being wanted by us, but we won't be specific at this stage. We don't want to drive him further underground."

"What an absolute fuck up all this is." Mark closes his eyes. He never swears.

"I'm going to get off the phone Mark. I'll get this sorted, then I'll be round to see you. In the meantime, I'll keep you posted every step of the way. Where will you be?"

"We should stay here in case he brings her back." Much as I can't bear just to pace around the house, I can't be anywhere else either.

Mark nods. "I agree. We'll be here Sir – you've got the address, haven't you? Keep me informed the minute you hear anything."

As he disconnects the call, his phone bleeps. His gaze moves from the screen to me. "Claire's on her way round," he says. "Apparently she's got something to tell us."

"Oh God. What now?" Tears I didn't realise I was crying are rolling down my face. The man I married, who I thought I could trust, is being hunted down by the police and a national missing child alert is about to go out to find Heidi. Who'd have suspected that Will could ever be deemed a danger to his own daughter? I grab my phone and try calling him for what feels like the millionth time. It's still off.

"It's only me." Claire calls into the hallway several minutes later. "The report has just been on the radio."

"I can't help worrying they've wasted too much time already." I glance up as she enters the lounge. "This should have been done at least an hour ago."

"To be fair Eva, at first, I was certain he'd bring her back.

But that was before we found out what else he's done. I can't get my head around what's going on."

"Me neither. Is Alysha alright?" Mark's leaning against the wall nearest to the front window, intermittently looking out.

I haven't drawn the curtains and keep imagining that I see headlights outside. When Claire pulled up, I hoped beyond hope it was Will bringing Heidi home.

"Alysha doesn't know anything about Heidi, does she?" Mark adds.

I close my eyes. "God knows what we'll tell her about all this. She adores Will."

"Brenda's making a fuss of her. She's having sausage and chips and she's fine." Claire smiles. "But you're probably best keeping her at home tomorrow – until you're ready to tell her something. She's bound to find out what's going on through one of the older kids at school."

"Where's Janet?" I pick up my phone and put it down again, unable to stop myself from checking it. "I'm glad you didn't bring her with you. She might be your mum, but..."

"That's what I'm here about, actually." Claire sinks to the sofa, drops her head into her hands and then looks up again. "I'm not quite sure how to tell you both this..."

"What?" Mark appears to have aged ten years this evening. We all have.

Claire wraps her arms around her knees, as though she's giving herself a hug. "It seems our dear mother knew all along."

"Knew *what* all along?" I drop into the armchair facing her.

She stares at the floor. "How Will's been spending his Saturday nights."

"You mean all the killings?" Mark's voice rises a notch. "She can't have."

"She's known about every one of them for the whole two years he's been at it." Claire's voice is flat. "I feel like throwing myself in that river right now."

"So it's definitely him then? How did she know?"

"Will must've confessed to her at some point. How else could she have found out? How could the rest of us not have suspected anything?"

"Do you think she had any part in it all?" I raise my eyes from the carpet to Claire's face. "Maybe it was a double act."

Claire shrugs. "Who knows?" Then she laughs, but it's hysteria, rather than humour. "It's official, brother dearest." She rises from her chair and slaps Mark on the shoulder. "We're part of the sickest and most warped family in the whole of Yorkshire. Who'd have thought me and you would be the sane ones?"

"I can't talk about this until I get Heidi back." Claire and Mark exchange glances as I raise my voice. "And I don't give a shit about your mum or your brother. They can both rot in a prison cell for all I care. Heidi's the innocent one in all this." I get to my feet and start towards the door. "I can't just sit here waiting. It's time I got out there and looked for her myself."

"You're going nowhere. You're in no state to drive." Claire catches me as I try to get past her. "We'll take care of you Eva. Heidi's going to be fine, I promise."

"You can't be certain of that. None of us can at the moment." I'm crying yet again. *What good is crying going to do?*

Claire rises from the sofa and pulls me towards her.

"How can your mother have known what a monster he is and not said a thing or even reported anything?" I weep into her shoulder. "All those lives. Totally innocent lives."

"From what I can gather from speaking to her..." Claire smooths my hair. "It seems to be about how it would reflect on her."

"What do you mean?" I pull back.

"To be the mother of a son who's so evil and capable of what he's done. It's all about what people might say about her – and what they might do to her. Oh, and you won't believe this..." Claire smiles, making me wonder what on earth there could be to smile about.

"What?"

"She even said that no other man would ever want her if the truth about Will was to come out."

"I don't understand why she moved back up here," Mark says. "She must've known this would be the case one day. You can't do what he's done and get away with it forever."

"It didn't seem like it was going to come out, did it?" Claire's voice is soft. "Jonathan Ingham took the guilt for all those river deaths to the grave with him. Will was cleared."

"I can't bear to hear that man's name any more today." Mark drops his head into his hands. "After everything he's taken from me."

"But what's our brother taken from all those other families?" Claire says softly. "How the hell are we going to live with this? People might believe we're like him."

"This is Will's doing. This is his shit, not ours. We can't let him take us down with him. Not in any way whatsoever." Mark stabs his finger into the chair arm as he speaks.

"But our own mother knew he was killing these women all along. I can't take it in."

"Have you told anyone else yet?"

Claire shakes her head.

"You should make a statement. That needs doing straight away." Mark's back in police mode again. "I'll let DI Jones know. He'll be on his way by now, anyway." He reaches for his phone. "Quick, stick Sky News on. I've had a text to say it's going out at 8pm."

I hold my wrist to steady my hands enough to press the right buttons on the TV remote. Apart from the biscuit I ate at the prison, I've had very little to eat today. I've been firing on adrenaline, but suddenly my blood sugar feels like it's dropped.

I grab a banana from the fruit bowl on the coffee table. Hopefully, I'll keep it down.

"*Police are this evening asking the public to keep a lookout for William Potts, aged forty-one, and his daughter Heidi Potts, aged eight, missing from the Alderton area of Yorkshire.*

There is a warrant out for Mr Potts's arrest, which was issued two days ago, after he breached his conditions of bail following a domestic incident.

Mr Potts, a serving police officer, collected Heidi at 2:45 pm this afternoon from Hawthorne Primary School in Alderton. Because of his bail conditions, this was unauthorised and unknown to the mother of Heidi Potts. After being unable to contact him since her collection, concerns are growing for Heidi's safety and their whereabouts are urgently sought."

This can't be happening.

"*Heidi has long, blonde hair, which she was wearing in bunches. She has blue eyes and freckles. Her navy blue school uniform bears the Hawthorne Primary School logo. She was wearing navy woollen tights and black t-bar shoes. She has a distinctive pink princess coat.*"

A sob catches in my throat at the description of her.

"*William Potts is six feet tall, of medium build and has short, dark hair. Both are pictured on the screen now, and it is imperative that we find them as soon as possible.*"

The tears flow faster as the Disneyworld photograph flashes up on the screen.

"*Mr Potts is said to be possibly dangerous and should not be approached by any member of the public. Instead, vigilance is sought in looking out for them, and we request that anyone who sees Heidi and William Potts should contact Yorkshire Police on 0800 101101 or call 999. We will keep you updated on this story.*"

"Story." I shake my head. "This is no story. We're bloody living it. Shit." I glance at the clock again. "It's actually over five hours since he took her. What if she's hungry? What if she's cold?"

"DI Jones is here." Mark walks from the window to the lounge door. "I'll speak to him in the kitchen about our prison visit and then Claire, I'll send you in to make a statement to him about Mum's recent revelation."

"Mum." She spits the word out like a glob of stale chewing gum. "She's no mum of mine after this."

Their voices echo from the hallway so I rise from the chair. "Come on Claire. We'll all sit in the kitchen. You need to listen in to what Mark's going to say to DI Jones about the visit and I need to hear what you've got to say about *her*."

"It's two hours past Heidi's bedtime now. Where will he have taken her? Claire, you must have some idea. Has he got any friends that you know of?"

"Eva." She slides from her seat and kneels in front of me on the carpet. "When all's said and done, Will's a lot of things but he's also Heidi's dad. He'll keep her safe, I'm sure of it. But in answer to your question, no, I can't tell you of any friends."

"He's always been a loner." Mark's back to pacing the floor. He's making me dizzy.

"It's no good you saying that he'll keep her safe. We know what he's capable of now, don't we?" My voice is a wail.

"But panicking is not going to get us anywhere, is it? We've got to stay calm."

"Stay calm? I can't stay calm in here. I need to be out there. Mark, will you drive me around? Claire's right, I probably shouldn't drive. I'm too wired."

"OK, I'll wait here in case there's any news." Claire leans her head against the back of the chair. "Take your phone with you and I'll ring you the minute I find anything out."

CHAPTER 24

Two days have passed. Night has become day, then night, then day again. I think it's Friday. I think it's the afternoon. The curtains are staying closed as Mark's cul-de-sac is swarming with reporters. My stomach is churning like a cement mixer. I've forced down bits of toast, sandwiches and the odd shot of brandy. It doesn't seem as though I've slept. Claire made me shower yesterday and left a clean pile of clothes outside the bathroom for me.

Janet is in custody, having been charged last night with 'conspiracy to pervert the course of justice,' after keeping quiet all this time with what she knows about Will being the 'river killer.' There was a sea of reporters at the magistrates' court this morning. Thank God they've remanded her. Who knows, she could end up sharing a cell with Pat Ingham.

Actually, that's really unlikely - they'd probably not even be allowed in the same prison given that Pat killed Janet's son all those years ago. Not only that, Pat's husband, DCI Jonathan bloody Ingham killed Lauren, Janet's daughter in law, and seriously injured Claire.

On the surface of things, any sympathy should be with

Janet, but because of the mother she's been over the years and the dreadful secrets she's kept, they should throw away the key. At least Pat has remorse and empathy for what she's done.

Part of me wanted to face my mother-in-law in the courtroom this morning, but when it came to it, I couldn't cope with seeing her. If I'm honest, I never want to look at her face again. According to DI Jones, she's been thoroughly interrogated to see whether she knows where Will and Heidi are. Mark told me that leniency has been touted in return for information, but she was still giving nothing away. Her house has been turned over to see if they've been there. But there's no trace.

I must have tried ringing Will around two hundred times in the last forty-eight hours. I can't understand why he hasn't got word to me that Heidi is safe. He knows exactly what he's putting me through. So far, there's been nothing, no sightings, no contact, nothing, since he collected her from school on Wednesday. All there has been is the discovery of his car, left on a side street a mile from Heidi's school. And a cold trail from there. It's like they've disappeared into a vacuum. I'm not sure how to go on without her. It's agony.

"Mark's rung again." Brenda passes me a cup of tea as I get downstairs. "His team has spent the morning checking all the CCTV at the rail and bus stations. He says he's looked at that much grainy footage, that he's cross-eyed. But there's still no news."

"I've an idea how you must've felt, now." I drag a comb through my wet hair. "Losing Lauren, I mean."

Brenda raises her gaze to the photograph of Mark and Lauren's engagement. They're so alike, Lauren and Brenda. "Lauren might have been in her thirties, but she was still my little girl. Anyway, you haven't lost Heidi." She pats my hand as she sits next to me. "We can't give up – they're out there somewhere."

"What do you make of what Janet's done?" I sip at the tea Brenda made me. "I still can't take it in."

"I always suspected she wasn't wired right." Brenda sniffs. "But I was polite to her for Mark and Alysha's sake. How any mother could live with knowledge like that about her son, I have no idea. All those poor women – and she could've stopped him."

"How does she live with herself?"

"She's got as much blood on her hands as Will, if you ask me."

I nod. She's right. "And he's still out there. With my daughter. It's Saturday tomorrow. I just hope they've got police all over that river."

"Have you spoken to your mum again Eva?"

"She hasn't really grasped what's going on. I've mentioned about her being in the early stages of Alzheimer's haven't I?"

"Yes. A time or two. Is there any chance Will could turn up there with Heidi?"

"I doubt it. Even when Mum was well, she didn't really approve of him. They've always just tolerated one another."

"Families, eh?"

"I've told Mum's neighbour what's happening, and she's keeping a lookout until Heidi's found. Like I say, I can't imagine them turning up there, but then Will isn't exactly predictable, is he?"

The prospect of him arriving at Mum's house and causing trouble doesn't bear thinking about.

I try to keep busy by sorting laundry in the hallway. But folding Alysha's dresses only reminds me of how I should be folding

Heidi's. If Will hasn't sorted anything for her, this will be her third day in the same clothes. Suddenly, a blast of cold air and loud voices pursue Mark through the door.

"Will you stay in the police after this Mark?" A voice booms.

Then another one. "How does it feel to know what your brother's done?"

"This is private property," Mark shouts before slamming the door. "They're like vultures." He kicks his shoes onto the shoe rack. "Lauren was never like that as a reporter. Preying on the misery of others."

"Any news?"

"There is actually." Mark slides his coat off. "At last. I was going to ring you but decided to come home instead."

"Tell me."

"It seems Will took out a hire car on Wednesday. We've been trawling through the local companies since there have been no public transport sightings."

"That's amazing." Brenda rushes from the lounge. "That's the first proper lead you've had."

"Well, we've had quite a few so-called sightings," Mark says. "But nothing that's amounted to anything. They're still sifting through it all though. Everyone is on it."

"Did he give his real name and driver number when he took the car?" My words pump out in gasps. "Did he have Heidi with him? Have they got him on CCTV?"

"DI Jones and another of my colleagues will be at the car hire firm by now. I'll be able to answer all that hopefully soon enough. The car's details should get circulated in the next news bulletin."

"Thank God." I sink onto the bottom stair. "I can't go another night driving myself crazy with worry."

. . .

Over the next few hours, Claire, Mark and Brenda take turns keeping me company and trying to keep me strong. As the hours ebb by, I know she's going to be out there for another night. She'll still be in her school uniform. She's got no other clothes with her. Will she be eating OK? Where is she sleeping? The sense of uselessness is so overpowering I could throw my head against a wall. I need her back with me. The void has become an excruciating physical pain.

I lie on the sofa, staring into the darkness. Brenda's taken Alysha and the dog to her house, away from this madness, and Claire's in the spare room. Mark offered me Alysha's room, but I can't sleep in a proper bed whilst Heidi's still out there. It's not as if I'm sleeping anyway. I spend the time drifting off now and then, mainly through exhaustion, but I've constantly got an ear open, waiting for someone to come to the door, or to telephone with news.

The reporters have given up for the day, but will no doubt be back as soon as it gets light again. I picture Janet in her cell. We haven't been told where she's been taken yet. I feel nauseous when I think of her keeping Will's horrendous secrets. There must be more to it than possible repercussions for being the mother of such a maniac. She's as sick as he is.

Sky News flickers in the corner of Mark's lounge. I've turned the volume down but can just about hear what's being said. Please, please, let this be the night they find them.

"*It's midnight and these are the headlines from Sky. Concern is continuing to grow for missing eight-year-old Heidi Potts, who was taken by her father, William Potts, from Hawthorne Primary School in the Yorkshire town of Alderton on Wednesday afternoon.*"

They're repeating exactly the same words that they've said every hour, on the hour since five pm, but I keep listening, hoping I'll hear something new.

"*Despite extensive police efforts, there have been no confirmed sightings of the father and his daughter, and as yet, the hire car details that were released earlier have not yielded any leads. The public are asked to watch out for a white Volkswagen Golf, registration AL18 7UD which was hired by William Potts from Alderhire Cars on Wednesday. There have been no matches through automatic number plate recognition, and it is believed that Potts may be travelling under false number plates. It is not known whether he and his daughter have remained in the Alderton area.*

Mr Potts is now wanted in connection with a serious police matter for which a sixty-two-year-old woman is being remanded in custody. Anyone with any information is asked to call 0800 101101 straight away. It is reiterated that Mr Potts should not be approached by any member of the public."

The photo I took in Disneyworld is flashed up again. Tears leak down the sides of my head and soak into my hair as I bury my face in the cushion. It's as though I'm drowning in misery. I can't confront anything until I get Heidi back safely, but after that, I must face the truth. That I've been married to a psychopath for all these years. And it's not too difficult to see where his traits were inherited from. Claire and Mark seem miraculously well adjusted to say they too were brought up by Janet, and grew up with Will. I can't imagine what I'd have done without them over the last couple of days. I'd have gone under if I'd been alone.

I'm woken by an almighty crash as glass splinters over me. I scream as a brick lands on the carpet, missing my head by inches.

Moments later, footsteps thunder on the staircase and the lounge light is snapped on.

"What the..." Mark strides towards the brick.

"Oh my God. Are you OK Eva?" Claire, still fastening her dressing gown, rushes towards me.

"Stay there sis. Get something on your feet. Eva, don't move. There's glass everywhere."

Claire returns with a dustpan and brush, now wearing shoes. "Double glazing is supposed to be unbreakable, isn't it?" She sweeps at the glass around me whilst I place the larger shards onto the dustpan.

"Keep still Eva. We need to get this glass up before you move anywhere." Mark turns to Claire then. "We never got around to getting new windows, did we?" He picks glass from the floor. "We've still got what they built the house with."

He says *we*, as though Lauren is still part of things. It must be incredibly difficult to become a single person again – though perhaps it's easier to lose your partner to their own death. In contrast, I've lost my partner to the murders he's committed, of fifteen others. This reality winds me, then my heart plummets even further at the realisation that there's still no news of Heidi. With the brick being thrown through the window, I've only just come back to awareness, and my heart still seems to be beating three times faster than what it normally would.

Mark is staring at the brick like it's diseased. "This could be the first of many bricks through the window. Or worse. Now it's leaking out about what Will's done, people will take their anger out on us. It's always the case."

Claire wipes at her tears. "We're victims of what he's done as well. Look at what I went through in February. I nearly died too. And we lost Lauren."

"I might be forced to move away," I say. "More for Heidi's sake than mine. You know how cruel kids can be. When word gets out about how deranged her father is, and what he's done. That's if I ever get her back."

Mark shakes his head as he continues to stare at the brick. "This is an utter nightmare. All of it."

"Can that be fingerprinted?" Claire nods towards it.

Mark shakes his head. "It's too porous. Look, we've got all the big bits of glass up." He gets to his feet. "You two sit in the kitchen, where it's safer. I'll put some board over this window then I wouldn't say no to a brandy if there's any left. My nerves are shot."

CHAPTER 25

MARK POURS water into the cafetiere, his eyes flitting to the lit up phone beside him. "She's persistent, I'll give her that."

"Who is?"

"Sara. I've asked her to give me a few day's space with all we've got going on, but she keeps on texting."

"What's the deal with you two, anyway?" Claire drops some bread into the toaster. "This is for you Eva. You're looking like a rake."

"I'm going to finish it with her." Mark walks to the fridge. "Not that there's a great deal to finish, but it's never sat comfortably, getting close to Lauren's best friend."

Claire and I exchange glances. It's a cross between *you don't say* and *thank goodness*. It's the nearest I've felt to normality in days.

"Did you get any sleep after what happened in the night? Pass me the butter, will you Mark."

"I think I did. I must have dropped off, eventually."

"Alysha's bed's comfy, isn't it?" Mark smiles. "I've fallen asleep there a few times when I've been reading to her."

Images of reading to Heidi fill my mind. "It doesn't feel

right, being in a comfy bed when... she's been gone for three nights now." Tears fill my eyes. "It's just... knowing for sure what a psycho I'm married to now – I can't shake the feeling that he's going to hurt her..."

"We're combing every shred of CCTV." Mark pads towards the table in his slippers. "You can't get anywhere these days without a camera eventually pointing at you. We'll find them, I promise you."

"Will's managed very well so far, though." Claire butters the toast. "Avoiding cameras, I mean. It's unbelievable what he's got away with."

"And it's Saturday again." I close my eyes. "Will's favourite night of the week. It's haunting me. How can anyone be married to a serial killer without ever suspecting?"

"I'm on shift tonight." Mark sits opposite me. "I only pray I'm the one to get him. He and my mother can live happily ever after at her Majesty's pleasure."

"It's just me and you left Mark." Claire sits as well. "We lost Dad, then Dean." Tears fill her eyes. "To be honest, Will and Mum might as well be dead after what they've done. Our family has been totally blown apart."

Mark looks from Claire towards me. "It's not only me and you left behind, as you put it. There's also Eva and Brenda, Alysha and Heidi. We're still a family."

"Sorry I didn't mean..." Claire slides the plate of toast in front of me. "I *do* think of you as family Eva."

"It's fine. Honestly. I know."

"I thought you didn't do nights anymore Mark?" She picks at her toast, clearly experiencing the same lack of hunger as me.

"We've all been drafted in tonight. Everyone. I need to ask Brenda to keep hold of Alysha."

"I'd have had her," I say. "But I can barely take care of myself."

"They're still searching for that car, aren't they?" Claire pushes her plate away. "Surely it can't be that hard to find a white Volkswagen Golf with false plates. There are cameras on most roads nowadays."

The day crawls by in a similar vein to the last few, and there's still no news. No leads. No sightings. And I can't shake this mood of foreboding. In the depths of my stomach, I sense that something is going to happen tonight. Therefore, I've persuaded Claire that we're of better use driving around and looking for them ourselves. Now that we've found out what sort of car he's driving. Brenda's waiting at Mark's house with Alysha and Biscuit in case Will miraculously turns up there. Brenda's been an absolute angel, as always.

Claire grips the steering wheel and yawns. "We've been driving around for over three hours. We're best leaving this to the police now. Besides, I'm starving."

"Can we drive round once more? Past your Mum's house and the Yorkshire Arms again."

She frowns. "Will won't be in the Yorkshire Arms with Heidi at this time of night. She wouldn't be allowed in, surely?"

"He might have got someone to leave her with." I shudder at the thought of my daughter being dumped on some stranger. Although, since yesterday, more hope has bubbled up within me. He wouldn't have rented a car if he was planning to do himself and Heidi in. And that he's changed the number plates means he wants to evade capture and carry on living his life on the outside. In his twisted mind, he must see some sort of future for himself and Heidi.

"Mark's calling." Claire glances at her mobile as it lights up in its holder on the dashboard. "Press the button, will you Eva? Hello?"

"It's me. Where are you?" Even in Mark's few words, I'm picking up from his tone of voice that something's not right.

"Driving around with Eva. Searching for white cars. We couldn't just sit at home, waiting."

"Are you driving now?"

"Yeah. We're going back soon though."

"Pull over."

Shit. Something's up. Fear claws at me.

"Why?" Claire glances at me as she slows the car.

"Pull over. I've got something I need to tell you."

She pulls the car up at the side of the road. I stare at the phone as I try to prepare myself for whatever's coming. I can't breathe. But surely, if it was news about Heidi, Mark wouldn't break it over the phone. He'd get us home first or to go into the station.

"What is it?" I can hear the wobble in my voice.

"It's Sara."

"What?"

"She's been pulled out of the river." There's more than a shake in his voice.

"What do you mean?" I reach for Claire's hand.

"It looks like she went in last night." He's crying.

"You mean, she's..."

"It's all my fault. If I hadn't shut her out. I should've been keeping an eye on her as well. I should've known she might be at risk from him."

"How's it happened?" Claire closes her eyes as she speaks.

Poor Mark. As if he hasn't been through enough.

"I don't know." His words are filled with anguish. "DI Jones has made me sit in the patrol car, away from it all. It looks the same as all the other drownings."

"But it was Friday last night. Was Sara out in the pub?"

"I've no idea. They only put the tent over her ten minutes ago. It's him though – it's got to be."

"But, but, if he's got Heidi with him..." What the hell has my little girl been subjected to? How will she recover from this?

"I don't know." Mark sounds broken. "I just don't know."

"Mark, you need to get yourself home. Where are you?"

"Usual spot. Carlton Bridge. They've pulled her out about half a mile from the Yorkshire Arms. Her body surfaced quicker than most."

Broken sobs erupt from him. DI Jones shouldn't have left him on his own. Not after everything he's been through.

"Her killer's our brother Claire. Our own flesh and blood. I think we're going to have to get away, start again somewhere else. How can we carry on living in Alderton now we've found out who our brother is?"

"Stay where you are Mark. We're not far away. We'll be there soon."

I press the button to disconnect the call. "He sounds as awful as he did when Lauren died."

Claire turns the car in the road. "And it's my brother who's done it. It's like being in the middle of some sort of horror movie."

"And my husband." Mark's right. There's no way we can carry on living in this town. But if I don't get Heidi back, I don't want to go on living, anyway. I drop my head into my hands. I don't know how Claire can get it together enough to even drive with all this going on.

"Poor bloody Sara." Claire stabs at the radio on button. "I want to hear if they're reporting anything yet. She was a pain in the arse, but..."

"Nobody deserves that. Do you really, really think Will's behind it?" I feel sick. He's evil personified. To think I faced him and vowed to spend the rest of my life with him.

She exhales a long breath. "He must be. Who else could it be?"

We pull up behind a crowd of people. Claire locks the car

and reaches for my hand. "Excuse me. Excuse me." We tunnel our way towards the cordon, ignoring the protests at our determination to force our way through.

"You can't go any further miss." An officer stands behind the tape, legs apart like a soldier.

"I'm Mark's sister," Claire says. "Sergeant Mark Potts. He's in a right state. I need to get to him."

I can see Mark silhouetted in the police car a few metres in front of us. I look into the officer's eyes. "And I'm his sister-in-law. Please let us through. That's his girlfriend who's been pulled out. He shouldn't be on his own. Not after what happened to him with Lauren."

"We need to make sure he's alright. Please."

"OK." He lifts the tape. "I'm actually a friend of Mark's. Go straight to the car though. And don't let any of them lot down there see you, or I'll get into trouble." He jerks his head towards where numerous white-swathed bodies flock around and within the tent like ants around a nest.

"Thank you." We duck under the tape and dash towards the patrol car. Claire slips in the passenger side, and I get in the back. It's a relief to slam the door against the clamour of the crowd.

Our sudden arrival startles Mark. He jerks his head from his hands. "I'm surprised they let you through."

"He said he was your mate. The bloke keeping everyone back."

Mark nods and points down to the riverbank. "Look at what he's done. He's our bloody brother Claire. What the hell are we going to do?"

She reaches for his hand. "You shouldn't be here, having to watch – this."

"Have you actually seen her?" I ask. "Sara, I mean." I say her name as though she's still alive. "Are you absolutely sure it's her?"

"Yes. I saw her. Briefly. Her sister reported her missing in the early hours. DI Jones wanted me to take a look – to make sure." I watch in the rear-view mirror as he closes his eyes for a couple of seconds, as if he's trying to blot out the memory. "Mine's not the formal identification though – her family will have to do that."

"I've no idea how you're still holding up." I reach forwards and rest my hand on his shoulder. He's shaking. How Will could do this to anyone is beyond comprehension, but to inflict this on his own brother...

"I don't know how any of us are." He cranes his neck to look at me. Blue lights circulate around us.

Whilst all the police are here dealing with this, they're not out there, searching for Heidi. That might sound selfish, but it's true. All the reading I've done on missing children suggests the more time that elapses, the less chance of them being found there is.

CHAPTER 26

MARK GRABS the radio from its holder on the dashboard.

"Sierra oscar one nine seven three."

"Come in."

"Sighting of white Volkswagen Golf, registration yankee delta one nine tango kilo charlie."

I sit bolt upright. They're going to get him. They're going to bloody get him. Claire and I glance at each other.

"Has the registration been called in to be checked?"

"It's registered to a silver Ford Focus which was SORN last year."

"Where's the Golf been sighted?" Mark turns the key in the ignition and revs the car.

I sit rock-like behind Mark. Claire looks back at me again, then at the crowd in front, probably thinking the same as I am. If Mark's going to pursue this car, how's he going to drive out of here.

"On the AIM, heading North."

"Which junction?"

"One moment Sarge. I'll find out the exact location."

There's a crackling before the voice returns. "It's at the

services heading towards junction seven. There are no patrols nearby."

At least he's stationary. But they haven't said for definite yet that it's him or whether Heidi is with him. Please. Please. Please.

"I'm onto it." Mark presses a button and the car's siren wails. He glances at us both as the crowd in front of us parts. "Are you two OK with this? I'm going to get bollocked for taking you with me, but right now, I don't give a shit. We're going to get him. We're going to get Heidi back."

I take a sharp breath as I'm thrown back in the seat.

"Come in one nine seven three. Confirmed sighting of white male and young girl. They're getting into the car."

This really is it. Thank God. She's with him. Now we need to get to them.

I grip the edges of the seat as Mark weaves in and out of the cars that give way for us. What the hell's going to happen when we catch up to Will? He'll see the blue lights behind him and then what? He's not just going to surrender himself – not with what he's running from. Nor will he have any idea that it's his brother, sister and wife coming after him.

Mark blasts his horn. A couple of cars aren't moving at all. It seems to take an eternity before we're out of the town centre and on the slip road, joining the motorway. *Please don't let Will do anything stupid.*

"One nine seven three. There are units en route South. We're installing them at all exits."

"One nine seven three to control. We're on the motorway, heading North from junction five."

Luckily, the voice on the radio doesn't enquire who 'we' relates to.

"You're only a few miles behind him Sarge. It's now been confirmed that he's been seen travelling from Derbyshire."

"He must have been at Mum's old house. Bloody hell."

I notice Claire's also gripping her seat. We've both got our seatbelts on, but a quick look at the dash tells me we're doing a hundred and twenty miles per hour. I've never travelled so fast.

"Control to one nine seven three. We've been in touch with a police negotiator, and also the therapist who's been working with the suspect. They're en route to the motorway but are some way behind you."

With the therapist breaking their confidentiality, I'm not sure his presence is a good thing – Will, of course could be more compliant, or it could completely push him the other way; it all depends on what he knows of his predicament.

"Hopefully, he'll come quietly. What's his current location?"

I'm in awe of Mark's professionalism given the fact that he's now chasing his own brother. I try to deepen my breathing – I've never felt terror like it. Please, please let my baby be alright.

"He's still on the A1M, heading North, and currently passing junction seven."

I watch as the speedometer creeps up to one hundred and thirty. I can't believe that Mark's driving at nearly twice the speed limit. He's not normally in traffic, so I doubt he'll have trained for this speed like Will had to. Will. When life was normal – or so I thought. My life since I met him feels like a complete lie.

We hurtle up the outside lane with the siren screeching and blue lights flashing. Vehicles in our path get out of the way, not that their drivers have a lot of choice. A collision at this speed wouldn't be pretty. The car eats up the motorway miles. We're going so fast that it makes me queasy to look out of the window. But I'm relieved to be here. Any minute now, we're going to catch up to him. Maybe he can already see the lights and hear the siren. If I was sitting at home waiting for news of all this, I'd be even more beside myself than I am here, amongst it. All we've got to do is stop him. He'll give Heidi back to me – he'll have no choice. I'll make him see sense, I'm sure I will. But we've got to get to him first.

"There!" Claire cries out several minutes later as she points at a car a few cars in front. "That's a white Golf, isn't it?"

I squint at the car ahead. It's difficult to make anything out at this speed.

"Come in control," Mark says into the radio, slowing abruptly. I don't know how he can drive at the speed he's at and conduct a coherent conversation as well. "Can I have that registration again?" He swerves in and out of two cars in front and suddenly he's behind the Golf, but on the outside.

"Yankee delta one nine tango kilo charlie."

"We're right behind it." Mark pulls into the middle lane and flashes his headlights behind the white car. They'll be in no doubt who we're after now.

I gasp as it speeds up. I should've known he wouldn't give in easily.

"OK, he's not pulling over." Mark leans towards the radio. "Are the units in situ at the upcoming junctions?"

"All in place. Keep up with him."

"Is it definitely him Mark?" I still can't make the shapes out in front of me, and I think I left my stomach behind in Alderton.

"It's got to be. It's a white Golf with false plates and he's sped up the moment he saw us. Who else could it be?"

"Heidi will be terrified, being driven at this speed." Our speedometer's back up to a hundred and twenty and we know from the camera at the services that she's definitely with him.

Claire reaches back for my hand and squeezes it. "He drives like this for his living, Eva. She'll be safe. We'll have her soon. She's coming home with us tonight."

The Golf swerves around everything in its way. Some drivers pull onto the hard shoulder. My heart is literally in my mouth.

"Sierra oscar one nine seven three." There's a crackle and a pause. "We've set up a roadblock after junction nine."

"Thank God," I shout. "We've got to stop him. He's going to kill her."

"I can see it coming up," Mark yells above the increasing sound of the engine. After a few moments, I gasp as Will swerves sharply off at the junction. He pulls his car up in front of the two cars blocking the junction's exit. This is it. We've got him cornered. I watch in horror as he drives the car down the embankment. I scream as it rolls onto its roof, before landing back on its wheels.

Oh my God.

"Heidi!" I screech as Mark slams on the brakes. "Now what do we do?"

Mark pulls our car up in the space where Will was moments before and is back on his radio. I'm first out of the car, scrambling down the hill. No one is going to stop me. By now, the helicopter's up, and blue lights are heading towards us from all directions.

"Heidi. Heidi. Where are you?" I turn this way and that, disorientated in the darkness. The others don't seem to have followed me yet. I've no idea where I'm going.

"Eva. Stop." Claire sounds like she's some way behind me as I stumble along. "Don't confront him on your own."

"I've got to find them," I shout back. I've got to get to Heidi. Will must realise it's all over for him, and it's at this moment when he could do something dreadful. Really dreadful. I shiver and it's not with the cold.

"Will," I yell into the darkness, trying to make myself heard above sirens, engines and the rumble of the helicopter. "Please just give her to me. Will!"

There's still nothing apart from distant shouting and sirens becoming even louder.

I stagger further forwards, tripping through the thick

undergrowth. The distant voices of Mark and Claire sound as though they've gone in the opposite direction. I'm probably best confronting him on my own, despite what Claire shouted after me. I'll have a better chance at getting through to him. I pause, my breath echoing in my ears. Amidst the din that echoes around us, I'm sure I hear a rush of water.

I blink as the helicopter shines its beam over the adjacent river, before shifting back to the other side. Two figures become visible, standing by the water. One tall, one small. My husband and my daughter. If it's me and them, I can reason with him. I've got to. I lurch forwards. Weeds or whatever my feet have been getting tangled up in become pebbles. I imagine this being an area that a family might stop for a picnic in the middle of a long journey on a sunny day. We used to be a family. What an absolute fool I've been.

"Will. Please." I get within a few yards of them and pause. "Please, please give her to me. I'm begging you."

"Mummy!" I see the outline of Heidi in the darkness. She's trying to let go of Will, but he tugs her back and grips her to his side.

"Don't come any closer, do you hear me?" His voice is a snarl and I realise I'm now confronted with the monster he really is. This is a moment that will haunt Heidi too. I pray that he's looked after her over the last couple of days and that she hasn't seen anything too horrendous.

"Why, will you throw me in there as well?" My eyes are adjusting to the darkness. "Like you did with the others?" I would gladly let him throw me in if it means he'll let Heidi go. There are enough emergency services here, hopefully they'd fish me out. And if he kills me, so be it. As long as whoever looks after Heidi ensures neither Will nor Janet ever comes within a country mile of her. Ever.

"You've really gone and done it, haven't you, you stupid bitch? Why couldn't you leave well alone?"

"Just give me my daughter."

"Please Dad. I want my mum." Heidi tries again to pull away from him. It's heartbreaking.

"You're staying with me, have you got that?" His voice hardens as he looks down at Heidi then back up at me. I've inched closer but we're still several feet apart. I want to rush forward and just grab her, but some instinct is stopping me. I know what he's capable of.

"Don't make this any worse than it is already Will."

"How can it be any worse? Anyway, you're the one who's done this to me. You're the one who retracted your alibis and grassed me up about the computer searches. I know all about it. You stupid, stupid bitch. You don't know how much damage you've done."

"It wasn't only down to me Will. They've got other evidence. It isn't my fault."

My fault. What the hell am I on about? How is any of this my fault? And how the hell did I ever think I could reason with this, this maniac? I have to get Heidi away from him. And if he throws himself in the river after that – well, the world will be a much better place.

Flashing lights and voices are edging closer. I don't know whether that makes things safer or not.

CHAPTER 27

An officer dashes from the undergrowth through which I've emerged. Two men follow him, their feet crunching on the pebbles.

"William Potts."

I turn and see several more people have gathered behind us.

"You're under arrest. Let go of the child. Drop to your knees and put your hands behind your head."

"Stay where you are. All of you," Will hisses. "I'm telling you. Don't come any closer."

"I want my mum," Heidi sobs.

I step forwards. This is breaking my heart. I've got to get her away from him, no matter what it takes.

"That goes for you as well, bitch. Get back." Without taking his eyes away from me, he bends to the ground and begins filling Heidi's pockets with pebbles.

"What are you doing?" She looks to be trying to tug herself away again.

"You keep still or you're going in that water, do you hear me?"

"Get the hell away from her." I lurch towards them. But the

men behind are onto me straight away, dragging me back. Will steps away from us, but nearer to the river, dragging Heidi with him. Her sobs are something that will live with me forever, however this ends up.

"I'm warning you. All of you." He points from one of us to the other, before bending to the ground again. More stones rattle into the pink princess coat which Heidi has always loved. When I first bought it for her, I had a job to get her to take it off - even when she was indoors.

"I repeat. William Potts. You're under arrest. Let go of the child at once. Drop to your knees and put your hands behind your head."

"You heard what he said Will." One of the other men steps in front of me.

"You!" Will stares at him and for a split second lets go of Heidi. Then he instantly grabs her again. "What the hell are you doing here!"

"Who are you?" Clearly Will knows him.

"Daniel Hamer. Will's therapist." He uses air quotes as he says the word therapist. "I was asked to attend by DI Jones. See if I could talk him down for the sake of the kid. Really, I'm here to make sure he gets what he deserves."

"I thought I could fucking trust you." Will's filling his own pockets with stones now. If he's trying to frighten me even more than he already has in the last few days, it's working. My daughter weeping beside him is more than I can bear. But I dare not move. Someone will save her. These are trained people. Someone will catch him off guard. They must have a plan. Why aren't they doing anything? Something? They should have dogs, tasers, whatever. And where are Mark and Claire? Perhaps they're back there, amongst the group of people I can sense behind me, but don't have the courage to turn around and look at. Somehow, I'll get Will off guard and I'll make a grab for Heidi.

"Suzannah thought she could trust you that night." The bearded man jerks his head back towards the crowd. "When she agreed to let you walk with her for a taxi. Come here love. There's nothing to be scared of anymore. He's the one who's scared. Look at him."

I turn now, following Will's gaze to a woman who steps out from amongst everyone else. As she comes closer, I recognise her as the woman from outside court – the one who gave Will a business card. It must be the same woman who rang me earlier this week, Suzannah.

Mark and Claire are standing on either side of DI Jones. They're probably under orders from him. Maybe they're like me, too scared of putting a foot wrong and placing Heidi in any more danger than she's already in.

"You might recognise me better in these familiar circumstances," she says, leaning into Daniel. "In the dark. At the side of a river."

My eyes have grown accustomed to the darkness and I'm close enough to see the fear on her face.

"Two years ago, wasn't it Will? I was one of the lucky ones. Good job I'm a triathlete, isn't it? Or else I'd be in my grave now like the rest of the poor sods you've ended."

"Did you really think we were going to let you get off with what you've done, you freak?" Daniel puts his arm around Suzannah. "Since I found out you were being investigated and then Suzannah recognised you, I've made it my mission to bring you down."

"So you tricked me, you mean? You recorded me talking last week, you arsehole. All those meetings were a pretence. You should be struck off."

Daniel laughs. "It's you that's about to be struck off. Struck out. Whatever. I don't envy you once you're put behind bars." He laughs again. "A bent copper that's got the deaths of all those women under his belt. You're going to have a rough old ride in there."

"Two of them were nothing to do with me. I wasn't even in the country." Puffs of air leave Will's mouth as he spits the words at Daniel Hamer. "What have you got to say about that?"

I'm close enough to Daniel and Suzannah to catch her whisper to him, "don't say anything else." He squeezes her arm. The look that passes between them tells me they know something about the mother and daughter who died whilst we were away. That's not for me to worry about right now though. I need to get Heidi away from Will. That is all that matters. The poor mite is still in her school uniform. I can't wait to put her in the bath and get a warm drink down her.

"Mum. I'm frightened." Her teeth are chattering.

"Will. Please. I'll do anything. Just give her to me."

"You've got the chance to do the right thing here." Suzannah stands next to me. "How can you do this to your own daughter? Look at her. What are you doing to her?"

"I'm a good father," he snarls. "Don't you dare judge me on that."

"Please Dad."

"Will. Please let her go."

"No chance. If I haven't got her, I've got nothing. There's no point in me carrying on without her."

Suzannah steps in front of me now. "Will, I'll swap places with her. Let her go to her mother. I'll come and stand with you instead. You can do whatever you want with me this time. Just let your little girl go."

"Let your daughter go to her mother Will. You're making things worse for yourself." The man who arrived with the officer and Daniel speaks now. He must be the negotiator. A fat lot of negotiating he's done. He wants sacking.

"How can things be any worse?" Will's voice rises and breaks like a wave at the foot of a cliff. I know the signs. He's going to lose it. And who's going to bear the brunt? Suzannah, myself or Heidi?

"Get back here." Daniel lunges for Suzannah as she rushes at Will.

My attention is averted to a thundering of boots down the embankment. Everyone twists to the direction of the noise. "Armed police," one hollers. "Get down on your knees. Now."

I hold my breath. A deafening scream pierces the momentary silence. My daughter is hurtling through the air.

All goes into slow motion. Her limbs flail in all directions and she lands with a sickening splash in the depths of the river. My own scream rips through me as I dart towards the river's darkness.

There's an ear-splintering bang. Followed by Will's anguished roar. Then a second deadening slap of a body hitting water. Seconds seem to elapse before everyone surges forward. I'm in first, wading into the river, but several pairs of hands pull me back. Someone wraps a blanket around me.

Time slows even more as I watch police divers rush to where Heidi hit the water. I sink to my knees. Please God. Please God. Why didn't I wrench her from him? Why was I such a coward? Please God. Please. It's so cold tonight. We'll be lucky if her heart didn't stop with the shock of the cold. And she can't swim.

I watch and wait, frozen to the spot. There's nothing I can do. Claire's at my side. She's talking to me. I don't hear what she's saying. She tightens the blanket around my shoulders.

What feels like a lifetime passes. My baby. My baby. She can't die. I can't go on without her. She has her whole life in front of her. Getting her ears pierced, birthday parties, her high school prom, sleepovers, exams. "Heidi!" I shriek into the night air. "Please, somebody – find her!"

· · ·

Mark's dragging her to the edge of the water. In the helicopter's light, I watch as he lays her out on the pebbles. She's not moving. She's really not moving. "No!" I scream again. Claire and I spring to her side at the same time as two paramedics.

As she's rolled over, she gurgles then splutters. "Mum!" Her voice is a croak. Thank God. She's breathing. She's alive. Mark is spluttering as well. He's saved her life. She's survived. Another paramedic darts towards us with foil blankets. I sink to the floor beside her, hot tears flooding my cheeks. Thankfully, tears of joy and relief have replaced my recent tears of anguished pain. Whatever she's been through these last few days, I'll get her through it. She'll get all the help she needs.

"Did you hit him when you fired?" DI Jones's voice booms behind me. "This manhunt does not stop until we get him, do you hear me? All of you! I want dogs, I want lights, I want more units. Get these two to hospital straight away. I want him found. Shoot him again if you have to, but I want him found. Quickly!"

"She's going to be fine," the paramedic says as she buckles Heidi's stretcher straps. "A night in hospital for observation, I reckon, then she'll be back home where she belongs with her mummy, won't you sweetheart?"

Heidi nods, her eyes swimming with tears, before whispering, "where's my dad?"

I shake my head. "They'll find him love. For now, we only need to worry about getting you warmed up and sorted out. I'll stay at the hospital with you tonight."

I jump as the ambulance doors are slammed. I don't think I'll ever stop jumping. It's going to take more than a warm drink and a few blankets to help Heidi overcome the ordeal she's lived through. Whether Will lives or dies tonight, this is going to take some coming back from. For all of us.

Claire's in the other ambulance with Mark. She said she'll

find us when we get to the hospital. Mark seems alright, but DI Jones has ordered that he gets checked over.

As we drive away, through the darkened windows of the ambulance, I notice that there are more vehicles pulling up. A van saying *dog unit*. Another saying *underwater search unit*. And a third ambulance.

Before you go...

Thanks for reading Drowned Voices - I really hope you enjoyed it and will consider leaving me a review on Amazon and/or Goodreads as this makes such a difference in helping other readers find the book.

Join my 'keep in touch' list to receive a free book, and to be kept posted of special offers and new releases.

Find out more about me via www.mariafrankland.co.uk and find out more about my other psychological thrillers by visiting my author page at Amazon.

Drowned Voices is the second book in the Dark Water Series. First in the trilogy is Undercurrents, and third in the trilogy is Emergence.

BOOK DISCUSSION GROUP QUESTIONS

1. What does the term police corruption mean to you?
2. How might the characters' lives progress from the end of this story?
3. Discuss the mother and son dynamic that exists between Janet and Will.
4. Could the situation have played out any differently if Eva had given in to Will's demands for a second child?
5. Explore Will's fantasy of having a son.
6. Discuss Pat Ingham's imprisonment. To what extent do you agree with her being punished, twenty years on?
7. Talk about the reasons why Will walked away from Pat Ingham's accusations and was originally cleared of all wrongdoing?
8. Discuss the factors that conspired to bring him to justice.
9. What involvement could Daniel Hamer and Suzannah Peterson have had in the deaths of the

mother and daughter whilst Will was on holiday, if any?

10. Discuss the websites Will had been visiting in the time leading up to him going on the run.

11. In what ways did Will's attentions towards Suzannah Peterson differ from his general opinion of women?

12. Discuss each character as to whether you see them as a victim.

13. Why might families of perpetrators be targeted by the public for their crimes?

14. What role did alcohol play in this story?

15. Discuss the relationship between Mark and Sara and why others might have been against it.

16. Talk about the possible effects of this story on the two young girls involved, Alysha and Heidi. How might the damage to them be minimalised?

IN HIS SHADOW - PROLOGUE

It takes between four and ten days after death for a body to reach putrefaction. In March, in a warm spring cellar, I would expect things to be doing their worst towards the earlier end of that spectrum. Today is day eight.

The odour of death assaults me as soon as I step into the hallway. I reach forward for the light, which blows no sooner than I have touched the switch. No! The fuse box is in the cellar. I should have done this before it got dark, but I've been putting it off all day.

I edge through the kitchen, burying my nose and mouth into the neckline of my jumper. The smell is like nothing I've ever encountered – bad eggs, curdled milk, sewerage and decaying meat all rolled into one. As I reach the cellar door, I pause, trying to get some breath into my lungs without my senses connecting to my inhalations.

The walls between this house and the terrace it backs onto are so thin, they might as well be made from papier mache. Once a shop downstairs and a large residential dwelling upstairs, it seems the developer took the cheapest option and built something barely stronger than a stud wall between the two resulting homes.

I listen for signs of life from the house behind.There shouldn't be any, but a slim chance exists that the last person I would want to see could turn up there. Nothing. Only the gasps of my own breath. Beads of sweat soak the skin beneath my jumper. Instinctively, I release my chin from it, inadvertently succumbing to the inevitable stench that now has its chance to launch its assault, causing my stomach to lurch and my mouth to fill with saliva. I swallow, hard. Although, I could get away with throwing up now, unlike a week or so ago. In fact, it could be viewed as an expected reaction.

I reach out for the door handle and slowly wrap my fingers around it, allowing the chill of the steel to cool my sweating palm. If only I could leave things as they are. But there's no way. I'll have to deal with this. Before long, passers by will able to smell what I can smell as they walk along the street outside.

I don't know how long I stand, rooted to the spot, steeling myself as I sway through indecision – do I throw the cellar door open, or edge it ajar an inch at a time?

Before I've even got it halfway, a swarm of plump bluebottles fly at my face. I jump back, yelling, spitting them out and swiping at them. There's no way I can go down there. No way.

There's only one course of action I can take. The one we agreed on.

Available via Amazon

INTERVIEW WITH THE AUTHOR

Q: Where do your ideas come from?

A: I'm no stranger to turbulent times, and these provide lots of raw material. People, places, situations, experiences – they're all great novel fodder!

Q: Why do you write domestic thrillers?

A: I'm intrigued why people can be most at risk from someone who should love them. Novels are a safe place to explore the worst of toxic relationships.

Q: Does that mean you're a dark person?

A: We thriller writers pour our darkness into stories, so we're the nicest people you could meet – it's those romance writers you should watch...

Q: What do readers say?

A: That I write gripping stories with unexpected twists, about people you could know and situations that could happen to anyone. So beware...

Q: What's the best thing about being a writer?

A: You lovely readers. I read all my reviews, and answer all emails and social media comments. Hearing from readers absolutely makes my day, whether it's via email or through social media.

Q: Who are you and where are you from?

A: A born 'n' bred Yorkshire lass, with two grown up sons and a Sproodle called Molly. (Springer/Poodle!) My 40's have been the best: I've done an MA in Creative Writing, made writing my full time job, and found the happy-ever-after that doesn't exist in my writing - after marrying for the second time just before the pandemic.

Q: Do you have a newsletter I could join?

A: I certainly do. Go to www.mariafrankland.co.uk or click here through your eBook to join my awesome community of readers. When you do, I'll send you a free novella – 'The Brother in Law.'

facebook.com/writermariafrank

instagram.com/writermaria_f

tiktok.com/@mariafranklandauthor

ACKNOWLEDGMENTS

Thank you, as always, to my amazing husband, Michael, who is my first reader and is vital with my editing process for each of my novels. His belief in me means more than I can say.

A special acknowledgement goes to my wonderful advance reader team, who took the time and trouble to read an advance copy of Drowned Voices and offer feedback. It was because of their urgings that this sequel to Undercurrents was ever written.

I will always be grateful to Leeds Trinity University and my MA in Creative Writing Tutors there, Martyn, Amina and Oz. My Masters degree in 2015 was the springboard into being able to write as a profession.

And thanks especially, to you, the reader. Thank you for taking the time to read this story. I really hope you enjoyed it.

Printed in Great Britain
by Amazon

42700637R00169